ABOUT THIS BOOK

ON her deathbed, Charles Dickens's wife asked her daughter to give Dickens's letters to the British Museum "so the world may know he loved me once".

That the world might have found that hard to believe is hardly surprising. In his later years Dickens built a wall in their bedroom to keep her out, forced her to visit his eighteen-year-old mistress to quell rumours, and tried to have her committed to an insane asylum.

He eventually banned her from their home and children, and set about destroying her reputation to protect his own from scandal. No two people were ever less suited to each other, had less in common or understood each other less, he told the papers.

This calculated portrayal of their incompatibility, crafted by Dickens to minimise his indifference and cruelty, has survived for nearly two hundred years.

Yet his own letters tell another story: that Catherine had once been his 'ever dearest Kate', the object of a love 'which no alteration of time or circumstance can ever abate'.

What other evidence forces us to challenge Dickens's control of the narrative?

In her paradigm-shifting new book, Annie Elliot shows Kate asking the same question. In the twenty-four hours following her husband's death in 1870, we see her revisiting the life they spent together, sifting through his correspondence, reliving their pains and joys, and laying ghosts to rest.

After having been silenced by Dickens's exploitation of the law —but also by her loyalty to him—about what really passed between them, this is Kate's opportunity to find her voice.

Part novel, part imagined autobiography, *Mr & Mrs Charles Dickens* is a poignant portrait of a woman struggling to make sense of what became a one-sided love that constrained and nearly destroyed her.

Drawing on extensive research and documentation, *Mr & Mrs Charles Dickens* fulfils Kate's last wish, restoring her to history as more than Dickens's discarded wife, giving her an identity of her own, and granting her the dignity, individuality and intelligence that she was denied in life.

ENDORSEMENTS

'ANNIE Elliot writes with great sympathy for Catherine Dickens. In a novel structured through shifts in time and a converging past and present, Elliot foregrounds Catherine's sense of loss in her marriage and her ability to counter and overcome that loss.'

Lillian Nayder, Professor and Chair of English at Bates College. Author of *The Other Dickens: A Life of Catherine Hogarth*

'A READABLE and convincing insight into the thoughts and feelings of Catherine Dickens in the twenty-four hours after the death of her husband. Based on thorough research, Annie Elliot provides us with an understanding of both the love and misuse experienced by this caring wife and mother throughout her twenty-two years of marriage to Charles Dickens.'

Christine Skelton, Emeritus Professor of Education, University of Birmingham. Author of *Charles Dickens and Georgina Hogarth: A Curious and Enduring Relationship*

'ANNIE Elliot's exciting debut *Mr and Mrs Charles Dickens* had me hooked from the very beginning. I love a literary historical novel and especially one that illuminates an untold story. In this instance, Elliot has done a great deal of research and woven into her writing many literary characters—all well drawn and memorable—without in the least weighing it down, making this almost a Dickensian novel in its own right. She has also been adept at depicting the increasingly intolerable domestic burden Kate shoulders. I genuinely cared about Kate and was incensed by her treatment. Highly recommended.'

Alison Woodhouse, author of *The House on the Corner*

'METICULOUSLY researched and beautifully crafted, Annie Elliot's novel gives life and voice to Kate Dickens, and brings her out of the shadows to which she was relegated by Dickens's dominance and cruelty. Kate deserves to be read and understood in this moving, illuminating and thoroughly enjoyable account.

Becky Docton, author of *The Ruins*

MR & MRS CHARLES DICKENS

HER STORY

'So The World May Know
He Loved Me Once'

A novel by

Annie Elliot

ENVELOPEBOOKS

ABOUT THE AUTHOR

ANNIE Elliot has a BA (Hons) in Literary Studies and an MA in Creative Writing. She has worked in local government and as a newspaper reporter, and taught communication. She has written a booklet to help teachers understand the difficulties faced by dyslexic children. Her short stories and flash fiction have won acclaim in literary competitions and she has been longlisted for the Mslexia Novel Award. She writes and performs monologues.

At university, her tutor, the late Fay Weldon, described Annie Elliot as a natural writer and her work as 'completely brilliant'. Struck by her talent for the acerbic and moving, the author and screenwriter Nikesh Shukla, host of the *Brown Baby* podcast, complimented her on her 'comedian's eye for detail and absurdity'. The naturalist, author and broadcaster Stephen Moss described her bitter-sweet style as funny and tragic.

Mr & Mrs Charles Dickens is Annie Elliot's debut novel. Her website is www.annieelliot.co.uk.

Love is not love which alters when it alteration finds.

WM. SHAKESPEARE

Dedicated to Catherine Dickens
née Hogarth
and to all women ill-used by men

Published 2026 in Great Britain and the USA
by EnvelopeBooks
A New Premises venture in association with Booklaunch

12 Wellfield Avenue, London N10 2EA, England
116 West 73rd Street, New York, NY 10023

www.envelopebooks.co.uk

Cover design by Stephen Games | Booklaunch

A CIP catalogue record for this title is available from the British Library.

Edited and designed by Booklaunch
EnvelopeBooks 34
ISBN 9781915023742

MR & MRS CHARLES DICKENS

HER STORY

'So The World May Know He Loved Me Once.'

FRIDAY, 10TH JUNE 1870—5:45 AM

MRS Dickens—Kate—always starts her day with thoughts of her husband: where he is, how he is, what he is doing, who he is with —but, strangely, he does not enter her head this morning. Perhaps, at some deep level, she is aware that the connection between them has been severed, although she has no sense of foreboding and is happily planning a dinner party. Her three older children and two of Charles's best friends, John Forster and Angela Burdett-Coutts (the wealthiest woman in England) have been invited and Kate is determined to make it just as splendid as all those in the past.

As she sits up in bed this bright and early morning, the bill of fare is uppermost on her mind: whether to serve pigeon, lark or snipe. Thank heaven for her son Charley and his lovely wife. Kate might only boil an egg and they would say that it was delicious and must have been laid by a golden goose. They always praise her curried seafood sauce too, but can she trust her cook to choose only oysters harvested fresh from the sea?

Raspberry and currant tart served with Italian cream will serve as a reminder of the family's very happy times in Genoa twenty-six years ago. Very happy? No, she must be honest. Not all their time there had been happy and if her ever-watchful husband, Charles, gets wind of the party she is planning, he will doubtless put pressure on their daughters not to attend. Mamie may bend to his will: she may not even be available. She seems to spend a lot of time away, visiting friends in the country these days. It might be better for all concerned if she didn't come after the spectacle she made of herself last time. Charley practically had to carry her out. But their younger sister, Catherine, will probably defy Charles and put in an appearance. If so, Kate will chalk it up as a little victory, something from which to derive a surge of satisfaction.

Asparagus soup is one thing they all enjoy but it is rather late in the season so it may be past its prime.

Kate has backache—a reminder that, at fifty-five, she is very much past her prime: no longer a lamb but a tough old piece of mutton. A walk to the shops will ease the pain and she will be able to take advice from her friends in the fishmongers and greengrocers on what is both fresh and inexpensive, after which she will guide Cook accordingly.

She shuffles to the edge of the mattress, rocks forward onto her feet and waddles across the room to settle down on the commode. The overnight water in the washstand has stayed warm. A lightweight cotton frock is all she will need today. She struggles to untie the rags entangled in her thin grey hair, shakes her droopy ringlets free and creeps downstairs, taking care not to wake the servants.

Black beetles scuttle across the flagstones as she pulls up the kitchen blind. What was it Charles had called the hedgehog that they kept to gobble them up in the basement of their first house in Doughty Street? A character from Oliver Twist? Yes: Bill Spikes. Charles is so good at thinking up names for all his characters—the real and the imaginary. Their fiery-tempered second daughter has been known as Lucifer Box for so long, no one now remembers that she is named Catherine, after her mother. In the early years Kate had been Charles's 'little mouse' or 'darling pig'. These days he'd be more likely to call her a fat old sow.

She consults her best-selling cookery book, foregoes breakfast, and sets off early to avoid crowds and pickpockets.

The stench of the street afflicts her as she opens the front door. Gloucester Crescent may be newly built but the drains still leave much to be desired and the smell causes her eyes to water. This makes her look as if she is crying but that would be a false impression, for she is not unhappy. Not too unhappy. She still has hope, accepts the cross the Lord has given her to bear and has learned to count her blessings.

The road is busy even at this early hour with ladies and gentlemen setting off for a turn around Regent's Park. Later in the day, others will make a trip to the Zoological Gardens. Kate does not like to see animals confined in cages.

She strays into the road.

'*Watch out!*' a coachman shouts.

Kate jumps back onto the pavement, and winces as pain shoots up her spine.

A passenger with mutton-chop whiskers frowns at her through the brougham's open window.

'Take care, Madam! You were nearly done for,' he says.

Kate begs forgiveness and tries to explain that her mind was elsewhere, but she is drowned out by the stamping of hoofs on cobblestones. The beautiful bay carriage horse snorts in complaint at being pulled up so sharply, and turns her regal head towards Kate. Long dark lashes sweep flies away from conker-brown eyes. Her tail lifts haughtily as she deposits a steaming pile of dung at Kate's feet. Kate pinches her nose against the smell.

A gypsy woman steps forward. 'Nosegays!' she croaks and holds one out. Her face is as brown as the horse's harness and just as leathery.

Kate smells the lavender. It turns her empty stomach. Bile rises and leaves a bitter taste in her mouth. She turns to walk away but the determined old woman blocks her path.

'Sprig of lavender? Freshly picked this very mornin'.' The woman smiles, revealing a graveyard of teeth. Kate averts her eyes but accepts defeat.

'How much?' she asks, and sighs.

'Three farthings, usual, but I'm a-feeling partic'la' generous. Sunshine's brought out the best in me—so a ha'penny to you, on account of your narrow hescape,' she says.

Kate takes a penny from her purse, hands it to the woman and waits for her change but receives two sprigs of lavender instead.

'Sure to bring you *double* the luck,' the woman says and pockets the coin in her tatty black skirt.

It is a price worth paying to be free to walk away.

'*Mind your back!*' the coachman shouts and whips the horse's well-groomed rump. It looks down its nose at Kate, flares its nostrils, tosses its gleaming black mane, swishes its tail and sets off at an extended trot.

Kate wants to shout out that although they live apart, she is still the wife of one of the world's most famous authors. But as usual, she says nothing. After thirty-four years of marriage she is accustomed to staying silent but has learned to express herself in other ways. Today she chooses to raise her right arm and hurl the lavender into the mound of manure.

A thin woman with an even thinner child stops beside her. 'Why did that lady throw away the pretty flowers?' the girl asks.

The woman shrugs at the girl. Embarrassed, Kate hurries off. She looks back over her shoulder to see if they are following her and nearly collides with a man selling newspapers. He's barking out the news. She doesn't quite catch it. 'Dickens is what?'

'Newspaper, lidey? Dickens is dead! Read all abaht it!'

Kate gasps. It cannot possibly be true! She tears open her purse, thrusts a penny at the vendor and turns to the story:

> LONDON, FRIDAY, JUNE 10.
> There is not a home in the United Kingdom in which the sad news of to-day will not be received with the deepest and most heartfelt regret, while across the Atlantic and amongst the distant populations in our vast colonial possessions a similar feeling will be experienced. Mr. Charles Dickens is dead. The distinguished novelist, who was 58 years of age, was seized with a fit of paralysis at his residence, Gad's-hill House, Rochester, on Wednesday evening. Throughout yesterday Mr. Dickens remained insensible, and died at twenty minutes after six o'clock last evening.

Kate's parasol slips from her hand and clatters to the ground. Her husband had collapsed two days earlier, and no one had told her. 'Georgina must have been with him,' Kate mutters. 'She should have sent for me. When all is said and done, I am still his wife.'

Kate would have saved him. He'd always overworked: in recent years he looked like a man in his eighties. How much better his life would have been had he not replaced her with her sister. Kate had eased her husband's load, managed his household, ensured he ate well, supplied him with his favourite cheese on toast, nursed him through his countless ailments, soothed his nightmares, acted as his secretary, kept his books, stopped the children from disturbing his work and responded passionately to him both in an out of the marital bed. Always a loving wife in every respect.

And now she will never see him again—not in this world—and he will never come back to her, as she has yearned for him to do. There will be no remorseful letters from him, owning up to having made a terrible mistake in ostracising her. There will be no knock at the door. No bouquet of roses. No hope. From now on, she will only have memories to sustain her: memories of his exuberance, his laughter, his passion, the fun they had, the love they shared.

Yes, the love. Despite his denials, she is sure that Charles did love her—once.

Kate clings to that thought but feels herself spinning and her legs giving way. Charles Dickens no longer exists, and she is no longer a wife but a widow. As she falls into a swoon she is aware of noisome breath and the stench of lavender.

She cannot recall walking home but remembers her maid, Matilda, saying that she looked as if she had seen a ghost, and asking permission to bring her some brandy.

'Yer sister must've known,' Matilda says on her way out to fetch the bottle. 'Yer 'usband was at death's door. Why didn't she send word? Finding out like that! The shock could've killed you.'

Yes, her little sister Georgina would doubtless have been beside Charles. Was this another in a long line of betrayals or was it, more innocently, an example of her sister's lifelong inability to understand how other people felt? The warning signs had been there since she was six.

Kate shivers. She closes her eyes but cannot shut out the icy winter frozen in her head.

December 1833

SCREAMS echo throughout the house again. My sister Mary has heard such sounds five times during her fourteen years on this earth but she still cries and puts her hands over her ears. The consternation is all new to Georgina but she seems oblivious to our mother's distress and runs around the kitchen echoing the shrieks and laughing.

I take my sisters' hands and lead them out into the frozen garden. In the distance Edinburgh Castle looms over the city, a fortress of hard grey rock against a hard grey sky.

'Let's sing "Ring-a-Ring o'Roses" and dance around to make a circle in the snow,' I say, as if nothing is amiss.

'Ring-a-ring o'roses, A pocket full of posies, A-tishoo! A-tishoo! We all fall down,' I bellow and try to skip lightly but find myself lolloping as I tug the two girls behind me. We throw ourselves to the ground and I force out an unconvincing laugh.

'We're not allowed to dirty our frocks,' Georgina says, frantically shaking slush from her hand-me-down dress, blissfully unconcerned by the emotions that surround her.

'Don't worry, my dear. You won't get into trouble today,' I assure her.

Delighted, Georgina smiles and makes a start on verse two.

'The cows are in the meadow, Eating buttercups . . . '

'Let me die!' comes a cry from indoors.

'Sing up!' I shout, trying to drown out the sound.

'I want to die!' our mother shrieks.

Mary tries to sing but her voice is swallowed by her sobs.

'The cows are in the meadow,' Georgina insists, 'Eating buttercups, A-tishoo! A-tishoo! We all jump up,' and she scrambles to her feet and bounds about like a spring lamb. Mary stays down. Try as I may to raise her, she is a dead weight on the cold dank grass as our grandmother arrives to tell us we have another brother, and a new sister too, and that they are to be called Edward and Helen.

'Twins! How is Mama?' I ask.

'She's quite well.'

Grandmother takes off her blood-stained apron.

'And the babies?' Mary asks still sitting on the grass.

'Both doing well,' Grandmama says. 'You may come up and see them in a wee while.'

Georgina dances over.

'Why didn't you let Mama die?' she asks as if her mother's fragility in labour is a matter of clinical curiosity.

Grandmama's mouth drops open. Her hand flies to her chest. She steps back.

'That's a dreadful thing to say. What on God's good earth made you ask such a wicked question?'

'She said she wanted to die and it's saintly to help people do what they want,' Georgina says.

No one knows what to say so we all say nothing.

Friday, 10th June 1870—9:30 AM

KATE is thankful that she has her old maid to take care of her, but now is not the time to discuss family grievances, not even with loyal Matilda, whom resembles a careworn old turkey, with her little grey head, wobbly red neck and big bosom.

'Do drink yer brandy, Madam,' Matilda says. 'It'll 'elp the shock.'

Kate is seated in an expansive wing chair by the hearth, propped up by cushions. She swirls the brandy around the glass in a golden vortex. She takes a mouthful and feels the warmth of it embrace her like a devoted husband. Charles had been devoted—sometimes. She looks at the glass. It is as bulbous as a pregnant belly. Twelve times Kate's has swelled. That surely is proof positive of her husband's love.

'Should I send for yer son, Madam?'

The swirling brandy settles down. Kate swooshes it to the left, then to the right. With each turn, the liquid resists for a second and then reverses its spin. Old doubts creep in. Charles was very cruel at the end.

Kate takes a sip. He must have loved her. She takes another sip. And she has never been able to stop loving him. A third sip. A widow has to rally her resolve. She tries to recite the words of her favourite sonnet but no sound emerges from her moving lips:

> Let me not to the marriage of true minds
> Admit impediments; love is not love
> Which alters when it alteration finds.
> Or bends with the remover to remove.
> O no, it is an ever-fixèd mark
> That looks on tempests and is never shaken;
> It is the star to every wand'ring bark
> Whose worth's unknown, although his height be taken.
> Love's not time's fool, though rosy lips and cheeks
> Within his bending sickle's compass come.
> Love alters not with his brief hours and weeks,
> But bears it out even to the edge of doom:
> If this be error and upon me proved,
> I never writ, nor no man ever loved.

'Shall I contact yer daughters?' Matilda asks as she pours Kate another brandy.

Kate drinks, stares out at the garden and sees herself as a child, pulling petals off a daisy one by one. 'He loves me, he loves me not,' says the little girl. Her voice echoes down the years.

'What about yer mother?'

Kate must take time to reflect, to accept, to beseech the Lord for strength to bear this bereavement with fortitude, but she finds herself trapped in a maze of unanswered questions. Try as she may, she fails to settle. Instead she flits from one memory to another like a butterfly.

'I'll leave you in peace, then, but call me if you need my help,' Matilda says and walks quietly out of the room.

Kate tries to focus on the trees, full of summer leaf. What is she now? No longer the estranged wife living in his shadow. She is a widow. His widow. More than that: the widow of a world-famous man. Death has bestowed on her a new status. She will surely receive condolences from the Queen.

It occurs to her that as the widow of a world-famous man, she must dress the part—and she must do so now.

It is an effort to get out of a chair these days. Kate rocks from side to side, inching her way to the edge of the seat, and uses her arms to lever herself up. She winces but reminds herself that a little droop between the legs is a small price to pay for giving birth to ten babies.

She is unsteady on her feet as she shuffles out into the hallway, clutches hold of the banister, hauls herself up the stairs and takes off her dress.

Stiff fingers struggle to turn the key in the trunk in the corner of her bedroom. Dust motes dance as she lifts the lid. Kate sneezes. 'God bless me,' she says. Her mourning gown lies on its back, arms folded across its chest like an effigy on a tomb. The black silk gleams as she holds it up—and Kate gasps. She had forgotten that her wedding trousseau had been laid out beneath it. She drops the black gown and clasps the bridal dress to her heart, hugging it with all her might. Once a symbol of all the happiness to come, it has become a ghostly reminder of broken promises, of paradise lost.

'Til death do us part,' she says, proud that she was true to her wedding vows right up to the end. She lays the dress down gently in the trunk. 'May we both rest in peace,' she says and steadies herself while she steps into her widow's weeds. The fabric is cool on her skin but she struggles to fasten the waistband, and no amount of breathing in will help. She will have to let it out, but the ivory sewing box with her needles and thread in it was a present from Charles on their wedding day, and she does not want to awaken more painful memories. Not today. She is no Pandora. Matilda will see to it tomorrow. In the meantime, she pulls down the bodice and selects her best string of jet beads from the dressing table.

She studies herself in the looking glass. The necklace hangs around her neck like an albatross. Kate reminds herself that she has overcome many bereavements during her life: a little sister, a brother, three babies, a parent, four grandparents and her in-laws. All have passed away and yet life has continued just as it did before she was banished, twelve years back, from husband, home and children, like an innocent princess by a wicked stepmother.

'At what point did his love for me begin to wane?' she asks her reflection. Should wifely intuition have alerted her? But what sort of a wife would she have been if she had suspected her husband? And, if she had suspected him, how could she have dissuaded him from acting on his misguided impulses?

She recalls being attracted to Charles from the moment she walked into her father's office at *The Evening Chronicle* and saw a man look round to observe who had entered the room.

January 1834

'AH, there you are Kate, my dear,' Father says. 'Mr Dickens, may I present my daughter, Miss Catherine Hogarth?'

He is in his early twenties, slim and fine-featured, impeccably dressed, and with piercing steely-blue eyes. They sparkle so. Waves of chestnut-brown hair fall across his broad, intelligent forehead. My fingers itch to sweep them off his brow. I look down and concentrate on removing my gloves in a vain attempt to compose myself, but my hands shake and fumble.

My father admonishes me. 'Catherine, where are your manners? Pray shake Mr Dickens's hand.'

'Please accept my apology, Mr Dickens,' I say. 'I cannot think what came over me. My father has told me so much about you but I didn't know . . . ' I trail off into an embarrassed pause. I didn't know what? I cannot believe that I was going to tell him how attractive he is. What am I thinking? Nothing. I've clearly lost my capacity for rational thought. My cheeks burn. I'm making a fool of myself. I wish I could escape and forget I had ever met him.

He smiles, takes my hand and presses it to his lips. They are warm. The heat spreads up my arm and through my entire body. There is a tickle between my legs. Shame on me! We have only just been introduced and my father is less than a yard away.

'I have heard much about you too,' he says, 'and I'm delighted finally to make your acquaintance, Miss Hogarth. Will you not be nineteen years old in a few months' time? I'm about to celebrate my twenty-second birthday and I'm arranging a small family gathering at my lodgings. I should be honoured to extend a cordial invitation to you to attend.'

Feeling faint, I steady myself by the edge of the desk and look up at my father.

'You may accept with my blessing if you wish, my dear,' he says. 'No doubt Mr Dickens will permit your sister Mary to accompany you?'

'Of course, Sir: I would be delighted to invite both the Misses Hogarth,' he says.

Well aware that a new party frock will be beyond our means, I wonder which of my existing dresses will be most pleasing to Mr Dickens and how to prevent my hair from falling out of curl the moment I untie the rags.

Mary comes to the rescue. Quite the needlewoman, she fashions silk flowers to embellish the neckline of an otherwise quite plain gown and coaxes my hair into resilient ringlets.

CHARLES leads the two of us into the parlour at his rooms in Furnival's Inn. 'I must introduce you to my mother,' he says at once.

A slight, dark-haired woman is seated on a stool in the corner of the room, beside a fiddler playing his violin. With a hooked nose like an owl's beak, she seems to be sniffing the assembled company for the scent of injured creatures to rip apart, and now she has me in her sights.

Charles guides us towards her. It is all I can do not to scamper for the door. I reach nervously for Mary's hand but Charles says, 'You don't need your sister now you have me to support you,' and pushes me forward. 'Mother, may I present the Misses Hogarth?' he says.

'Miss Catherine Hogarth, Mrs John Dickens, my mother. And this is Miss Mary Hogarth.'

Focusing on me, Mrs Dickens sinks her talons into my tiny paws.

'Maria! How kind of you to come,' she says.

Assuming she is struggling to hear beside the fiddler's scraping, I raise my voice and say, 'Mary is my sister, Mrs Dickens. My name is Catherine, but please call me Kate.'

'You have no call to shout,' Charles's mother says, curtly. 'I got the two of you mixed up, that's all. Besides which, Charles was courting a Maria for quite a while. Lovely girl. Made for one another. I hoped they would marry but no: another in a long line of bitter disappointments in my life. My husband has suffered trials and tribulations too. No doubt Charles has told you about when he was but a boy and his father, through no fault of his own—'

'Mother!' Charles says. 'This is not appropriate.'

'Ah, there I go again. Always in the wrong. That's me to a tee, Miss Hogarth.'

'Mary,' says Charles, 'perhaps you'd be good enough to entertain my mother. Come, Catherine: I want to introduce you to my father. Mary, I shall come back and rescue you in a moment!' And with that, he pulls me out of the harridan's grasp.

'That's it, off you go,' she reprimands. 'Don't stay to amuse me yourself, despite its being your birthday and your being obliged to me for the hours of agony I suffered bringing you into this cruel world . . . .'

Crestfallen at having made a poor first impression on the woman I pray will be my future mother-in-law, I try to redeem myself with a bright smile. My upper lip sticks to my teeth. My nose twitches in a vain attempt to release it. It's a wonder she doesn't throw me a piece of cheese.

Mr Dickens holds forth on a high-backed chair in the middle of the front wall. He catches sight of Charles and gesticulates wildly, as if greeting a long-lost son. The Red Sea parts as his disciples clear a path for us.

'Charles! My boy! And who might this charming young lady be?' he asks, kissing my hand.

John Dickens is an older version of Charles—the same twinkling blue eyes in a slender face and wavy brown hair though his is thinner on top. Charles has his father's sense of style too, although the older man's waistcoat is rather more ostentatious and his cravat has more knots than a hangman's noose.

'Miss Catherine Hogarth, father,' Charles says.

'A pleasure to meet you, Miss Hogarth, and I look forward to being introduced to your mother and father too. I hear he is a writer with connections to Sir Walter Scott, and an accomplished musician as well.'

A nod is obviously all that is required of me.

'A most cultivated man, not unlike myself, I fancy! I, too, have literary ambitions and have long thought of conducting an orchestra when I return from my Grand Tour of Europe.'

'How wonderful,' I say, enthusiastically. 'I would love to read what you have written and watch you perform on your return.'

'All in good time, all in due course,' he says, cheerily, and waves us away. 'Go and enjoy yourselves,' he instructs us.

I am pleased to see that Mary has managed to detach herself from the termagant and is dancing a reel with a handsome young fellow. Her usually pale cheeks are crimson.

'That's my little brother Frederick,' Charles says.

'Little? He's twice your size! How old is he?'

'Fourteen or perhaps fifteen—almost the same age as your sister, I imagine,' he says with a frown on his face.

Oh dear. I have caused offence.

'Let's hope he doesn't grow much more,' I improvise. 'His big brother is the ideal height and build.'

Comforted, Charles smiles.

'You and I are a perfect match,' he says. 'And your waist is so slender, my arm could encircle it twice. You are my little mouse.'

Frederick dances Mary towards us and she pants as they arrive. He doesn't wait for a formal introduction.

'Miss Hogarth, will you do me the honour of dancing with me?' he says, releasing Mary and holding out his hand.

Charles steps between us.

'I need a word with you, Brother,' he says and leads him out of the door.

Mary still hasn't got her breath back.

'Are you quite well, my dear?' I ask.

'Never better,' she grins. 'Fred is quite a character.'

'That's a relief, after their mother,' I say. 'What a terrifying person—but their father seems friendly, and he's a writer and musician just like Papa. Did Fred tell you he's about to undertake the Grand Tour?'

Mary laughs.

'Their father is a penniless clerk in the Naval Office and more likely to be off on a tour of Chatham Dockyard than the Grand Canal,' she says.

'Oh,' I say, deflated. 'Really?'

'Really what?' Charles asks as he returns.

'A . . . really good evening,' I reply and it's not a lie because I really am enjoying myself.

Mary winks at me and says she will seek out Fred.

'I expect he's in the kitchen helping himself to my brandy, along with all my other relatives,' Charles says.

He takes my hand and, with Mary not here to chaperone me, plants a kiss on my lips before leading me off to dance. A kiss! On my lips! This is the best night of my life. He is attentive, witty and charming—oh so charming—and I am completely under his spell. I am Titania, my eyes anointed with magical pansy juice.

FRIDAY, 10TH JUNE 1870—10:55 AM

KATE is tired of studying her reflection. The voluminous skirt of her mourning gown balloons around her. She is more black widow than fairy queen nowadays. She covers the looking glass with a scarf and turns away. Her necklace sways. She fiddles with it as if reciting the rosary but no amount of Hail Marys will save her today. Her fussing breaks the string. Black beads rain down. Kate lifts her skirts, unties her crinoline and steps out of it like a bird escaping its cage. She gets clumsily to the floor and crawls about on her sore knees, intent on retrieving all the stray pieces of jet and rethreading them as if rethreading the fragments of her life.

There is a tap at the door and Matilda enters. She stops dead as she takes in the scene.

'I'll do that for you, Ma'am, but let's get you up first,' she says and struggles to help Kate get to her feet. 'I actually came up to ask if you'd like me to accompany you on a little walk,' she says.

Kate shakes her head in silent refusal.

'It's a lovely day,' Matilda says, but blushes at her clumsy wording. 'I meant, the weather is fine.'

No doubt wishing to cover her embarrassment, Matilda kneels down to gather the remaining beads. Kate thinks of all the grates Matilda has black-leaded, fires she has laid, floors she has scrubbed and steps she has donkey-stoned in her long years of service in much grander houses than this.

With the broken string and beads in her apron pocket, Matilda pulls down her mob cap and hurries out. 'I'll get them re-threaded for you, Ma'am,' she says as she goes.

Kate sits on the bed and thinks back. She is nineteen years of age and Charles is with her. Her sister Mary and his brother Fred accompany the two of them to the theatre, both as spectators and performers. How enthusiastic she is to join Charles playing roles in amateur theatricals and operatics. Such fun for two young lovebirds.

Charles is always full of energy, Kate less so. On long walks through London's parks, he strides ahead, ever impatient for new discoveries. Kate cannot keep up with him and Mary has never been a brisk walker so Fred always takes one sister on each arm and the three of them skip along together singing at the tops of their voices. Charles always looks back and laughs, then rushes on.

Muddy shoes, slippery leaves, pouring rain, tedious tenors and unintelligible plot lines matter to her not one jot. Being in Charles's company is more than enough to make her giddy with happiness and she cannot conceal her feelings from friends and family.

The two Marys, her sister and cousin, both tease her mercilessly about her obsession with London's penniless young writer. She had confided to them the thrill she had felt during that first meeting and the two girls had rolled around on her bed, unable to contain their laughter, and she had felt foolish for being so unguarded.

February 1834

'OH, Mr Dickens, what a big goose feather you have on your quill,' my sister Mary says.

'Pray tickle me between the legs with it,' says my cousin Mary.

'Mary! Other Mary! Stop! Mother will hear you,' I beg, but they pull me onto the bed with them.

'He's a reporter? Good at shorthand is he? And what about longhand?' my cousin asks. She wiggles her fingers and tickles my ribs until I too am laughing hysterically.

'What wavy hair you have, darling Charles,' says my sister. 'Would you like to see my curls?' She cavorts around my bedroom waving her nightgown well above her waist, performing the scandalous French *can-can* with a wild abandon that I imagine is usually confined to Parisian dance halls.

A knock comes at the door.

Our mother enters, closely followed by Georgina, our seven-year-old sister. Caught red-handed, Mary freezes in a *tableau vivant*, bent over with her skirt over her head and bare backside in full view.

'I do not know what you think you are doing, girls, and I frankly do not wish to know,' Mother says, turning her disapproving gaze to each of us in turn. 'But whatever it is, you will stop forthwith. Have I made myself clear?'

'I would never ever do anything like that, Mama,' our little sister says. She places her hands on her hips and scowls at us. She is growing up fast.

'Of course you wouldn't,' Mother smiles and pats the head of her saintly little namesake. 'You are my good girl, Georgina.' Returning her focus on us sinners, she repeats, 'Have I made myself clear?'

The three of us nod in silent chagrin as they leave and close the door behind them.

'Georgina has a halo and you are my unholy Marys,' I say.

We bend double, hands clamped over mouths in a vain attempt to stifle another fit of giggles.

Friday, 10th June 1870—Midday

'LUNCH is ready, Ma'am,' Matilda says, and holds out a calloused hand. She heaves Kate up from the bed, takes her arm and guides her downstairs.

'Sarah has made yer favourite broth,' she says as she pulls out a chair in the dining room. 'Please try to take a little.'

Kate eases herself into the chair and lifts a spoon to her lips but the smell of boiled chicken bones makes her nauseous. The broth is the colour of wash-day water. Pearly globules of fat float around in it, catching the light. Kate's stomach heaves. Her spoon falls back into the bowl.

'I'm sorry, Matilda. Please tell Cook I'm sure it's as delicious as ever but I have no appetite,' Kate says.

'Perhaps a little bread and lard, then?' Matilda suggests.

Kate smiles to ease her maid's concern but leaves the slice untouched.

'Do try, Madam, or you'll make yerself ill,' Matilda pleads.

Kate looks but she does not see her maid. She sees a young Charles during their courtship, sitting hour after hour beside her sickbed, the very image of an adoring suitor as he administers Camphor Julep and Calomel, paid for out of his meagre salary. She recalls the touch of his hand on hers, his anxious face. She does not recall misgivings about the strength of his feelings. And why would she? Hadn't he moved lodgings to be closer to her? Talked of requesting her father's permission to ask for her hand in marriage? Told her nothing could lessen his love?

She gets up from the table, makes her way into the parlour, opens the bottom drawer of her writing desk and takes out a pile of letters tied up with a red ribbon. There is her name in her husband's handwriting. The words blur as her eyes fill with tears. Kate cannot accept that Charles will never write to her again, that he will never write anything to anyone ever again. He had written only six of the twelve monthly parts of *The Mystery of Edwin Drood*, and had never made any notes on how his stories would end, so nothing now will follow but blank page after blank page. Both his last novel and his death will leave mysteries unsolved.

Kate sits in the armchair next to the empty fireplace. She unties the ribbon and takes the first letter from the top of the pile. She has kept them neatly in order and read them many times, particularly during those first lonely days and nights after their separation. Surely so much correspondence shows how much she was once on his mind; but does it prove any enduring love?

She skims through the first paragraph where Charles expresses his desperation to see her. When she first read his words in May 1835 her spirits had soared as she believed his urgency equated to love. Now she discounts it as mere infatuation—but what of the rest of the letter, where this master of pithy and vivid writing admits that he cannot find the words to describe what he feels for her? The writing isn't just conventionally stilted: it's clumsy.

> If I were to say on paper how interested I am in the slightest word that concerns you, much more on so important a point as your health, it would look like egotism.

What is he trying to say? She reads on:

> Were I to express half my solicitude in your behalf it would appear like profession without sincerity, and were I to endeavour to embody the least of the feelings I entertain for you in words, it would be a useless, and hopeless attempt.

Why couldn't he write to her the way he talked when they were together?

> For each and all my dear Girl you must give me credit, until time has enabled me to prove the sincerity and devotion of the affection I bear you.

She had to give him time to prove his sincerity and devotion? Why did he need it? *She* didn't: she had been able to tell him right away how she felt. But there is some consolation in the last paragraph.

> Keep up your spirits above all things—if the consciousness of awakening sympathy and interest in the breast of any human being be a consolation in sickness, you may take my assurance that you possess both to an extent which you can hardly imagine —nor I describe.

Believe me
My Dearest Catherine
Ever Yours Affecy.
Charles Dickens

Well, this seems to be a genuine expression of love and it is reinforced the following month when Charles writes of his impatience to secure suitable lodgings so they may marry. He says he hopes that she was impressed, when they met the night before, by his 'repeated and solemn assurances of entertaining for you a love which nothing can lessen—an affection which no alteration of time or circumstance can ever abate'. Apologising for writing in haste, and on office paper, and by waning candlelight, he adds that,

> I have the vanity to believe that these professions must be gratifying to you, knowing the sincerity with which they come from me.

Kate hugs the letters to her chest, just as she had in those innocent days when her heart had nearly burst with joy at the thought that she would soon be the wife of such a talented, attractive man.

She unfolds the next letter. It is an invitation to visit his lodgings to cook him breakfast, with Mary as chaperone. How thrilled she had been at the opportunity to rehearse her wifely role, and asking for Mary to accompany her showed how noble Charles was to want to protect her good name. A wry smile passes her lips as she recalls how hard he fought her in later years when his good name was called into question. But she will not think of that: she is determined to enjoy reliving the day of that meeting.

June 1835

I KNOCK at the door of his lodgings. There is no answer. I try again, shrug and look to Mary. More practical than I, she turns the handle. The door is unlocked and opens. We step inside. The curtains are drawn across the small window at the front of the room but a single candle burns on the mantelpiece.

‘Charles,’ I call out into the gloom as I remove my hat and gloves, and prop my wet umbrella up in the grate. There is no reply. I feel my way across the room to the window—and stub my toe on the leg of the table. I curse in a most unChristian manner.

‘Catherine, for shame!’ says Mary.

I hope Charles hasn’t heard me. I pull back the curtains and look over my shoulder, in case he is sitting in the armchair by the hearth, ready to jump up and surprise us. He’s not there. I breathe a sigh of relief.

‘Perhaps he has been summoned earlier than anticipated to the office,’ Mary suggests. She sets down her basket on the table and starts to unpack the bread, butter, eggs and bacon we brought from home.

‘He works such long hours. Do you suppose my poor love could still be asleep?’ I ask.

‘You could try peeping in at his bedroom door,’ she says.

I creep over quietly and turn the handle slowly.

‘Charles?’ I whisper as the door creaks open. The windowless room is lit by candles. Charles is sitting up in bed with his nightshirt on, smiling.

‘You must be the new maid,’ he says. ‘Pray enter but do not try any tomfoolery with me, for the most beautiful woman alive already has my heart.’

I laugh and look back at Mary.

She smiles and gives me a nod. ‘I’ll busy myself setting the table,’ she says. ‘And slice the bread. And then boil the eggs. And perhaps fry some bacon. I’ll call you when breakfast is all ready but it may take an unusual amount of time.’ She is the most thoughtful sister.

‘You’ll find everything you need in the dresser,’ Charles calls out to her, adding ‘Your sister is an angel,’ as I enter the room.

‘I know,’ I say, ‘but she will get in terrible trouble if my father finds out she left us alone together—and in your bedroom!’

He reaches out for my hand and pulls me towards him.

‘Then we’ll have to make sure he doesn’t find out, won’t we?’

He releases my hand and pats the bed, indicating for me to sit beside him. There is mischief in his eyes.

What does he expect of me? Will he think me prudish if I behave with decorum or be disappointed if I relax my moral standards? The neck of his nightshirt is unbuttoned. Dark hairs are visible on his chest. It is all I can do not to slide my hand inside the white cotton and run my fingers through them.

'You would appear to be having difficulty breathing and your cheeks are flushed,' Charles says with a smirk. 'Are you finding my room too warm for your liking?'

'Yes . . . no . . . I . . . .' He must think me so gauche. Charles wants a wife, not a silly girl. I may not be of age but I should show some maturity. I take a step forward.

'You seem a little uncertain. Perhaps you have a fever.' He reaches forwards and places his hand on my forehead, then frowns and nods like a doctor assessing a patient. 'Ah yes, indeed. As a medical man, I prescribe that you remove a few clothes to make yourself more comfortable.'

Cautiously, I take off my wet coat—just my coat—and lay it across his bedside chair. There is no harm in that. The room really is quite hot, after all.

'Now doesn't that feel better, my dear?' he asks.

'Much better, Doctor. Thank you,' I say, playing along.

He pats the counterpane again. 'I prescribe also that in cases of fever, a little bed rest is necessary. It might be prudent for you to stretch out beside me for a while,' he says.

Before I can stop myself I find I am lying on the bed by his side, but this could not be construed as in any way compromising because I am on top of the blankets and still have my boots on.

'Other physicians in my consulting practice observe that your corset is too tight, which is likely the cause of your shortness of breath. We are agreed that you would feel very much more comfortable were I to unbutton your dress,' he says, unbuttoning my dress as he speaks. 'And your laces,' he continues, as he starts to undo my stays.

I take a deep breath and gasp as he gently pulls on the ribbons of my petticoat and cups one breast in his warm hand. I reach inside his nightshirt and fulfil my wish to run my fingers across his chest.

'Do you think you should be doing that, Miss Hogarth?' he asks. 'Pray remove your hands from my person or I may not be able to comply with the code of medical conduct expected of a medic of my high status, and the blame will be yours.' He takes my hands in his, pulls me towards him and kisses me. Our lips have met many times before but, being ever observed, we always kept our behaviour formal. Now I feel more than a tickle between my legs and hear myself panting—as my mother did when she was having the twins. A reminder of where this might lead is enough to bring me to my senses. With a superhuman effort I pull away.

Charles groans. 'You are a difficult, unruly patient,' he says, planting a kiss on my hand. 'Headstrong too.'

My trembling knees make it hard to stand up. My tingling fingers make it hard to make myself presentable.

'The Superintendent at the sanatorium advises that your honour and my sanity may be at risk if we don't marry as soon as possible,' he says. 'I just need to work hard and save enough to give us the best start in our life together.'

'I long for our wedding night,' I say and kiss him again.

He pulls me back onto the bed.

'Breakfast is served!' Mary shouts.

FRIDAY, 10TH JUNE 1870—2:10 PM

KATE must have dozed off in the chair for she has a crick in her neck and is embarrassed to discover a damp patch of saliva on her shoulder. She pulls her handkerchief from her sleeve and dabs at her dress, worried a water mark will stain the silk. She will, after all, be in widow's weeds for at least a year now, and maybe two in the circumstances.

The short nap has left her a little befuddled. Was she dreaming about that time she lay on a bed with Charles before they were married—the time he pledged to work hard to achieve financial security? Ah yes, that was one promise he never broke. Once they were engaged she rarely saw him. Left so often alone, she began to brood on whether he really needed to spend so much time attending debates in the Houses of Parliament or travelling to court proceedings or writing up his reports in the newspaper offices where her father worked. She wanted to seek his reassurances but did not know how best to phrase her request without sounding needy. It was never easy to question him. She just wanted to know that he loved her. She still does . . .

July 1835

'WHAT ails my little mouse?' Charles asks.

'What makes you think anything ails me?' I parry his question with one of my own, and remain at the other end of the room.

'There is clearly something troubling you,' he says. 'Pray tell what it is.'

I stare out of the window and sigh.

'If I have upset you I can but abase myself and beg your pardon most humbly, but I cannot think how such a thing might have happened, for we have not been together since Wednesday last week and I have written so many times since then to impress you with protestations of my unwavering devotion.'

'Hmmm,' I say as I bustle past him and busy myself with rearranging the ornaments on the mantelpiece.

'Is that the problem, my love? My absence? We must be honest with each other if we are to make a happy marriage.'

'If spending so much time away from me causes you so little unease, then I shall likewise bear it without complaint,' I say. I take the seat opposite him and brush imaginary dust from my skirt.

'But sweet mouse, you know I work only to secure our future and would much rather be in your company. It is necessity and necessity alone which keeps me at my desk. When I have saved enough money you may rest assured that nothing and no one will keep me any longer from your side.'

He kneels in front of me, takes my hand and kisses it.

I feel forlorn but try to minimise it. 'I'm so sorry I was a leetle weetle bit coss wiv you,' I say feebly, and look into his eyes. Tears drip onto my dress. He rises, pulls me to my feet and embraces me. Wrapped in his arms I believe we have come to an understanding.

FRIDAY, 10TH JUNE 1870—2:30 PM

HOW naive and foolish Kate had been to trust that that would be the end of the matter. Feeling reassured, she spent the next day looking forward to hearing from Charles while she busied herself sewing, paying calls on friends and helping her mother with the younger children. Little Helen had broken Georgina's cup and Georgina was refusing to drink out of anything else. Kate went to the shops and bought an exact replica, knowing Georgina would rather shrivel up like a prune than relent.

Time dragged until a letter from Charles arrived in the next morning's post. Kate retrieved it from the doormat and skipped upstairs to read it in bed and relish in private his loving words. She savoured the moment by slowly breaking the seal and kissing the paper which her beloved's hand had touched. Then she saw the salutation. It was not the usual 'My Dearest Kate' but 'My dear Catherine'.

Kate finds the letter now and relives the pain and fear she had felt when she first took in its words. Charles tells her that he is in pain and that, before going to bed, he has to share how he is feeling, however unkind or reproachful this may seem. He had hoped that their three weeks as an engaged couple might have been blissful but she has now upset him twice and he needs to bring this to a head.

> The sudden and uncalled-for coldness with which you treated me just before I left last night, both surprised and deeply hurt me—surprised, because I could not have believed that such sullen and inflexible obstinacy could exist in the breast of any girl in whose heart love had found a place; and hurt me, because I feel for you far more than I have ever professed, and feel a slight from you more than I care to tell.

Kate had objected to Charles's own behaviour, and had made her feelings clear, and he's not happy about it. He accuses her of 'strange behaviour' and of having 'a hasty temper' and instructs her, plainly, to control herself: such behaviour 'will never make you more amiable, I more fond, or either of us, more happy'. He goes on to accuse her of insincerity and says that he is ready to give her up:

> If three weeks or three months of my society has wearied you, do not trifle with me, using me like any other toy as suits your humour for the moment; but make the acknowledgment to me frankly at once—I shall not forget you lightly, but you will need no second warning.

His worry, he says, is that if she can behave with 'unkindness' as his fiancée, her behaviour will only worsen as his wife. He does not say this to make her angry, he says, and he is not angry, but he is hurt and feels slighted in a way he could not have been had someone else upset him. He wants to be sure that her love for him is as real as is his for her, and in complaining to her about her behaviour, he now finds himself more articulate about his feelings than previously:

> If you knew the intensity of the feeling which has led me to forget all my friends and pursuits to spend my days at your side; if you knew but half the anxiety with which I watched your recent illness, the joy with which I hailed your recovery, and the eagerness with which I would promote your happiness, you could more readily understand the extent of the pain so easily inflicted, but so difficult to be forgotten.

July 1835

SMARTING like a scolded child, I march downstairs to seek out my sister, who is helping Mama in the kitchen. I wait until Mother's back is turned, then wave the letter in the air to attract her attention. She grins, for she knows how much I look forward to hearing from my beloved, but her face falls when she sees my expression. She makes an excuse and follows me upstairs. I close my bedroom door behind us, fling myself into her arms and cry.

Between sobs I make Mary promise not to breathe a word to our parents, whose confidence in Charles's good prospects makes me fear that they will heap shame on me for putting my future with him in jeopardy.

Level-headed Mary calms me down. She sits on my bed and takes her time to read what Charles has written. While she reads, I pace up and down in an effort to dissipate my torment.

'Ouch,' I cry as I stub my toe on the leg of the washstand.

Mary, used to my clumsiness, does not even look up.

'Put on your spectacles,' she says.

'Charles disapproves of spectacles,' I say and limp from wall to window and back. 'He associates them with weakness and old age.'

After what seems an age Mary stands up and explains that she needed to take her time to digest the import of Charles's letter in full. She encourages me to take heart and tells me that she knows me to be every bit as good as Charles hopes I am and that, as his wife, I will be more than worthy of his affection and respect.

'How selfish I have been in thinking only of my wish for more of his time, and constantly putting pressure on him to call on me,' I say. 'There will be no more of it or it is plain that I will lose him. From now on I will think only of Charles and his needs, and bring him succour, not scowls, when he is good enough to break off from his labours. Forthwith I dedicate myself to preparing to be the best wife in the world. There will be no more cavorting with you and cousin Mary. I shall devote my spare time to reading the books on wifely devotion that Charles has recommended and promise that he will never have cause to admonish me again.'

Mary praises my resolve but warns there will be a price to pay. She says I will need to be not only subservient but also self-reliant, as she suspects that Charles will not rest from his efforts until he achieves fame and fortune.

FRIDAY, 10TH JUNE 1870—4:00 PM

DEAR Mary, wise way beyond her years. It has taken Kate decades to appreciate just how right her sister had been. She rolls her head from side to side to ease the crick in her neck, then checks her shoulder to see if saliva has left a mark.

Cook has made afternoon tea—a plateful of cucumber sandwiches and Kate's favourite madeleine cakes—but the bread turns to papier-mâché in her mouth. She gags but does not want to offend, so spits the mushy ball discreetly into her handkerchief, folds the cotton around it and tucks it up her sleeve to be disposed of later. They had eaten madeleines on the first day of their honeymoon, in a whitewashed cottage by the Thames in Kent. Their landlady's smiling eyes were so small and dark, it looked as if someone had pushed currants into her doughy face.

She does not want to recall their wedding day but with every blink an image appears: her little brothers and sisters running around in their Sunday best clothes; Mama and Mary encouraging them to behave; nine-year-old Georgina quoting rules of wedding etiquette to Edward and Helen, the two-year-old twins; blinding spring sunshine streaming through the lychgate; daffodils nodding their approval in a gust of wind; her father's eyes filling with tears as he walks her up the aisle; and Charles looking lovingly at her as he makes his vows. He truly loved her then, she is sure of that. And he had placed his trust in her when he had lain in her arms on their wedding night and confided his fears.

April 1836

MRS Craddock greets us at her front door. She is as stout and homely as a cottage loaf, with her round face and hair in a topknot. One grey strand has escaped. She winds it back into place and pats the bun on her head as if to check she's well baked.

'Mr and Mrs Dickens?' she asks.

This is the first time anyone has called us by this name. Charles and I smile at the acknowledgement of our newly married status. We say 'yes' in unison and laugh.

'Come in, come in,' our landlady says, taking off her apron and tucking it under her arm. 'I'll show you to your room.'

She huffs and puffs up the stairs like someone blowing to cool her soup. Our boots clonk on the bare boards. The room is spotless and adequately furnished with a double bed, washstand, chair and chest of drawers. There is a well-worn rug on the floor and a chamber pot under the bed.

Charles puts down our bags.

'This will do very nicely, thank you,' he says.

'It is nothing fancy but I hope you will be comfortable enough,' Mrs Craddock says. 'If you would care to follow me downstairs, there is tea in the back parlour.'

She catches us looking longingly at the bed and smiles. 'You must be tired after your journey. I'll light a fire to take the chill off the room while you eat. Then perhaps you'd like an early night? Weddings are all very well but they do take it out of you.'

'Indeed,' says Charles and he reddens. I take his hand and squeeze it as we follow Mrs Craddock out of the room.

Downstairs, we take our seats at a small table with a starched white cloth. Mrs Craddock pours tea into china cups and suggests we help ourselves to the sandwiches and cakes while she busies herself warming up our room.

We sip our tea. Little madeleine cakes are calling to me but I must not appear greedy so I resist the temptation to tuck in. Would Charles laugh and call me his little mouse if I nibbled away at the edges as I like to do before biting into the jam-soaked sponge and letting the sugary ecstasy explode in my mouth? How I would love to bite the cherry off the top and savour the sweet smooth surface of the coconut icing on my tongue. Instead, I hold off from taking that first bite and closing my eyes as I swallow it. Pleasures delayed can be pleasures doubled.

Charles leans across and kisses me.

'How long do you think we should wait before retiring for the night?' he asks.

'Let's eat quickly and yawn in front of her. She has already acknowledged that we may wish to go up early,' I say.

'Yes,' says Charles. 'I thought it was rather forward of her.'

'I saw you blush but I'm sure she had no wish to give offence,' I say.

'Men don't blush,' he says, stiffly.

'I'm sorry,' I say quickly, in an attempt to appease him. 'I only mentioned it because I felt my cheeks flush too.'

'You looked as if you were about to combust,' he objects, 'and perspiration broke out on your brow. It was unladylike.'

'I'm truly sorry, Charles. Shall we make a start on the food? Shall I pour another cup for you?'

He ignores me. What a careless wife I am, offending my husband within hours of making my vows. I refill his cup and pray he will take pity when he sees how my hand shakes. He pays me no heed. I pile sandwiches onto his plate before taking one for myself.

Mrs Craddock wobbles in like a jelly.

'Your room will soon warm up,' she says and looks at the untouched sandwiches on our plates. 'I suppose you've been too busy making eyes at each other to think about food but do eat up. You'll need plenty of sustenance in your bellies tonight, if I know anything about honeymoons.'

To my surprise, Charles's mood changes, and he laughs as if they are old friends and tucks into his sandwiches with gusto.

Mrs Craddock says, 'That's what I like to see—a man with a

healthy appetite.' She winks at Charles. 'I'll leave you to it, but call me if you'd like another pot of tea.'

I pick at a sandwich and try to gauge Charles's state of mind while he eats the rest. His brows are knotted and his forehead furrowed, but these may only be signs that he is deep in thought.

He smiles.

Tension falls from my shoulders.

'Something sweet, for my wife—the sweetest woman in the world,' he says and hands me a madeleine. I have lost my appetite but I eat to please him.

'Thank you, my dear husband,' I say and take tiny bites, to avoid spitting coconut crumbs over him.

Charles has eaten two madeleines and one chocolate sponge by the time I finish what he has been so kind to give me.

'Do you think we could sneak upstairs now without causing offence?' he asks.

It would seem that my tactless remark has not killed his desire to consummate our marriage.

Without hesitating, I suggest that it might be better to thank Mrs Craddock for the food and take our leave politely. Then it occurs to me that I should have agreed with him rather than immediately appearing to contradict him again.

'Very well, my love: you know best about domestic matters,' Charles says. 'I just preferred not to let her embarrass you again.'

I wasn't embarrassed but have now learnt to keep my opinions to myself.

'But we could sneak away, if you prefer. I don't want to risk your discomfort,' I say, and then grit my teeth again. I should not have said 'discomfort'. Another tactless remark. No wonder Charles is irritated.

Mrs Craddock appears in the doorway, blocking our escape.

'Would either of you like anything else?' she asks.

'No, we are quite replete,' Charles says, on behalf of us both. 'You put on a wonderful spread for us. We were just about to retire for the night.'

'Very well, my dears. Sleep well,' she says.

I breathe a sigh of relief at the lack of innuendo. Mrs Craddock smiles as we squeeze past her, and I think we have managed to escape. Then she ruins it by adding, 'when you do finally get to sleep!'

Charles laughs it off but rolls his eyes and glowers at me behind her back. I fear I really have ruined our wedding night by defending our licentious landlady and follow him slowly up to our room. He closes the door behind us with resolution and, before I can apologise again, he lifts me off my feet and carries me to the bed. This time he doesn't stop at unbuttoning my dress. He strips me naked and strokes my skin tenderly.

'You are so, so beautiful. I have dreamt of this moment many times but even my fertile fancy could not conjure such a perfect vision,' Charles says. 'Are you nervous my little mouse?' he asks.

I nod my head and then shake it, not sure what he wants me to say. Would it be too brazen to admit I am shaking with anticipation more than fear?

'You are bound to be confused but please rest assured: I will be gentle,' he says.

He starts to undress. I watch, unable to take my eyes off him. It is all I can do not to tear his shirt from his chest and pull him on to me but I know I must not. I must be completely passive and he must lead.

There is a groan of desire. Did it come from Charles or me? I do not have time to decide as he lies down on top of me and stoppers my open mouth with his warm tongue. True to his word, he pushes gently inside me. I gasp. Rhythm overwhelms us as our bodies knit perfectly together. There is more than a tickle between my legs now. It is as if a whole feather mattress has exploded. Charles grunts. I thrust my hips up and feel a thousand throbs. A warm glow of utter peace spreads through my body like the precursor to blissful slumber after a perfect summer's day.

Charles rolls off me. He covers his face in his hands and shakes. Tears trickle down to his chin.

'Whatever is the matter, my love?' I ask. 'Have I done something else wrong?'

He shakes his head.

I take my new husband in my arms and cradle him like a newborn baby.

'I'm so frightened,' he says.

'What do you fear?' I ask.

'Loss,' he says, 'but I can't expect you to understand'.

'I would like to try,' I say, and stroke his hair back from his brow.

'You cannot begin to comprehend what it's like to have a ne'er-do-well as head of the family, to be dragged out of school and set to work twelve hours a day in a stinking factory.'

'I do know something of your pain, dearest,' I say. 'We had to leave Scotland to avoid father's creditors. He had made some poor investments.'

'But you never suffered the degradation of visiting your father in a debtors' prison, did you?' Charles asks, insistent that his griefs have always ranked higher than mine.

'No, that is true, but we do not have anything to fear now. Everyone predicts your Pickwick story will make your fortune, so there really is nothing to worry about,' I say.

'Don't you see? The more I have, the more I have to lose,' Charles says. 'One day I will be dragged off to moulder away in Marshalsea Prison. "We knew you'd be back," the gaolers will say. "Like father, like son."'

'No one will say that, because it is never going to happen, Charles. I cannot change the past but I foresee a bright future and I can promise that come what may, you will never lose me. I made a solemn vow before Our Lord today to love, honour and obey you, for richer or poorer, and to forsake all others until death do us part.'

FRIDAY, 10TH JUNE 1870—5:30 PM

KATE guffaws at the irony: Charles had been the one who feared loss but, in the end, he was the one who had done the forsaking. Kate is not bitter; she has taken care not to allow herself to drown in her own bile. In fact, she feels sorry for Charles, lying alone in his coffin, no doubt fretting about being buried in a pauper's grave.

She chuckles to herself but then shakes her head slowly. Being rich and adored all over the world had certainly not proved to be the panacea he had yearned for. 'Poor Charles,' Kate says, for she knows that her sister Mary had been right. He had never escaped the spectre of the debtors' prison, and a thousand sovereigns, two thousand sovereigns, a never-ending stream of sovereigns had been insufficient to quell the never-ending fear of an empty purse which had weighed him down all his life.

‘Oh madam: you’ve not touched a scrap of food all day,’ Matilda says, as she clears away the cakes and sandwiches. ‘Shall I fetch you some warm milk?’

‘Yes, please,’ Kate says. How comforting the idea of warm milk should be but there is no comfort for Kate today. A cat yowls in the street but Kate hears it as a hungry baby crying for its mother’s breast. She wonders where the child is and to whom it belongs. The mother should see to it. The cries reach a crescendo. What is the woman thinking of? Kate pushes down on the arm of her chair and manoeuvres herself onto her feet. Hands on hips, she arches her aching back just as she did in the latter stages of her pregnancies. She cocks her head like a pet dog listening for its master’s return. Screams surround her. Kate sticks her fingers in her ears. There is no escape. The infant’s distress reverberates in her head. A band of toy soldiers beats its drumsticks against the inside of her skull. Desperate to find the baby, she looks under the table, in the dresser, behind the fire screen. She even lifts the lid on the coal bucket.

‘Here’s some lovely warm milk,’ Matilda says, setting the glass down on the table. ‘I’ve stirred in another drop of brandy to help ease your mind.’

‘Please make it stop,’ Kate pleads.

Matilda frowns.

‘Madam?’

‘The baby,’ says Kate.

‘Baby?’

‘It’s crying with hunger.’ Kate says. She wonders what is wrong with her maid.

Matilda looks at her mistress warily as she tries to hear what Kate is talking about.

‘I can hear Sarah downstairs bashing the dough for tomorrow’s bread, but she ain’t bashing no baby,’ she says.

‘Deaf as a post,’ Kate mutters.

Matilda takes Kate by the arm, and guides her back to her armchair.

‘I fear shock and an empty stomach may be playing tricks on you. Please drink up, Madam.’

Kate does as she is bid but does not find the baby’s screams any more tolerable. She nurses her head in her hands.

‘You are overwrought, Madam. Please try to rest a little.’

Kate wants to argue, to prove that there is a baby in urgent need of feeding and comfort, but she does not have the strength. She nods, closes her eyes and sees her newborn son.

Charley kicks his frog's legs, clenches his tiny fists, throws back his bald head and bawls.

January 1837

'IF at first you don't succeed, try, try and try again. They don't all latch on straight away but he'll soon get the hang of it,' my mother says.

'Our Fred was a hungry baby. No matter how much I fed him he still screamed for more,' says Charles's mother.

I reach out and take my son but, just as before, he thrashes around in my arms and shakes his head left and right as if denying my maternity.

With one hand my mother-in-law supports the baby's head while pushing my shoulders forward with the other, so my bare breasts tilt downwards. Mother pinches the pink area around my sore nipple and, with the split-second timing gained from years of experience, thrusts it into my baby's mouth just as he turns towards me. It feels as if he has the teeth of a tiger but I resist the urge to pull away. Charley bites down with his gums and, to my great relief, begins to suckle.

'There you are,' Mother says. 'Practice makes perfect!'

'Girls are easier,' says Mrs Dickens. 'Pray for a daughter next time.'

'I'm not having any more children,' I say.

Their laughter is short-lived as Charley spits out my nipple in disgust, turns his head away and begins to wail again. I wail along with him.

'Now, now: don't take on so,' Mama tells him. 'My poor girl has really been through the mill: not a wink of sleep with you fretting since the moment you were born.' She turns to Mrs Dickens. 'And a day and night of suffering before that,' she reminds her.

'That's nothing: I laboured for five days and nights with some of mine,' says Charles's mother, gazing up to heaven with her head tilted and chin in the air like a long-suffering saint, 'and I've heard tell of a woman whose pains went on for a week!'

‘A whole week? Are you sure?’ Mother asks.

‘Seven days and seven nights, without a word of a lie,’ Mrs Dickens confirms, pumping up my pillows with her fists.

Mother looks at me and rolls her eyes. We have both heard far too many of these horror stories from my mother-in-law in the past few months.

‘The poor woman was lucky to survive all that,’ Mother says.

‘Oh no, you have the wrong end of the stick there, Mrs Hogarth. The mother died in agony with the baby still stuck inside her,’ Mrs Dickens says triumphantly, never a woman to take kindly to surrendering the last word.

Mother sighs. ‘We should leave Kate in peace for a while so she can get some rest. Let’s wrap the baby up and take him for a wee walk.’ She leans down to take Charley from me and whispers, ‘Pay no heed to her tall tales.’

‘Yes, do stop fretting: you’re upsetting the baby and stopping the milk from flowing,’ Mrs Dickens says, unhelpfully. ‘Much more of this and we’ll have to send for a wet nurse before he starves to death.’

My eyelids are heavy but sleep won’t come. My breasts are madeleine cakes. Jam and desiccated coconut topped with a cherry have been replaced with flakes of dry skin and blood oozing from my cracked nipples, but I would rather die than let another woman feed my baby. If force of will can bring forth a plentiful supply of milk, Charley will be at risk of drowning in a white sea next time I suckle him.

Cracks in the ceiling form a spider’s web. I am a swaddled fly trapped in the middle, waiting to be consumed. Death would be preferable to this limbo-land of motherhood in which I had expected to take pleasure but can find none. It’s hard to remember ever taking pleasure from anything. I try to sit. Pain shoots up between my legs. I lie back again. Pain shoots up my spine. I am Snow White, held captive in a glass coffin, staring out.

Almost out of earshot a baby cries. Muscles, sinews and tendons tense, nipples rise and harden. The cries grow louder and louder until they are outside my room. The door opens slowly. I can hear nothing but screams. They ricochet off the walls and ceiling, and strike me like lightning bolts.

‘Are you asleep, my sweet Hen?’ my mother asks. She closes the door on the commotion behind her.

I shake my head.

'You and the baby both need rest,' she says.

'I'll try suckling him again. Perhaps he'll take his fill and settle down to sleep this time,' I say, but tears belie my effort at optimism. Mother wipes them away gently.

'We may have to think about getting you a wee bit of help,' she says.

'Yes.' I say.

Mother smiles and sighs as if relieved.

'You and Mrs Dickens helped me right through the birth. I'm sure you'll help me feed him too,' I say.

Her smile contorts to a grimace.

'Maybe we need . . . more practical assistance,' she suggests. 'Perhaps you could consider . . . '

Mrs Dickens strides into the room with Charley in her arms. A pale skinny woman with lank hair and spotty face scuttles in after her.

'This is Daisy, the baby's wet nurse,' my mother-in-law shouts over my son's screams.

'My baby doesn't need a wet nurse. I shall feed him myself,' I try to shout back but my voice sounds weak and unconvincing.

'Nonsense. This has gone on quite long enough,' Mrs Dickens says, joggling Charley up and down and patting him on the back with far too much force.

'Let me have him, please,' I beg. 'Give me one more chance.' I reach out my arms. She hands Charley to the woman who is named like a cow. 'No!' I screech. 'Fetch Charles. He won't allow this.'

'Charles has just paid Daisy a month's wages in advance on my advice,' Mrs Dickens says and smiles. 'It's a pity he didn't take my advice about who to marry, too. We wouldn't have had all this trouble with Maria Beadnell.'

I don't even have the energy to gasp at her cruelty. I hate her. I hate Daisy. I even hate Charles. But most of all, I hate myself.

My mother-in-law guides the wet nurse to the nursing chair—my nursing chair. She sits and unbuttons her bodice. I pray my baby will reject her udders but the little turncoat latches straight on to her as if she is his real mother and I'm the imposter. He gives little grunts of contentment. These are even more unbearable than the sound of him crying. I don't want to watch but can't look away.

My sister blocks my view.

'Let's get you cleaned up,' Mary says. 'I've filled the bath downstairs and stoked up the fire.'

She helps me out of bed and takes my arm as I shuffle towards the door. Spots of blood speckle my bare feet.

'She shouldn't be getting up for a month,' Mrs Dickens says.

Mary frowns at her but says nothing.

She steadies me as I step into the bath and lower myself gently into the warm water. I wince as it laps my nipples.

'Lie back,' Mary says, cradling my shoulders. My empty breasts float up to the surface like a pair of hollow haggises.

My little sister bathes me like a baby, supporting my head as she washes my matted hair, sponging away the ache in my neck, soaping my rice pudding of a stomach, sluicing the dried blood from my thighs and the clots stuck to the hair at the top of my legs. The bath water turns as red as a slaughterhouse floor.

'Up you come,' she says. 'I've warmed the towels. Stand by the fire and I'll pat you dry; then you can get back to your baby.'

'I'm not a good mother,' I say.

'Good mothers do what is best for their children, however hard it is for them. All will be well now,' she says. Buoyed by her words I tread a little more lightly as she takes my hand and leads me back to bed.

FRIDAY, 10TH JUNE 1870—6:00 PM

MARY was right. She always was. All was well, at least for a while. She had never left Kate's side during those early months, and had gone with the two of them when Charles had whisked her to Kent to revive her spirits with fresh air and give them both a much-needed break from his mother, who took great pleasure in constantly reiterating her daughter-in-law's many failings.

In Mrs Dickens's opinion, Kate had not coped well with the birth, which had been short and straightforward compared to how badly she had suffered during her own eight confinements. Then there was the feeding failure. She herself had never had a problem and could have wet-nursed twins along with her own babies, had she been called on to do so. And although she did not wish to cast aspersions—for who does?—she couldn't help noticing that Kate had evinced an unnatural aversion to a month of lying-in, something she was sure that Maria, her preferred choice of daughter-in-law, would have welcomed.

Matilda pulls out the footstall from under Kate's chair.

'Let me help you put your feet up, Madam,' she says, lifting them as she speaks. 'Look at your wonderful embroidery. So many bright colours and patterns. Shall I fetch your sewing box?'

'No,' Kate says, 'it was a present from my husband,' and then regrets making her maid blush.

'Something to read then? How about Elizabeth Barrett Browning? You always enjoy her poetry, don't you? I'd read it to you meself but I never learned me letters.'

'Thank you but I'm thinking about my sister,' Kate says.

'Not that Miss Georgina Hogarth, I hope?'

'Not Georgina. Mary—long before your time . . . '

And Kate is no longer a widow. She is back to being a young wife in Kent with a young baby and a young sister to help look after him. They are on one of their long walks and enjoying making fun of Mrs Dickens.

April 1837

'THAT'S not the right way to swaddle him,' Mary says, mimicking my mother-in-law's voice. 'Maria Beadnell would never make that mistake!' She stops to rest at the brow of a hill. 'Maria is blessed with perfect maternal instincts—unlike some I could mention.' My sister nods her head knowingly in my direction and giggles.

I play along. 'You've bound him too tight! That's not nearly tight enough! Don't pick him up when he cries. You're making a rod for your own back, my girl. Give him some laudanum: that will soon get him off to sleep. It never did mine any harm. You need to drink more to get the milk going. A few pints of ale are sure to do the trick. You should get him out in the fresh air no matter what the weather. Snow and ice will put roses in his cheeks. Maria's cheeks were always rosy.'

Mary laughs but struggles to catch her breath.

'Let me carry Charley. He's quite a plump cherub now, thanks to Daisy,' I say.

'Ah yes, dear, dear, darling Daisy. Did I mention it was me who persuaded Charles to take her on? He always listens to his mother,' she says. 'Such an obedient son.'

'He'd do anything to shut her up,' I say and take Charley from her. 'You look tired Mary: shall we turn back now?

'I'm fine,' she says. A gull screeches overhead as if it doesn't believe her.

'There is quite a chill breeze coming off the river this morning. Do speak up if you've had enough,' I say.

'No, no: I've got the lovely comforter you knitted to keep me cosy,' she says. 'Let's give Charles a little longer to get on with his writing undisturbed. He always seems under so much pressure these days with deadline after deadline.'

'He pushes himself to the limit. He's never content. He wants a bigger house and more servants. I'll be much more use to him, now I'm out of confinement,' I say.

'One step out of that bed before the month's up and your insides will drop right out of you,' she says, wagging her finger in my face.

'Maria would never have dreamt of putting a foot to the floor for at least six months,' I add.

'You mark my words, Catherine! I've seen it happen with my own eyes, time and time again.'

I laugh but feel a little guilty. 'We really shouldn't mock Mrs Dickens. Her heart is in the right place and she's had a hard life.'

'Yes, we are wicked, wicked women,' Mary says. She sticks her fingers up either side of her head like devil's horns.

'Everyone thinks you so saintly. They'd have such a shock if they saw you now,' I say.

'I'm an angel,' Mary says, flapping her arms. 'I only have to spread my wings and I'll fly straight up to heaven.' The comforter billows out behind her as it catches the wind.

Charley squirms in my arms and whimpers.

'St Mary, I'm sorry to call you back down to earth but I fear our time is nearly up. Someone is beginning to think about his next meal,' I say and pat Charley's back.

'Did I hear Charles say that Clover is booked to come again at eleven?' Mary asks.

'Yes! I can't believe he's found another wet nurse with a cow's name. Maybe I'd have less trouble if Mother had called me Buttercup?'

'But then I would probably be Bluebell,' Mary says. She moos, bends forward and swings her hips slowly from side to side, for all the world like a cow swaying her way to the milking parlour.

The sound of our laughter soothes Charley back to sleep.

'I've just written to cousin Mary to tell her that he really is the most darling boy, and grows sweeter and lovelier every day, and although he is my own I had to admit I never saw a dearer child,' I say.

Mary takes Charley from me and kisses his forehead. 'I'm to be his godmother soon so he's my darling boy too,' she says.

FRIDAY, 10TH JUNE 1870—6.45 PM

'SHE loved Charley so much,' Kate says.

'Who did, Madam?' Matilda asks.

'My sister Mary,' Kate says. 'I've been thinking about her a lot today. She stayed with us when we were first married and wrote to tell our cousin Mary how happy we were. I have the letter here: my cousin thought it might ease my sorrow. She says, "I have just returned home from spending a most delightfully happy month with dearest Catherine in her own house! I only wish you could see her in it, and sincerely hope you may some day or other." She says I make a most capital housekeeper and that I am as happy as the day is long: she even says that Charles and I are more devoted than ever since our marriage, if such be possible. She's very impressed with Charles: she calls him "such a nice creature" and says he's very clever and always busy with his writing and courted incessantly by the literary world. As for our lodgings in Furnival's Inn in Holborn—"not exactly a house but a suite of rooms opening from one to another"—which Charles has held onto until the end of his three-year tenancy, she says we have furnished them "most tastefully and elegantly", "the drawing-room with Rosewood" and "the dining-room with Mahagony furniture". "M-a-h-a-g-o-n-y"! Mary's spelling was never perfect but I could always rely on her. She looked after me when Charley was born, came with us to Kent when he was just a few months old, and helped with the move to Doughty Street and lived with us there.'

'She sounds like a proper sister, not like that other one. Never right what she did—your own flesh and blood an' all,' Matilda says. 'If you don't mind me sayin',' she adds.

Kate does not mind for Kate is not really there. She is off to the theatre with Mary.

May 1837

'MAKE haste, you two. The carriage awaits and it looks like rain,' Charles shouts from the hallway.

'We are on our way, Dearest,' I shout back, as Mary hands me my umbrella.

I lower my voice and whisper in her ear, 'The play has received mixed reviews so we must take care to reassure Charles of its merit.'

'Of course, of course,' says Mary.

'It's a farce, so we must laugh loudly at every opportunity. Some critics failed to be amused by it.'

'You can rely on me,' Mary replies. 'Ha! Ha! Ha! Ho! Ho! Ho! Will that do?'

'Absolutely not!' I say, but cannot stop laughing with her.

'What is so humorous?' Charles asks as he helps Mary up into the carriage and steadies me as I trip on the steps.

'I was outlining some of the background to the production,' I say, which I was.

'And I find farces hilarious,' Mary says and winks at me.

Charles frowns as I snigger.

'I hate to dampen your spirits, my dear, but you should know that my mother and father have accepted my invitation to accompany us this evening,' he says, sitting opposite us in the carriage and studying my countenance.

I smile and say, 'I'm sure we will all have a most enjoyable evening together.'

'Most enjoyable,' Mary echoes. She pulls her skirt down over her boots, smooths out the creases, wriggles closer to my side and gives me an imperceptible nudge.

'Just like your play will be,' she adds with perfect comic timing.

A puff of air escapes my mouth.

Huh!

A chortle threatens to follow. I wrap my arms around my chest and hold my breath. Mary elbows me in the ribs.

Huh! Huh! Huh!

I dare not look at her as she is sure to wink at me again, so I turn to look through the window. A dog cocks his leg up a lamppost as I mimic a sneeze.

Achoo!

'I do hope you don't have a cold coming,' Charles says. 'Perhaps you should come and sit next to me Mary, dear. We wouldn't want you to catch it.'

Mary sneezes too.

'I fear it is too late to save me!' she says and wafts a hand towards him, like one of his stricken heroines.

'I will come to your rescue,' he says as he reaches for it, eagerly. Her infection, unlike mine, provides him with an opportunity for heroic sympathy.

'You must write a starring role for Mary in your next play, Charles,' I say.

'I must,' he nods. 'She is certainly the most talented of you Hogarth girls.'

Mary releases his hand and squeezes mine. She holds onto it tightly as we reach St James's Theatre.

Mr and Mrs Dickens are already seated in the front of our box. My father-in-law sits with his legs stretched out in front of him. His bent arms form a triangle as he leans back to cushion his head on a pillow of interlaced hands. My mother-in-law is scrunched up beside him as if compensating for his over-abundance. He greets us with a condescending wave but doesn't get up, and pulls her back down as she attempts to stand. We squeeze into the red velvet chairs behind them. Charles sits squashed between Mary's skirts and mine as the curtain rises.

True to her word, Mary laughs loudly throughout the performance—although not always in appropriate places—and sings along to 'A Hunting We Will Go'.

Gentlemen in the audience below us cross their legs one way and then the other and adjust collars they now find uncomfortably tight. Ladies tug at their sleeves and stroke the feathers in their bonnets as if encouraging them to take flight. Cues for laughter are met instead with muttering. Charles has an expression of unconcern fixed on his face, but I fear what may happen if someone takes it into their head to walk out of the performance and thank the Lord that the play is but thirty minutes in length.

The curtain comes down.

'Bravo Charles!' I say and clap loudly, to try and distract him from the muted applause coming from the rest of the audience.

Mary and I rise in the hope of making a quick escape to spare Charles any further embarrassment but, as the lights go up, Mr Dickens Senior gets to his feet. He leans precariously over the edge of the box and gesticulates to those exiting from the stalls below us.

'My Lords, Ladies and Gentlemen,' he says in a voice much louder than the leading man has managed.

Mary looks at me aghast. I roll my eyes and take Charles's left arm. She follows my lead and takes his right.

'You may not be aware that *Is She His Wife? Or, Something Singular!*—this phenomenal one-act play, or burletta, to give it its correct title, that you have been extraordinarily fortunate to have witnessed being performed before you this evening—was in fact written by my son, the one and only, Mr Charles Dickens, the Inimitable Boz! Yes! The very same, very famous, world-renowned author of *The Pickwick Papers*, who is now enthralling readers with each instalment of his poor-little-orphan-boy story, *Oliver Twist*. And, not only that, but he is with us tonight, right beside me in this very theatre! May I present to you the one, the only, Mr Charles Dickens!'

Shoving his wife aside, he pulls Charles towards him and Mary has to grab the back of Mrs Dickens's dress to save her from plunging over the edge of the box. The men and women below us stand in the aisles, raise their arms and applaud like obedient seals at feeding time. Charles looks ill at ease. Their initial half-hearted response will have cut him to the quick, but still he waves, smiles and takes a quick bow. His father bows so low that he hits his head on the edge of the box and is still bobbing up and down as the applause fades and the audience makes its way to the exits.

Out in the rain, Mr Dickens makes a show of feeling in his pockets but finding them empty.

'Could we not squeeze them into the carriage with us?' I ask.

Charles shakes his head and gives his father enough coins to hire a cab.

'He'll probably keep the money and make us walk home,' Mrs Dickens says, bitterly.

I hand her my umbrella.

The ride back is sombre. Charles doesn't say a word. I cannot think of anything to lighten his mood and Mary seems equally at a loss.

He strides through the front door.

'I don't know about you two but I need a brandy and water, or at least a glass of wine,' he says and makes his way down to the basement without waiting for us to answer.

Mary and I go up to the drawing room. I try not to look at her but she catches my eye, winks and hums 'A Hunting We Will Go'.

'Stop it!' I say but Mary has flipped the mood in that way that only she can, and she gallops around the room, holding her skirts above her knees. We both laugh.

'You must come and see the 'orse,' she quotes from the play and drags me around behind her.

'Stop! Charles will catch us if you're not careful,' I say. We perch sedately on the sofa as the door opens and there he stands, carrying a tray with three filled glasses.

'I've sent the servants off to bed. Did I hear banging?' he asks.

'That must have been me poking the fire,' Mary says and gives me another wink.

I gulp down the wine to drown my mirth.

'Steady on, my dear,' Charles says.

'Thirsty,' I say.

Mary says she feels a little tired and is ready to retire.

'I'll come and check on Charley,' I say.

We part with a kiss outside her bedroom.

'Want to come in and see the 'orse?' she asks, as I make my way up to the nursery.

I stop half way up the stairs and look down at her, shake my head and laugh.

'Sleep well, my wicked little sister,' I say.

She neighs, tosses her head and closes the door.

Charley lies peacefully in his crib. His billiard-ball skull is starting to sprout his father's brown wavy hair but he has my more rounded cheeks and what Charles calls my little rosebud mouth. I yearn to pick up my perfect baby, but resist the temptation and content myself with tucking in his blanket and blowing him a kiss.

'God bless, you precious boy,' I say, setting the cradle to rock gently and tiptoeing out.

A strange cry stops me at the top of the stairs. It didn't come from the nursery so I hurry down. Charles is already at Mary's door.

'You heard it too?' he asks, turning the handle.

'She's probably up to some foolery,' I say, as we walk in.

Mary lies on the floor.

'Mary!'

I kneel down and pat her pale face.

'Help me get her onto the bed,' Charles says.

He cradles her in his arms as we call her name over and over and over again.

No response.

No response.

No response.

'Wake the servants. Send for the doctors,' Charles says.

I want to stay with my sister but I do what he asks, then return and kneel beside her bed, praying.

The doctors arrive, frown and shake their heads. They say that Mary's heart is failing and that there is nothing they can do.

This cannot be true. Mary is young and full of life. Minutes ago she was galloping around and laughing. There must be something they can do to save her.

Charles puts some brandy to her lips but it runs down her chin.

We keep vigil.

We watch over her like powerless guardian angels.

Pray, pray, pray for the Lord to spare her.

I would ask Him to take me in her place but Charley needs me and so does the new life growing inside me.

At three o'clock in the morning my sweet sister's heart beats no more. She dies in my husband's arms.

'So perfect a creature never breathed. She had not a fault,' Charles says. He takes the ring from her finger and cuts a lock of her hair.

Grief stabs me. I clutch my stomach, bend double and hobble

towards the door. Alone in our bedroom I take a towel from the washstand to stem the blood that's flowing down my legs. Stab, stab, stab in the stomach. I howl and crawl around on all fours, leaving a trail of gore behind me.

Hush! Hush!

I must not disturb Charles. He has more than enough to bear.

As I stand, clots of blood fall to the floor like lumps of liver ready to be fried but swaddled inside one of them is a tiny grey sac, and I know my baby has gone to Heaven with my sister.

Friday, 10th June 1870—7:10 pm

MATILDA takes a seat opposite her mistress, folds her hands in her lap and keeps quiet. Kate rambles.

'We had made plans to go back to the cottage when the warmer weather came, blissfully unaware that Mary would not see that summer . . . She gave so much love to everyone that her heart gave out . . . She died in my husband's arms . . . He took the ring from her finger and placed it on his own hand and there it has remained. I have no doubt it will go to the grave with him . . . My mother was so grief stricken, I feared for her sanity . . . It was all my husband could do to keep her from the room where Mary lay in her coffin . . . .

'When we separated, Mother gave me the letters Charles had written to her at the time. Do you want to see them?'

Kate does not wait for an answer. She sifts through the pile of correspondence.

'Here we are,' she says, waving a letter at her maid. 'Listen to this. He writes that he wishes she had gone out for a walk. "You cannot think how much it would please me," he says. "It is really time you made the effort. If it were painful at first, you would very soon find ample compensation in the additional strength and cheerfulness which I am sure it would give you."

'I was shocked that he could write that to a mother whose seventeen-year-old daughter had just died. And that was not the end of it. A few months later he wrote again, insisting she should think of "the many remaining claims upon her affection and exertions, rather than give way to unavailing grief". Perhaps I should have said something but, as usual, I kept quiet. Too late now. Should I have spoken up?'

'That's really not for me to say, Madam, but I do know you need to stop taxing yourself with all this and take some rest,' Matilda says and places a cushion behind Kate's head.

Old habits die hard. Kate remains silent about her husband's numerous shortcomings and doesn't tell Matilda about her own grief and how it caused her to lose the baby she was carrying.

'The next letter I wrote to my cousin Mary was to ask her to take my sister's place as Charley's godmother,' Kate says. She rests her head on the cushion and closes her eyes.

She feels an arm around her shoulders and a hand on her wet face. She tries to persuade herself that it is Mary. There is such comfort in the touch that, for just a little while longer, she won't open her eyes and destroy the illusion. Then, with her next inhalation, she detects the unmistakable scent of her firstborn baby. Kate smiles.

'Charley,' she says.

'Yes, Mother. I'm here now,' he says.

Kate risks opening her eyes and there is her son, no longer a screaming baby but a fully-grown man—with her nose, her rounded face and her soft blue eyes beneath his father's wavy brown hair.

'Charley.' She says his name again.

He takes her hands in his.

'I'm so sorry, Mama. I have only just been able to get away,' he says. 'Lucifer Box will travel tonight and be with you early tomorrow morning.'

Stubble scratches her fingers as she strokes his cheek.

'Do not concern yourself on my account. I am quite well,' she says, unwilling to distress her son.

'Your maid said Aunt Georgina didn't send you a telegram?'

Kate does not trust herself to speak, so just shakes her head.

Charley frowns.

'You collapsed in the street when you found out about father?'

'I felt a little dizzy.' This is not a lie. She had felt dizzy before her legs gave way.

'And you arrived back at the front door on the arm of a gypsy?'

'Did I?' Kate really cannot remember. 'How kind of her to take pity on me.'

'And how kind of you to say that, Mama, but Matilda had to buy a sprig of lavender to get rid of her. Cost her tuppence!'

'I'll get my purse,' Kate says, upset at the thought of all those who would now seek to profit from her misfortune.

'Don't worry, I've already recompensed her.'

'Thank you, Charley, and thank you for your concern. I am at fault for trusting my sister when I should know better by now.'

'I have never condoned her behaviour but at least she sent word to me and the others, and it is possible that shock may have affected her judgement on this occasion,' Charley says.

'Oh no! Did my poor Charles suffer? I cannot bear to think of him dying in pain.' Kate kneads her skirt as if she's about to bake bread.

'Father was having dinner at Gad's Hill Place with Aunt Georgina when he took ill. She said he slipped down onto the floor and fell into a deep sleep. I was summoned and ensured he had the best doctors but nothing could be done to save him. He lingered on for twenty-four hours but without recovering his senses. They said it was apoplexy.'

Kate shakes her head slowly.

'Over-exertion—that's what killed him,' she says. 'I wish I could have made him rest. I should have been by his side at the end. I would have told him how dearly I loved him.'

'He wouldn't have heard you, Mother, but I'm certain he never doubted the strength of your feelings. Rest assured that father died peacefully.'

'Praise the Lord for His mercy,' Kate says.

'I left a copy of today's *Times* in the hall. I'll fetch it so you can take comfort from the obituary.'

Kate nods, although she has often been scarred by what is printed about her and doubts she will find much comfort today.

Charley returns and hands her the newspaper.

'Shall we sit together on the sofa?' she asks.

Charley nods and helps her up. She stands painfully, takes his arm and leans on him, grateful that he slows his pace to match hers as they make their way, step by step, across the room and sit side by side. She spreads the newspaper out on her lap and reads:

> One whom young and old, wherever the English language is spoken, have been accustomed to regard as a personal friend is

suddenly taken away from among us. CHARLES DICKENS is no more. The loss of such a man is an event which makes ordinary expressions of regret seem cold and conventional. It will be felt by millions as nothing less than a personal bereavement. Statesmen, men of science, philanthropists, the acknowledged benefactors of their race might pass away, and yet not leave the void which will be caused by the death of DICKENS. They may have earned the esteem of mankind; their days may have been passed in power, honour, and prosperity; they may have been surrounded by troops of friends, but, however pre-eminent in station, ability, or public services, they will not have been, like our great and genial novelist, the intimate of every household. Indeed, such a position is attained not even by one man in an age. It needs an extraordinary combination of intellectual and moral qualities to gain the hearts of the public as DICKENS has gained them. Extraordinary and very original genius must be united with good sense, consummate skill, a well-balanced mind, and the proofs of a noble and affectionate disposition before the world will consent to enthrone a man as their unassailable and enduring favourite. This is the position which Mr. DICKENS has occupied with the English and also with the American public for the third of a century. It has been his peculiar fortune to appeal to that which is common to all sorts and conditions of men, to excite the interest of the young and the uninstructed, without shocking the more refined taste of a higher class and a more mature age. Thus the news of his death will hardly meet the eye of an educated man or woman who has not read his works and who has not been accustomed to think of him with admiration and friendly regard.

He was born in February, 1812, and has consequently not long attained his fifty-eighth year. As men live and work now, this is an age which would give the hope of many years of successful exertion, to be succeeded by a period of honoured repose. But we have this consolation, that the life of Dickens has been long enough to allow full scope for his genius, and to enable him not only to earn, but to enjoy his fame. In this respect his career has been extraordinary. He was one whose marvellous powers were developed early, and he attained the highest eminence in the first years of his literary career. It is certainly a wonderful phenomenon that a book like "*Pickwick*," the pages of which overflow with humour, and are marked in every sentence with the keenest observation of men and things, should have been produced by a young man of 24. After the light but clever "*Sketches by Boz*," DICKENS began "*Pickwick*" in 1836, and finished it in the course of the succeeding year. We are inclined to think that this, the first considerable work of the author, is his masterpiece; but, whatever may be the world's decision on this point, it can hardly be doubted that the prize must be given to one of the group of fictions which he produced within the first ten or twelve years of his literary life. "*Nicholas Nickleby*" teems with wit, and the characters, with one or two exceptions, are life-like in the extreme. "*Oliver Twist*" everybody knows; "*Martin Chuzzlewit*" is excellent, and the American portions are not only the most amusing satire that has been published in the present age, but fill us with wonder that the peculiarities of thought, manner and diction of a people should be so surely seized and so inimitably expressed by a young writer who had been only a few months in the country.

When young in years he showed the mental balance of an experienced writer. And yet what freshness and vigour there were in those wonderful serials which, about the time the present QUEEN came to the throne, changed the popular literature of the day! When that young, unknown author appeared on the field he was at once hailed as the new chief of popular fiction. It is a long time ago, but our older readers will remember the excitement caused by the "*Pickwick Papers*." The shilling numbers of "*Boz*", carried everything before them. They were read here by tens of thousands, though the reading public 30 years ago was not what it is now; and they were reprinted in every possible form in America. In fact, half the newspapers in the States transferred them to their columns bodily the day after their arrival. This popularity they fully deserved. They are among the few books of the kind that one can return to again and again, or, having opened at any page, can read straight on, carried forward by a sense of real enjoyment. The characters of DICKENS have been accepted by all men's discernment as the true reflection of human nature; not merely of manners or costumes. SQUEERS is to everybody the low, tyrannical schoolmaster; BUMBLE the representative of parochial pomposity; Mrs. GAMP is the type of her vulgar, hard-hearted sisterhood. Perhaps a more signal proof of the genius of DICKENS is the manner in which his style and diction have penetrated into the ordinary literature of the country. So much has become naturalized and is used quite unconsciously that it is only by re-reading those earlier works which most impressed his

> contemporaries that one becomes aware how great has been their influence.
>
> We cannot conclude these remarks without paying a tribute of the moral influence of the writings of which we have spoken. Mr. DICKENS was a man of an eminently kindly nature, and full of sympathy for all around him. This, without being paraded, makes itself manifest in his works, and we have no doubt whatever that much of the active benevolence of the present day, the interest in humble persons and humble things, and the desire to seek out and relieve every form of misery is due to the influence of his works. We feel that we have lost one of the foremost Englishmen of the age. There are clever writers enough, but no one who will take the place, literary and social, that belonged to him. It was but the other day that at the Royal Academy banquet he made the best speech of the evening, in matter, language, and manner. His powers as an actor are well known, though, of late years, they have been only exhibited in the narrower field of public readings. He was made to be popular, and, even irrespective of his literary genius, was an able and strong-minded man, who would have succeeded in almost any profession to which he devoted himself. We can but condole with the public on his sudden and premature loss.

Kate gets to her feet, flapping the newspaper angrily in her hand.

'Moral qualities?' she says and rips the paper in half.

Charley leaps to her side.

'Mother!' he shouts as he tries to restrain her but there is no stopping Kate.

'A well-balanced mind?'

Rip

'A noble and affectionate disposition?'

Rip

'An eminently kindly nature?'

Rip

'Full of sympathy for all around him?'

Rip

'Desire to seek out and relieve every form of misery?'

Rip

'Strong-minded? Well at least they got that one right!'

Pages from the *Times* lie shredded on the carpet.

Kate looks at her son vacantly as if nothing has happened.

'You'll be able to fill next week's edition of *All the Year Round* ten times over with obituaries like this, all written by men—always men—who only saw one side of your father. I think,' she says and pauses for a moment to deliberate; 'I think it is time I set the record straight, starting with the visit to America.'

Charley stays silent.

Kate stares at her son but doesn't see him. A raven obscures her vision.

October 1841

'WE need money and I need a break from writing novels,' Charles insists as he stomps up and down the parlour. Grip, his pet raven, struts along behind him.

'Charles, my love, we can manage and you can take a break without travelling to the other side of the world,' I say trailing after the malicious bird.

Charles turns so sharply that we almost collide. Grip flutters onto the back of the sofa to avoid being crushed between us and fixes me with his gimlet eyes.

'Perhaps you would care to explain how I am to write about America without setting foot in the country?' Charles asks. 'Shall I stare at the red, white and blue flag for inspiration? Say red is for the blood shed in their war of independence? Well?'

'Well? Well? Well?' Grip asks.

'White for the snow on the Rocky Mountains? Blue for the waters of the Atlantic Ocean?'

I step back. Charles steps forward and prods me in the chest.

'Would you have me pluck a feather from a chicken, stick it behind my ear and imagine I'm a Red Indian?'

With one eye on the bird I take a seat on the sofa and pat the cushion to my right. 'Pray, sit beside me, Charles, so we can discuss this matter calmly,' I say.

He ignores my suggestion but Grip, apparently disturbed by the mention of feathers being plucked, jumps from the back to the arm of the sofa. Stiff as a clockwork toy he twists his head and looks at me quizzically, as if wondering why I'm bothering to argue with his master, who towers over us both like an oak tree.

'There-is-nothing-to-discuss!' says Charles, stabbing out each word with his right forefinger, while he rests his left hand on his hip. 'I-am-going-to-America! You-are-coming-with-me! You-promised-to-honour-and-obey!'

'Obey, obey, obey,' Grip nods approvingly.

'I would follow you willingly to the ends of the earth, my Darling, but what about our children?' I ask.

He taps his foot.

'Arrangements can be made,' he says emphatically.

'How long would we be away?' I ask quietly.

Charles shrugs his shoulders. 'Just a few weeks,' he says, as if time is immaterial.

The longcase clock in the hall seems to contradict him. It chimes and strikes the hour.

'Dong, dong, dong,' Grip tolls.

'Each day will seem like a year to little Charley,' I say, hoping the crack in my voice and the reminder of his four-year old son will make Charles think again.

'Children are adaptable and we'll be back before he even notices we're gone,' he says, flapping his hands as if to wave away my concerns.

Grip takes fright, and hides beneath the sofa. He makes screaming noises, just as the children do when he pecks them.

Mentioning Charley hasn't made his father reconsider but maybe thoughts of the little ones will. 'What about the girls—and baby Walter? They are too young to be left with strangers for weeks on end,' I plead.

Charles sighs. He raises his eyes as if appealing for divine help.

'Are you being deliberately obtuse?' he asks. 'They wouldn't be "left with strangers". Fred has already offered to keep an eye on them and the Macreadys will help too.'

Clearly, it has all been already arranged behind my back and I am the last to know. This is hurtful but it will not further my case to say so.

I try a different tack. 'Fred is a wonderful uncle and there is no denying that they love to play with him but, let us be realistic, Charles: he can barely look after himself, let alone four young children—and as for Macready, he's never off the stage these days, and Kitty is busy with her own little ones.' I reach for his hand but Charles turns away and storms off like an enraged bull.

'Whine as much as you like,' he shouts from the hallway. 'I have made up my mind.' He storms out of the front door, slamming it behind him.

'Bang! Bang! Bang!' says Grip.

'Do be quiet,' I say. 'When you screech your last, he'll rush out, buy a replacement bird and feed you to the cat before you're cold.'

Grip holds his head high, flaps his wings and flies out of the window in search of his master.

'I'll come to America with you,' he'll squawk. 'We don't need her.'

FRIDAY, 10TH JUNE 1870—7:25 PM

'I DIDN'T want to go,' Kate tells Charley.

'I know, Mother, I know. Please don't distress yourself.'

'I told him you were too young to leave. Your father said a few weeks but he knew all along it would be a good six months.'

'Six months . . . !'

'When I argued, he sent his friends to persuade me.'

'Forster and Macready? That's just the sort of thing he'd do.'

'And then there were the books. Just the way it was before we were married.'

'Books, Mother?'

'About a wife's duty. One of them was a true story. A poor woman's husband was wounded at the battle of Waterloo. The husband died. It made me cry.'

'I can see how it would do that, Mother. Are you quite well? Shall I ask Matilda to fetch you something?'

'You could fetch the portrait. I commissioned it especially.'

Charley looks in the sideboard drawer. He finds a picture of his father as a young man and hands it to her.

Kate looks surprised.

'Not that one! He gave me that one when we were engaged. I want the one of you, Mamie, Lucifer Box and Walter. Maclise painted it before we sailed. I showed it to everyone we met, kissed each of your images every bedtime and slept with it under my pillow every night we were away.'

Charley searches the sideboard. A plaster Pickwick figure rests on top of a picture frame. He holds the portly little gentleman up to show his mother but it falls from his hand and smashes on the floor.

'I'm desperately sorry,' he says, picking up the pieces and placing them carefully on the side table. 'I'll try and glue them back together.'

'No matter,' Kate says. 'I have a box full of them in the attic, along with Pickwick canes, Pickwick hats, Pickwick coats and Pickwick cigars. The obituary was right in that regard: people couldn't get enough of him. Your father was mobbed all over America. Admirers even tried to snip cloth from his coat. He soon wearied of it.'

Charley slides the picture frame out carefully.

'Is this the right one?' he asks.

'That's it.' Kate takes it from him and kisses the four little faces through the glass.

'When your father fell ill with a fistula not long before we were due to depart, I hoped he would call off the trip, but with my tender care as his nurse, amanuensis and secretary after the operation, he recovered in time. Such irony! Five days later my grandmother died, and my twenty-year-old brother George two weeks after that. My heart longed for me to stay and console my mother but your father would not hear of it. If I loved him, I was duty-bound to accompany him, he said. I did love him and, despite everything, I still do.'

'I know you do, Mother, and you have told us many times over the years how hard it was for you to leave us and undertake such an arduous journey. Father loved you and wanted you with him. It would not have been practical to take four young children with you. In that he was right. And he often told me what a wonderful travelling companion you were.'

'Did he? Truly? Charley, do you think he ever did love me? I have been asking myself that a lot today. I did my best to be a good wife, before Ellen Ternan took centre stage, but how could I compete with a professional actress less than half my age?' The thought of Ellen brings Kate's warmer feelings for her husband to an abrupt end.

'Try not to think about all that today, Mother.' Charley pats her on the shoulder and smiles. 'Father is dead and we have all survived unscathed.'

It dawns on Kate that it is her son who is acting, now.

'You don't remember, do you?' she asks.

'Remember what, Mama?'

'You don't remember what happened when we got back?' Kate holds her breath and clutches the portrait tight to her bosom.

'We were all very pleased to see you and grateful for your safe return,' Charley says.

Kate says nothing.

'And I think that was when Aunt Georgina moved in with us.'

Kate feels as if she has turned to stone.

'But I really should be getting home now, if you're sure you can spare me.' He kisses her cheek.

Kate inhales deeply but doesn't look up at Charley. She stares instead at his face in the portrait and sees her little boy smile as she enters the nursery on her return from the USA.

July 1842

'CHARLEY!' I shout, and run towards him with arms outstretched, ready to give my lovely boy the biggest hug of his life. He jumps off his rocking horse and races towards me but stumbles. 'I'm too glad!' he says and falls to the floor.

I'm in danger of tripping over my feet in my rush to reach him.

'Up you get,' I say. 'Charley? Come now, this is not the time for playacting . . . '

His eyes roll back into his head and his little body judders.

'Charles!' I scream.

Charles quickens his pace towards us. Fred runs over. He picks up Charley's limp body and lays him on the sofa. I sit with my precious son's head on my lap and stroke his hot forehead.

'Is he going to die?' I ask Charles.

He kneels beside us. 'Of course not, but I'll send for Dr Morgan and Dr Elliotson. They're the best in the land.'

FRIDAY, 10TH JUNE 1870—7:40 PM

'ELLIOTSON explained that joy had overthrown your system, affected your brain and brought about the seizure. Your father concluded that you were a very queer fellow, quite different from your sisters and brother, and too sensitive—like me,' Kate says.

She looks around the parlour. No one is there. Perhaps it's just as well. Her son hadn't needed to hear any of that. She has no recollection of saying goodbye to him, and hopes she didn't neglect to kiss his cheek, wish him farewell and send her love to his wife and precious little children, as she always does.

Four little faces gaze up at her from the portrait. She can hear Charles gloating that he was right: that there was never any cause for concern, that Charley remembers nothing and that the other children remember nothing too, but Kate knows that some harm is so hard to bear that it lies buried deep beneath the memory, burrowed into the very heart of one's being.

Kate mops her brow. She finds the heat oppressive. Matilda brings her a glass of lemonade and asks if there is anything else she can fetch, but Kate wants only peace and quiet now, so she can think about other foreign trips. She may have lost the American battle but she congratulates herself on winning a different war, two-and-a-half years and another son later. Sales of *Martin Chuzzlewit* had been disappointing, so Charles had decided to save money by moving to Italy for a year and earn extra money by writing about the trip. But this time, there was no question of leaving the children behind, and Charley, Mamie, Lucifer Box, Walter and baby Frank were all to go with them.

Letting Devonshire Terrace for twelve months had been a nightmare. The tenants insisted on moving in before the Dickenses were ready to sail, which meant that the whole family—along with their servants: Anne, Charlotte and Jane, the cook—had been forced to pack up and move into temporary lodgings for a few weeks, before packing again for the voyage.

As their carriage trundled through France in stifling heat, Kate had consoled herself with thoughts of their anticipated destination: the Villa di Bagnerello, with its high walls overlooking vineyards and the Bay of Genoa. After a journey of two weeks they were welcomed by a pink-painted house infested with a thousand fleas. Shortly thereafter another bloodsucking parasite would threaten to leech the life from her marriage.

July 1844

DUST falls from the walls as my lady's maid, Anne Brown, beats the beds. Her hair and eyes have always matched her surname and now her skin is turning brown too.

'Don't worry, Madam, I'll soon get the little blighters under control,' she says and coughs.

Lucifer Box pulls at my skirt and complains in a loud voice that she cannot speak as her throat is still sore, although I'd promised last night that she'd feel better this morning if she was a good girl and went to sleep.

'I want to go home!' she shouts.

I want to go home too. In fact, I had never wanted to leave home, but I can't say so, so I hoist my little girl up onto my hip and walk over to the window. 'Look at the lovely view of the sea we have here. We don't get that in smelly old London,' I say.

'When can we go home?' she asks. Sea views are obviously not a priority for Lucifer Box.

'Look, the sea is the same colour as the pretty stones in Mama's engagement ring,' I say. 'Do you remember what this colour is?'

She feigns innocence by opening her eyes wide, looks straight up at me and says, 'Bluey green?' knowing full well the answer is 'turquoise'.

But she is only four years old and homesick and poorly, so I don't take the bait and say, 'Yes, clever girl; and the special name for that is?' to give her a second chance.

'Bluey green,' she repeats. Lucifer Box was named Catherine after me but earned her unholy nickname from inheriting her father's hellish temper along with his looks and temperament, particularly his determination to get his own way at all costs.

'Well done. That's a very good description of turquoise,' I say, and smile to show she cannot rile me into submission.

She wriggles off my hip, slides down to the floor, walks over to Anne, smiles up at her sweetly and says, 'My throat is so sore I can't speak. Please will you take me home?'

Anne stops beating the bedding, scratches the flea bites on her arms, and says she would if she could but that this house is home for now.

My devilish daughter runs from the room screaming, 'Take me home! Take me home! Take me home!' at the top of her non-existent voice.

Frank wakes from his morning nap and starts to cry.

Charley calls up from the hallway, 'Are you all right, Mother?'

I reach the top of the staircase just as Lucifer Box reaches the bottom. She knocks over Walter who screams even louder than his sister and Frank put together.

Mamie comes in at the front door. Hands on hips she assesses the situation, helps Walter back on his feet, tells Lucifer Box to stop being a baby and goes off to comfort Frank. We were right to christen her 'Mary', after my dear sister, for she has a calming influence on everyone. The door to Charles's study is flung open. He flies out, his face as puce as his flea bites.

'How in God's name do you expect me to work in this pandemonium?' he shouts.

Lucifer Box says nothing. Charley looks at me. Walter concentrates on rubbing his sore knees.

'I'm sorry you were disturbed, Charles. Georgina and I will take the children down to the bay soon,' I say.

'I'd rather your sister stayed here to help me, but take her if you're incapable of managing alone,' he says.

The commotion has woken Fred. He runs down the stairs in his nightshirt, like a ghost whose haunting shift has expired, and the children rush up to him. He tousles Charley's hair and lifts Walter onto his shoulders.

'Uncle Fred, Uncle Fred, will you please take me home?' Lucifer Box pleads.

'I'm not Uncle Fred. I'm Fearsome Fred the Pirate and I'm going to take you all down to the sea, so we can sail away on my pirate ship,' he says.

Charley claps his hands. Walter copies him and nearly falls off Fred's shoulders. My dear husband storms back into his study and slams the door.

'It looks like the captain won't be coming on board today,' Fred says. He grabs my arm and hoists it above my head. 'But who have we here?' he asks. 'It's the first mate! She'll keep us all in order.'

'Right, me hearties: let's get ready to go,' I say and do a little jig as I take Lucifer Box's hand.

Fred lifts Walter down from his shoulders. 'Anyone not shipshape by the time I'm dressed will be forced to walk the plank,' he says and runs back upstairs.

'Me? Plank?' Walter says in the wobbly voice he uses when asking if there are monsters under his bed.

'No, no plank for Walter. You are my very important cabin boy,' I say and kiss his cheek as I pick him up.

Charley cringes as Charles's study door opens, but it is only Georgina.

'I hear we are off to the seashore. Let's make a trip to the outhouse before we go.' She pulls Lucifer Box away from me and lifts Walter out of my arms.

I seem to have been cast adrift and so I go to fetch Frank.

Charley brings me my parasol. 'Let's go outside and wait for them in the sunshine,' he says. 'I'll carry Frank for you.'

Fred sings sea shanties all the way to the bay. The children join in with their own interpretations of the lyrics and the tunes. Lucifer Box's throat seems to have made a miraculous recovery.

Charlotte puts down rugs. I lay Frank down and he waggles his legs like an upturned crab. We sit in a circle and I unpack the picnic Jane has prepared for us. I give Walter a piece of pie, but he drops it in the sand and cries.

'Never mind, watch this,' I say and throw the wasted pastry up in the air. A seagull swoops down and catches it in its beak. Walter laughs, takes another slice and drops that in the sand too.

'Feed bird, Mama,' he says.

'Once more only and then you must eat all the rest like a big boy,' I say.

Three gulls swoop and fight for the second slice. The children cheer the winner. Baby Frank coos his approval. Georgina says gulls must not be encouraged and shuts the lid of the hamper. With a squawk of resentment the birds fly off to follow the fishing boats.

Fred strips off his shirt and says he's going for a swim. The children want to go with him but he says they must stay on the shore and look out for sharks.

'Be sure to shout if you see one,' he says as he rushes headlong into the water and swims off.

Four little faces watch his progress with their hands shading their eyes.

'I'm sure that's a shark's fin,' Charley shouts.

Lucifer Box runs up and down the beach. 'Where, where?'

'Don't be silly,' Mamie says.

Walter rushes up to sit on my lap. He sucks his thumb.

'Don't worry. There are no sharks. It's just a game,' I say and rock him gently, to and fro. He closes his eyes and his whole sleeping body sags like a sack of flour in my arms. Sunlight sparkling on the sea, the gentle shush of waves, the chatter of children and murmurs of adult conversation lull me almost to the point of slumber but my head jolts up as Charley shouts for Uncle Fred, and the others join in a chorus of 'Uncle Fred! Uncle Fred!'

It's a struggle to get to my feet with Walter in my arms. He joggles about as I run to the water's edge, hoping this is all part of the shark game. Georgina and Charlotte follow in my wake.

Fred is a long way out, bobbing up and down, his head breaking the surface of the water and then ducking below it.

'Help! Help!' I shout, just in case he's not playacting. Everyone joins in.

Walter wakes with a start.

'Shark!' he shouts.

'No, there's no shark,' I say, and set him down.

Fred waves his arms like a maniac and disappears again. This is no performance. He's drowning in front of my eyes.

I cup my hands to the sides of my mouth, and scream so loudly and so long that my head starts to spin, but I fill my lungs and scream and scream and scream again.

Fred floats face down.

A burly fisherman rows to the rescue.

Too late?

Is it too late?

Strong arms drag the limp body on board as if merely landing an outsize catch.

The children are crying. Should I ask Georgina and Charlotte to take them back to the villa or would that cause even more distress?

'Let's all say a silent prayer for Uncle Fred,' I say.

'Uncle Fred,' says Walter and hiccoughs.

As the boat nears the shore Fred sits up and a stream of water pours out of his mouth. It is clear our prayers have been answered.

My skirts cushion my fall as my legs give way.

Fred jumps out of the boat. The children run into the water to meet him.

'Come out of there at once! Your clothes will be ruined,' Georgina shouts but no one takes any notice of her.

Fred picks up Walter, holds Lucifer Box's hand and kicks his foot to spray Charley and Mamie. 'Did you see the size of that shark Fearsome Fred fought off?' he asks.

Walter looks up at Uncle Fred and over to me. I smile and shake my head.

'Don't worry, he won't come back to this beach in a hurry now he's met a real pirate,' Fred says.

FRIDAY, 10TH JUNE 1870—8:00 PM

THE lemonade has not been touched. Kate shivers and rubs her upper arms, not because she is cold but at the thought of what was to come with their next move.

Should she take off her wedding ring, now she is no longer a wife? What about her engagement ring, with its turquoise stones? She cannot bring herself to do so. The turquoise has lost its lustre. She rubs the rings against the black silk of her dress, as if trying to conjure a genie, and wonders what her three wishes would be. Her first is to bring Charles, her baby and all her loved ones back from the dead. With the second she banishes Ellen Ternan and Augusta De la Rue from ever appearing in their lives. With the little actress and the perpetual invalid out of the way, she doesn't really need to bother the genie again but, just to be on the safe side, she uses her third wish to ask for her husband's love and to change fate so that she'd never lost it.

If only that Italian summer had not faded so fast; if only the encroaching autumn had not dampened the family's spirits along with the villa's walls; if only Charles had not been forced to admit they could not spend the winter in Villa Bagnerello; if only he had not moved them into town and into the orbit of the De la Rues.

At first Kate had believed a magic wand had been waved to transform all their lives for the better. Palazzo Peschiere, with its frescoed walls, grand *sala*, sea views, fishponds and beautiful gardens, had seduced the whole family. Walter no longer had nightmares about sharks, and Frank thrived—thanks to Valentina, his new wet nurse and the latest in a long line going back to those early days with Daisy. Charley relaxed as much as he ever could in his father's company, and no longer spent his days watching out for Kate's welfare. Mamie felt free to relinquish some of her big-sister role and became more of a little girl again. Lucifer Box rarely asked to be taken home, even when friends from England visited. Best of all, romance had re-entered her marriage. Compassionate days were now complemented by passionate nights.

In the twilight of this first day of widowhood, Kate's mind is illuminated by Italian sunlight.

September 1844

WARM air strokes my sun-kissed skin as I take my husband's arm and stroll with him along the harbour wall. Inky waves caress the sand below. Sleepy boats rock to-and-fro, clinking music from their chains in the dark evening. Along the shoreline, restaurants beacon their welcome. Charles and I will sit on a terrace with silhouetted diners and sip liquid sunshine.

Friday, 10th June 1870—8:02 pm

CHARLES revelled in his role as an English nobleman on a Grand Tour of Italy and Kate was glad to become once again his intrepid travelling companion—climbing the Leaning Tower of Pisa, throwing sugar plums to crowds during the Roman Carnival, attending high mass at St Peter's, watching ballerina Fanny Cerrito perform, ascending to the peak of Mount Vesuvius.

But the magic interlude vanished back in Genoa when Augusta De la Rue, with her dark hair and dark rings under her eyes, made her appearance at one of their dinner parties and a shadow fell across their union once again.

There had always been dinner parties. Kate has lost count of how many they gave and attended over the years. She loved to plan the menus and put their guests at ease but she also enjoyed seeing Charles in his element, telling stories and spellbinding the great and the good at their table. Moments before their arrival he would be stomping around, complaining about the cost of wine and resenting his wasting precious writing time on toadies and humbugs. But as soon as the toadies and humbugs were seated around him, it was as if a curtain rose and he was transformed into his pseudonym—Boz the Inimitable, the consummate performer.

Kate tries to remember who else had been present on that fateful De la Rue evening. Charles was always in charge of the guest list and was charm personified when issuing invitations he later regretted. Among their regular guests were the British consul-general, Timothy Yeats Brown, and his wife Stuarta; Charles Gibbs, a Genoa-based banker whom Charles had befriended during that summer stay in 1844; and Sir George and Hester Crawford—but was this the first time the Swiss banker Emile De la Rue had been invited, along with his English wife Augusta? Kate is not sure.

It was definitely December because Charles had just returned to Italy after a brief trip back to England to read the latest draft of *The Chimes* to friends, and was in high spirits from their positive reaction. Plum pudding was probably on the menu but definitely goose, as their cook, Jane, had fretted that the delay caused by the late arrival of Mr and Mrs De la Rue would dry the bird out.

Kate recalls looking at the two empty chairs at their dining room table, and at the clock, and wondering how long Charles would make everyone wait for his new friends to make their appearance.

December 1844

EMILE De la Rue enters, red-faced. He apologises profusely for inconveniencing everyone but explains that his wife suffers from the vapours. Although she very much wanted to attend, her courage has failed her and she remains rooted to a seat in the hallway. He fears he will have to escort her home.

Charles immediately offers his services as a master of

mesmerism, and is out of the door before Emile can stop him. This, I realise, is the moment my husband has been waiting for. Having studied under the eminent Dr Elliotson and been impressed with how he had treated Charley's emotional reaction when we returned from America, Charles has always looked for someone of his own to save.

Emile takes his seat, mops his brow with a napkin and knocks back a glass of wine. Without Charles, the atmosphere in the room deflates like a hot air balloon relieved of its burner. An awkward silence ensues. I encourage the guests to help themselves to more Burgundy, excuse myself and slip out to have a word with Cook, who is likely to become distraught now we are being made to wait even longer.

I don't wish to interrupt Charles, of course, and know he will be peeved with me if I do, but I have to cross the hallway to gain access to the kitchen and, I confess, I would like to catch a glimpse of him ministering to his patient, but Madame De la Rue is no longer seated on the hall chair. There is no sign of my husband either. He must have escorted her into the grand *sala*, wishing for a more private consultation in impressive surroundings.

In the kitchen, sweat is dripping off Jane as she stirs a steaming pan with a wooden spoon. She looks around, drops the spoon, says 'it's a disaster' and bursts into tears. I wipe my soup-splattered dress, shush her and suggest she take the goose out of the stove, so it can be sliced and covered with a serving dish to keep it warm and moist. I reassure her that the plum pudding can continue to simmer away without either drying up or drowning, as it is protected by its muslin shroud. It is the soup that is the main concern. Keeping it hot has caused quite a bit of evaporation; Jane laughs when I suggest we solve the problem by renaming it 'potage'.

I return to my seat in the dining room just as Charles and Madam De la Rue make their triumphant entry. It feels as though they have been gone an age, but it's probably been no more than thirty minutes.

Charles is neither a tall nor a well-built man but he looks positively statuesque next to the pale, twitchy pixie at his side. I am appalled by her red dress—such a gaudy, attention-seeking colour—and wonder if she wears curly-toed elfin shoes beneath its hem. I dislike the way she looks up at my husband admiringly and dislike even more the way my husband smiles down at her and strokes the hand she has seen fit to rest on his arm. In truth, there is not much I can find to admire in Madame Augusta De la Rue. She is adorned with far too many flounces and frills for a simple dinner, and this leads me to question if the equally ostentatious diamonds round her tiny neck are genuine or paste.

Our guests applaud the happy couple, congratulate Charles on whatever he did for Madame De la Rue, and salute the pixie-woman herself on her courage in joining us. Because of their delay, the soup is spoiled and I am left with a bitter taste in my mouth. The taste becomes even more bitter when Charles rearranges the table plan so that Augusta can sit beside him, and I fear she will monopolise his attention.

FRIDAY, 10TH JUNE 1870—8:45 PM

KATE'S presentiment was correct. Her husband neglected her and all their other guests, and spent the entire evening engrossed in conversation with Augusta. After that night she was never far from his side. Kate twists her wedding band around her finger. Round and round it goes, along with her thoughts of Charles and how she fought long and hard to break his obsession with this strange De la Rue woman.

March 1845

'JEALOUSY is unbecoming, Catherine,' says Charles distractedly, his quill in his hand. 'Augusta is an invalid and in need of my help.'

I walk up to his desk. 'Perhaps you could concentrate on me for a moment, rather than on your writing, Charles.'

He looks up. 'May I remind you,' he says in his melodramatic way, 'that if I fail to produce an Italian travelogue, this family will fail to eat.' He concentrates on dipping his nib into the ink.

'Day and night, Charles, for months on end, you have given that woman your undivided attention, with never any thought of writing an Italian travelogue,' I say, facing him across his desk.

'My work is always on my mind,' Charles replies, quickly adding 'along with you and the family, of course. When I included a pet raven in *Barnaby Rudge*, I did so to remind the children of Grip.' His quill feather flutters as if ready to take flight.

'He was never their pet,' I laugh. 'We all lived in fear of that bird, and its replacement, but you cared not a fig because you were obsessed with it, just as you are obsessed with your latest little pet.' I lean towards him until we are almost nose to nose. He leans back from me and says, 'Mesmerism requires absolute concentration.' His quill hovers as it travels from inkwell to paper.

'And I don't, Charles? I'm your wife.'

Ink drips onto his manuscript.

'Now look what you've made me do!' Charles shouts.

I offer him a sheet of blotting paper. He snatches it from me without any thanks.

'You always do as you wish, with never a thought for the rest of us,' I say.

'What would you have me do? Stand by and watch Augusta suffer when I have it in my power to cure her?' He scrunches up the stained blotting paper and throws it towards the wastepaper basket, but it falls short and lands on the floor.

I stomp over and snatch it up. 'Her husband says she no longer experiences hallucinations and hasn't had a headache for some months,' I snap. 'He is very grateful to you.' Charles does not answer. He only listens when I sugar my words with praise, so I add, 'You have done a wonderful job, my Dearest, but please let that be an end to it. I need you too.'

'Augusta has responded well but there is still more work to be done. Now she feels able to confide in me, we have begun to explore many other things that unsettle her. The poor woman has not slept well for weeks.'

'She hasn't slept well for *weeks*? I haven't had a full night's sleep since the first of your five children was born eight years ago, but I have to carry on. I have spent whole nights walking up and down in the nursery with one baby in my arms and another in my belly, ensuring that your sleep is not disturbed. Why don't I get your care? Why are you more concerned about someone else's wife?'

'I arranged for a wet nurse to feed our babies to stop you starving them to death,' he replies.

Such spite. Such venom. I squeeze the ball of blotting paper hard to resist the temptation to throw it at him. 'You did, over my head,' I say, 'and, as you are well aware, it is one of my greatest regrets. I begged for another chance to feed Charley.'

Charles places the quill in its stand and folds his arms.

'What I meant is that you had help, but Augusta relies on me alone.'

'Then it would seem that Augusta and I have something in common. We're both unable to depend on our husbands for support,' I say and before I can stop myself, I fling the blotting paper ball at him. I know I should be ashamed at such an undignified, unwifely display of rage but, instead, I want to pat myself on the back. I have shown courage in the face of intimidation, something Charles would once have applauded me for. What his reaction is today, I dare not wait to see but scamper away before I can find out.

Friday, 10th June 1870—9:10 pm

KATE is proud of her younger self, but a little ashamed of what she did next. She can't believe she found it in herself to deceive Charles but was she really at fault for snatching a few crumbs from Augusta's table when the opportunity was set before her on a plate?

'Shall I sit with you again for a while?' Matilda asks.

'No, thank you,' Kate replies. 'I need to concentrate.'

'Concentrate, Madam?'

'Today's news has given me much to think over,' Kate tells her maid.

'Very well, but try not to trouble yourself with vexatious thoughts,' Matilda advises. 'They never do no one no good.'

Kate says she will try not to mope but feels that there are thoughts that must be dealt with—scabs that need picking—before she can rest. Her current preoccupation is Augusta De la Rue but she knows that, eventually, she will have to turn her attention to Charles's first love, Maria Beadnell and his last, and to decide, once and for all, whether she was nothing more than an interlude between two greater loves.

April 1845

CHARLES and I are rattling along in an open carriage. The wind is bitterly cold. I slip off my muff to brace myself against the side, but my fingers are too numb to hold onto it. It blows out of my hands and goes skimming across the road.

I expect Charles to raise his eyebrows in exasperation but he is preoccupied with Madame De la Rue as usual. Though we are now hundreds of miles south of Genoa, their minds are about to meet in the astral realm. He has agreed to calm her into a trance at eleven each morning. He will use mesmerism to restore the flow of the magnetic fluids circulating through her body. If I had the opportunity, there would be other mechanisms I would use to control her magnetic fluids.

I call on the cabbie to stop the carriage so I can retrieve the muff, and jolt in pain as we hit another rut and come to a halt. As I stand, the world goes white and whirls around me as if we have been engulfed in a snow storm. Oh no! Not a dizzy spell! It might be because I stood up too quickly but I know only too well what else it can portend, and the last thing I want is to have to warn Charles that another baby is on the way. He would hate that—and blame me.

I sit back down to stop myself swaying, shut my eyes and take deep breaths. This attracts Charles's attention.

'Are you quite well, my Dear?' he asks.

Unable to speak, I open my eyes but the harsh wind makes my eyelids flutter like a butterfly.

'How astonishing,' he says.

With no speech and limited vision, I reach out in his general direction and wave my arms around helplessly.

Charles grabs my cold hands, kisses them and breathes warm air onto my fingers.

'I astound myself,' he says. 'I never knew the extent of my powers until this moment. I seem to have mesmerised you, along with Augusta. It is miraculous!'

For the first time in months I have my husband's undivided attention. How welcome this feels. If only I'd known that all I had to do was gasp for breath, flutter my eyelashes and flail my arms, I would have done it sooner.

'You are obviously extremely susceptible,' he says. 'I had never realised.'

I suck in my lips and bite down, to stop myself laughing at the irony.

'We are so attuned,' he continues. 'I was focusing on someone else but you could not help but be affected by me.'

One more deep breath, another little flutter of my eyelashes and then I will swoon into his arms, in earnest hope of remaining there forever.

FRIDAY, 10TH JUNE 1870—9:35 PM

KATE had refused to return to Italy the following year. She savours the memory of Charles's having to make excuses to Augusta and having to explain that his wife had not been well during their previous stay and that they would be decamping to Switzerland instead.

But Kate knows that no victory over Charles is ever truly final. Nine years later she gave her blessing to his bachelor tour of Europe, only to find that Genoa, and therefore Madame, had been included in his itinerary. After the visit he wrote home, assuring her that Emile De la Rue had always been generous and affectionate when enquiring about her and the children, and that on meeting Augusta after all this time, she had asked warmly about Kate, and begged to be remembered to Mamie and Lucifer Box and Georgina.

Charles blames the rift between the two women on Kate's misguided jealousy, and is of the opinion that the time has come for *her* to put matters right. Writing from Turin on 5 December 1853, he says that Kate's attitude is not amiable, not generous and not worthy of her. He says she has it in her power to write to Augusta 'at once' to say that she had learnt about her sufferings from him and has felt impelled to respond. Tell her, Charles says,

> that if you should ever be thrown together again by any circumstances, you hope it will be for a friendly association without any sort of shadow upon it.

Understand above all things, he adds, that 'I shall never ask whether you have done it.' In fact, he would never mention the subject again. But

> if you could do this without any secret reservation in your own mind, you would do an unquestionably upright thing.

In writing warmly to Augusta, he says, Kate would feel better about herself, and her warmth would be well received by both De la Rues. But it would need to be done because she wanted to, in her heart, having reflected on his words. If done merely to appease or please him, 'it would be utterly valueless and contemptible.'

Charles ends his letter by saying he expects to be home in a few days, and that Charley, now in Leipzig, will be joining them for Christmas—'and if I may judge of his weather by ours, he will have a mighty cold journey of it.' He hopes also that, on his return, he will find that she has prepared the mantelpiece with Christmas ornaments.

Kate wishes she could have refused to obey Charles's thinly veiled command but recognises that she had known deep down that her position was not as secure as it had once been. Charles's letter says otherwise, of course. He tells her that, thanks to him, she has been made 'proud and honoured' in her married life, and been given 'station better than rank', as well as being surrounded with 'many enviable things'. That, he says, is 'the plain truth'.

But he had been tricksy: that was the plain truth.

'Of course you wouldn't have needed to ask if I'd written what you prescribed for me, Charles,' Kate mutters. 'The De la Rues would have reported to you the moment my olive-branch landed on their doormat.'

Black beetles scurry around in her head, scattering the moment they are interrupted but gathering again when she closes her eyes against the light and sits alone in silence.

Without asking, Matilda brings Kate a glass of brandy.

'I've stirred in a little laudanum to help you relax, Ma'am. Can I bring you anything else?' she asks.

Kate knocks back the drink, hands her maid the empty glass and shakes her head.

'Very well then, I'll leave you in peace,' Matilda says.

The tincture has the desired effect. Kate remembers what it was like to feel secure that summer in Switzerland, with Charles and the children, while Augusta and Emile were far away in Italy. A tune comes to mind. She hums the first few bars. The music fades and she tries again. This time snatches of lyrics accompany the melody. Something about feeling sorrowful at heart and a boat heading for the rocks? She wracks her brains—'The Lorelei'!

> The air is cool and the twilight is falling
> and the Rhine is flowing quietly by . . .

Charles sang it to her as they sailed up the Rhine, sitting on deck, warmed by the late spring sunshine. Fairytale castles slid by on the wooded shore as they approached their new home in Lausanne.

The house Charles had rented for the summer was set on a hillside, in extensive grounds bordered by woods. It was spacious and offered wonderful views of Lake Geneva below and mountains above. Charles spent the summer working, of course. Charles always worked but, without the De la Rues on their doorstep, Kate was happy. Happy enough.

July 1846

CHARLES'S study door is shut. I tap on it. There is no response. I creep in quietly so as not to disturb him. He does not look round but gazes out at the lake. One of the windows is open but the room is still as hot as an oven.

'I've been up to the stream,' I say and hand him a glass of spring water.

'Bless you, my Dear,' Charles says, putting the cool glass to his forehead.

I massage the stress out of his shoulders and kiss his hot neck.

He gulps down the water.

'You are an enchantress with a magic touch but I am not to be seduced,' he says and picks up his quill. 'This magic feather will make you disappear, lest I am tempted to neglect my work.'

He tickles me under the chin with it.

'I will not be banished until you have shared all your imaginings with me,' I say and straighten two piles of paper on his desk. One is headed 'Dombey & Son'; the other says 'The Battle of Life'. He pushes my hands away.

'No, no, no—neither is ready to be scrutinised, but you will be the first to see the result of my labours when they are complete, and it is my ardent hope that I will have earned a positive review for both.'

'You earned a very positive review from me last night,' I say, and giggle.

'You are a scarlet woman: be gone!' he says and chases me from the room.

FRIDAY, 10TH JUNE 1870—10:15 PM

THE children had been happy too. Charley was away at school during the week but they had made the most of their outings after church on Sundays with festivals, boat trips and hikes.

Little Lucifer Box was not quite so volatile now. But Kate cannot stop herself smiling as she remembers the girls' governess—long, thin and sharp-featured—wiping away strawberry jam and sticky red crumbs after suggesting that Lucifer Box was eating too much cake at her seventh birthday party.

Walter was about five years old then and Frank nearly two-and-a-half. Alfie was teething and she would carry him around the garden and into the woods to try and settle him. How he had chortled to see his older brothers building dens. The bigger boys played at being soldiers with rifle sticks on their shoulders and would rush out to ambush her and the baby. She tries to block out these thoughts because she knows that, one day, the game would become harsh reality for Walter.

Rosemont: the name of the Swiss house comes into her mind. Hill of roses. Charles brought her flowers—but when was it? Kate feels the need to answer her own question, as if facing interrogation in a witness box. She pleads innocence but the barrister in her brain will not spare her.

Roses? Was it roses? Red roses? Perhaps she will find the answer in the garden. Too many hours of sitting motionless have taken their toll. Kate's back is stiff as she eases herself up and makes her way outside.

The sun has set but white roses defy the gloom. Solitary male bees lie silent now, under flower petals. With antennae at rest they are curled up as cosy as contented babies; Kate, though, is still on high alert. She sniffs the air, like a dog scenting a buried bone. Heady perfume fills her head with visions of Charles. He holds a bouquet of red roses for her. When was that? And were the flowers meant as evidence of his enduring love? Kate is back in court.

'No, m'Lord, the case for the prosecution will show that this cannot be proved,' the QC says to the judge. He turns to Kate. 'I put it to you that, rather than symbolising undying affection, the flowers in question were in fact an admission of guilt.'

Kate knows this is true. She sits down on the garden bench and thinks back to their cold house in France. Paris in November of that year had been quite a shock after that scorching Swiss summer.

November 1846

HOW blue my fingers are. Clapping my hands will get the blood circulating. Anne drops the fire iron she has been using to scrape ice off the inside of the bedroom window.

'I'm sorry to startle you,' I say. 'I've just come up for a thicker shawl.'

'No matter, Madam.' Anne takes a shawl from the chest of drawers and wraps it around my shoulders. 'It's perishing today but I've got a good blaze going in the parlour. Mr Dickens and your sister are in there at this very moment, going through the accounts.'

'That will put a smile on Georgina's face,' I say.

'Yes: she loves nothing more than neat columns of figures,' Anne replies.

'Apart from my husband,' I call over my shoulder as I hurry back downstairs. 'She's very fond of him.'

Charles and Georgina sit side-by-side, with a ledger resting on their knees. They don't look up as I take a seat by the fire.

'From what you've shown me, it's clear that this place is costing far too much to run,' Charles says. 'The heating bill alone will soon send us all to the workhouse.'

Georgina turns the page. The ledger wobbles on their knees. Their hands meet as they reach out to steady it.

'It certainly does drain your resources,' she says.

They are too engrossed to see my eyes roll. If only my little sister would take the trouble to look back at all the entries I have made over the years, she would see that this is nothing more than Charles's relentless insecurity, and that we are more likely to end up living in a palace than on the parish. *The Pickwick Papers* alone brought in two thousand pounds and the serialisation of *Oliver Twist* earned him twenty guineas a month, although he always joked that he should have asked for more. I snorted with laughter the first time he told me this. I now clamp my hand over my mouth to stop myself laughing out loud at his preposterous concerns but fail to contain my mirth. My husband and my sister look up at me like a pair of disapproving bookends.

'This is a serious matter, Catherine,' Charles says.

Georgina nods in agreement and frowns, as she always does when anyone laughs.

'I'm sure we don't need to worry too much, Charles. Go back a few pages, Georgina, and you'll see that *Nicholas Nickleby* brought in three thousand pounds. So did *Barnaby Rudge*. As for *The Old Curiosity Shop* . . . ' But I am interrupted by a hullabaloo from the nursery upstairs.

'A timely reminder that the ever-increasing size of our family is another drain on my finances!' Charles shouts. 'I fear there are far too many Dickenses,' he adds, and waves the ledger at me.

'I'll go and pacify the children,' my sister says.

Charles smiles at her.

'Thank you, my dear Georgy,' he says.

I pull my shawl down to cover my stomach, having been made sharply aware that this is not the most propitious moment to announce the happy news that a seventh child is on the way.

Friday, 10th June 1870—10:50 PM

DID Charles regret wishing for a smaller family when she was fighting for her life a few months later? Did he fear that he had invoked some dark force when they lost not just one but two babies? Black magic had certainly seemed to descend on her and the children after his outburst in Paris.

First it was Charley. Against her wishes, the poor boy had been sent back to attend school in London, where he promptly caught scarlet fever. Was it guilt that drove Charles to insist they rush back from France to be near him, even though fear of infection meant they dared not visit? Anyone could see that she was not the only parent frantic about their firstborn, and overjoyed when he was spared.

Kate picks a pure white rose and holds it to her nose. The soft petals brush her lips like a tender kiss. Charles had bought roses to console her for the loss of a baby—but which baby and when?

April 1847

SOMETHING is wrong. These are not the same false starts that preceded Walter's birth. Mother and Mrs Dickens say I need to give myself more time, as if twenty-four hours in agony with no sign of progress is nothing.

Blood pours down my legs. I scream and beg for mercy. Mother takes my hand.

'It's probably better if you don't bear down just yet, my little Hen,' she says. Her voice is calm but there is fear in her face.

Another spasm of unbelievable pain engulfs me, accompanied by a primordial need to push. I squeeze my eyes shut, grind my teeth and dig my finger nails into my hands to resist the urge.

'Charles is wild with anxiety,' Mrs Dickens tells my mother. 'He has sent for two doctors and one of them is Charles Locock—yes, *the* Charles Locock, the very same Charles Locock who serves as obstetrician to Her Majesty the Queen.'

Two doctors? I must be at death's door if Charles is willing to pay for two top consultants.

'I've told her to try and keep the baby in a while longer but she feels she needs to push and I can't get through to her that she's losing a lot of blood,' my mother says.

'Stop it at once or you'll both be dead,' my mother-in-law shouts in my ear.

I don't want to die but my body has a will of its own and I am powerless to fight it. I am racing along in a carriage, alone, on a terrifying life-or-death ride. White light invades my sight, there is a hiss and then silence.

'AH, you're awake. Let's see what's going on here, shall we?' I am being addressed by a man with grey hair and grey whiskers. He phrases his words as a question but I know from his manner that I will have no say in the matter.

'Don't let me die,' I plead. 'Please save me and the baby.'

His cold hands prod, poke and shove my stomach.

Another pain pushes me beyond the bounds of human endurance.

A voice screams, 'I can't take any more! Let me die!'

'Don't you shout at Dr Locock like that!' Mrs Dickens barks at me. 'I'm sure Queen Victoria would never raise her voice, even if she were about to lose her baby and bleed to death.'

The doctor looks at her impatiently through his bushy grey eyebrows. 'Quite,' he says, as if all the women he has ever attended at childbirth have queenly manners. He looks at me and wags his finger.

'Now you listen to me, my Girl: the baby is breech presentation. That means upside down. We must turn it or I will have to use forceps.'

He reaches into his bag, extracts a pair of long tongs with sharp teeth, waves them under my nose as if threatening me with torture, and places them on the bedside table. They lie there like a hungry crocodile ready to snap. I'm about to beg him not to use them but his pummelling takes my breath away.

'You push from the top on that side, Davis, and I will work from the bottom over here.'

Two side-on silhouettes set to work on my stomach like prize fighters in a shadow puppet show. My poor baby will not survive this onslaught and I doubt I will either. I am no match for these two brutes.

'Try to compose yourself,' Dr Davis says.

'She's not listening to you, Doctor,' says Mrs Dickens, and then shouts, 'Compose yourself!' in my ear, 'or they'll be dragging the baby's dead corpse out with those metal teeth and you'll be split in two like a slaughtered pig.'

The doctors step back and we all watch with fascination as my stomach churns, heaves, rolls and re-forms, like a mountain after an avalanche.

I grunt like a boar. With the whole force of nature blasting through my body, nothing will now stop me bearing down. Another grunt. Another almighty push and then a blissful release from pain. A baby as scrawny as a skinned rabbit slithers out into his paternal grandmother's arms, and squeals in protest at his topsy-turvy start in life. Mother throws her arms around me.

'I thought I was going to lose you *and* the baby,' she stutters between sobs.

'May I leave you to deal with the placenta while I break the good news to Mr Dickens?' Dr Locock asks his colleague.

'Of course, Sir,' Davis says.

Mrs Dickens thrusts her newborn grandson into my mother's arms and she's off across the room like a racehorse. Dr Locock may be Queen Victoria's obstetrician but the good doctor is no match for my mother-in-law. In a couple of paces she has outflanked him and disappeared out of the door.

'Charles! Charles! It's a boy,' she calls. 'A pathetic little shrimp of a thing but alive!'

'Give me a little cough,' Dr Davis says to me. 'Then we'll stitch you up and make sure you're all set for your next confinement.'

'Never,' I say. 'I'm never going to do this again.'

Mother takes out her handkerchief and dries her eyes.

'Never say never: you said the same thing when Charley was born,' she reminds me.

'But I really mean it now,' I say. 'I can't go through this again.'

'Nonsense!' Mrs Dickens is back. 'Come in, Charles,' she says.

Dr Davis quickly covers the after-birth with a towel. Mother uses her damp handkerchief to wipe red smears off the baby's head. I pull the top sheet over my blood-stained nightdress.

Ashen-faced Charles stands in the doorway, his head in his hands.

FRIDAY, 10TH JUNE 1870—11.35 PM

IF there were no flowers on the day that Sydney was born, Kate wonders when the roses came.

A tiny glow comes down the garden towards her.

'Oh there you are, Madam,' says Matilda, shielding a candle flame with her hand. 'I've been looking all over. I've turned down yer bed. Is there anything else I can do before I retire?'

Kate shakes her head, and says her maid may rest easy. Kate will lock up.

Matilda offers to leave the candle but Kate is content that the stars alone illuminate her thoughts.

Guilt stalks her. It knows that new widows are easy prey. It knows they torture themselves over a husband's death, reviving one regret after another until they pool, like drops of mercury. As Kate sits alone in the dark evening, guilt picks away at partially healed scabs until old wounds open and bleed again.

She closes her eyes and shakes her head. Miscarriages. A baby's death. The loss of a son. All her fault.

Guilt savours the taste of her tears.

'God punished me for wishing I was not pregnant,' Kate says, although it had only been a few months since the horror of Sydney's birth, and eight pregnancies had taken their toll and, most important of all, Charles was not happy to hear the news that another baby was on the way. But, nevertheless, there is no excuse. She is as guilty as Charles.

Guilt reminds her how excited she was about returning to her homeland to hear her husband give a talk in Glasgow. They were going to stay with Sir Archibald Alison on his country estate, and then with Francis Jeffrey, their friend in Edinburgh, and be home in good time to celebrate Charley's eleventh birthday at their annual Twelfth Night party.

Plans, plans, plans. Kate now knows how futile they are. She had planned to be with Charles forever. Such vanity.

December 1847

ANOTHER stab in my stomach. I hold my breath and stare out of the grimy train window. Rain obscures my view of Glasgow. I make a pact with myself. If I pray, and don't move, all will be well.

Stab, stab, stab.

Please God forgive me. I didn't mean what I said. I do want this baby.

Jab, jab, jab.

The Lord is my shepherd; I shall not want. He maketh me to lie down in green pastures; He leadeth me beside the still waters. He restoreth my soul.

Gasp.

Charles lowers his paper, tearing himself from the troubles in Ireland. His eyes narrow. He frowns. I seem to have aroused his suspicion that there may be troubles closer to home.

I cross my legs, fold my arms over my stomach, lean forwards and smile.

He is not fooled. 'What troubles you now, my dear?' he asks.

'A touch of indigestion.' Perhaps saying so will make it so.

'You look pale. I'll open the window. Fresh air will put some colour in those cheeks,' he says.

Rain spatters my face. Smoke billows into the compartment. Charles coughs. The train shrieks a warning. Its whistle drowns out my screams. We enter a tunnel. Darkness descends. It is the same pain I suffered after Mary died. I fear the same outcome.

Another whistle. Grey light, grey smoke, grey rain, red blood. Charles finds me curled up like a foetus on the carriage floor.

'Kate! Kate! Is this what I suspect it to be?' He kneels beside me and takes my hands in his.

My silence is confirmation enough.

'Not on a train! We must get you off at the next station. We cannot risk someone entering our compartment and witnessing this embarrassing spectacle.'

He pulls me to my feet. My knees buckle and I slump onto the damp seat. Charles tries to close the window but it sticks halfway up. A smut catches him in the eye. Rain runs down his face. I want to imagine he is crying.

Friday, 10th June 1870—Midnight

THERE were no tears from Charles, no flowers and no guilt. He said his mother had wasted floods of tears over failures of this kind and that Kate must put on a brave face whilst they were guests of Sir Archibald. What a relief it had been to catch the train a couple of days later and be on their way to their friend Francis in Edinburgh. But, when the train's whistle blew, Kate had panted so fast, she feared she might faint.

Kate has made many journeys by train since then but whenever she hears the sound of the whistle, she sees a tiny ghost swaddled in a copy of *The Glasgow Times*.

January 1848

'HAPPY New Year,' Charles says, as if nothing has happened. Francis suggests I should rest rather than joining their shopping trip, but my husband insists I am as hale and hearty as ever.

Cracks appear in the brave mask that I wear on my face as grief, guilt and pain drag me down. I trudge from shop to shop, overwhelmed by weariness, and struggle to ignore the dull ache low down where the baby had been. I soldier on until the pavement rises up and hits me in the face.

A BLINDING headache wakes me. My vomit erupts over my husband as I sit up. A man in a white coat tells Charles that this is often the case. All had not come away as it should, but he has administered chloroform and rectified the situation.

Saturday, 11 June 1870—Five past midnight

KATE will take time, now, to grieve for all her losses. She is determined. Four months—four months was all she'd had to mourn in secret for the baby she had lost on the train before she was pregnant again.

She had told Charles she was tired but her tiredness had counted for nothing with him. She had told him she was sore but this seemed not to register with him either. She had said she was red-raw but he was not concerned. She was, after all, his wife; she had marital duties.

She did not say anything about the more frequent trips to the water closet and the little leaks when she sneezed, but she did complain that her back ached and he had seen that she could not stand straight, but it made no difference. Charles demanded his conjugal rights, regardless of her discomfort and the risk of another pregnancy, and so she resorted to feigning sleep and headaches and sickness. In spite of that, Henry still came along the following January.

By then Charley was about eleven, Mamie ten, Lucifer Box nine, Walter six, Frank four and Alfie three. That made little Sydney sixteen months when they set off to Broadstairs for the summer. With so many memories of happy family holidays there, Kate made up her mind to celebrate each union—and the consequent pregnancies—as proof of Charles's love.

Her determination to think well of Charles—to shroud herself in comforting illusions—has long since become impossible but, to keep her spirits up, she will try to concentrate on those sunny days, to brace herself for another loss, for she now remembers why he had bought her roses.

August 1848

CHARLES chases the children round the garden. It's wonderful to see him relaxed and carefree. Georgina sits under a tree in the far corner with Sydney on her lap. He wriggles off and toddles away as fast as his little legs will carry him but trips. Completely unconcerned, he jumps up, toddles some more, trips again, jumps up and toddles off anew. Now Mamie picks him up. He squeals in delight as she runs around with him in her arms. Alfie races after Frank but cannot keep up.

'Wait me!' he shouts.

Charles roars.

'M-m-monster coming!' Frank warns the other children.

Walter stops running, turns, and heads straight for me.

'Shark?' he asks.

'No, there are no sharks here!' I say. 'It's just Papa playing a game.'

Lucifer Box feigns a fall.

'Eat me up, Papa. I'm not scared,' she cries. But Charles is focused on catching Charley, who is too fast for him. I raise my hand to shade my eyes.

'Run, Charley, run!' I shout as Charles gains ground.

'Stick your foot out, Lucifer Box!' he shouts.

She does and Charley tumbles. He wipes his eyes but laughs. Charles casts a shadow over his eldest son as he pulls him up.

'You'll never be a match for me, young man,' he says.

There is a flash of lightning and a rumble of thunder.

'It's going to rain cats and dogs,' I say.

'Don't be ridiculous,' Georgina replies. 'Animals do not rain from the sky.'

I don't want the children to be soaked while I try to explain to my laborious sister the function of hyperbolic imagery in English idiom, so I ignore her and suggest we all go inside and play a parlour game. Lucifer Box races past us all and rushes into the house.

'I'm first!' she shouts, as we trail in behind her.

My back is beginning to ache, so I sit on the sofa.

'Are you tired, Mama?' Charley asks, and sits beside me.

'You'd better watch out for the parlour bear,' Charles shouts. He snarls, hunches his shoulders and lumbers after Lucifer Box. She screams, Alfie screams, Frank screams. Walter runs and jumps up onto my lap. I laugh, stroke the hair out of his eyes, and shush the others.

Georgina comes in from the garden. She claps her hands.

'That's quite enough of that!' she shouts. 'You are all far too excited. Let's play charades. Shall I begin, Charles?'

'Aunt Georgina is right. You certainly are too excited,' Charles agrees, but mimics a dancing bear behind her back.

We all laugh. Georgina looks over her shoulder and Charles folds his arms and looks stern, as if he was doing no such thing.

'Do you want to perform the first charade, Charles?' I ask.

'No,' he says. 'Let's play "Animal, Vegetable or Mineral?" and you go first.'

Georgina stomps out.

'No, no—me, me, me,' says Lucifer Box.

'You always go first and I'm older than you,' Mamie says.

'Go on, Mama, you're good at this,' Charley says.

I look at Charles. He nods.

'Very well,' I say. 'It's an animal.'

'Shark?' asks Walter.

'No. Not a shark.'

'D-d-dog?' asks Frank and adds, 'woof woof'.

'No, but a good try and very good barking,' I say and smile at him.

'Doggie?' asks Alfie.

'Not a doggie either, I'm afraid,' I say, 'but that's another very good guess.'

'Me doggie,' Alfie says and crawls over to me.

'I can see you are a very nice doggie,' I say and pat him on the head.

'How many legs does it have?' Lucifer Box asks.

'Two.'

Walter frowns. 'Not a bear?'

'No.' I put my arms around him. 'It's nothing to fear.'

Lucifer Box sidles up to us, puts her face next to his as if she is going to kiss him, but then bares her teeth and growls. Walter screams.

'Lucifer Box!' Charles wags his finger at her. 'Leave Walter Young Skull alone.'

'You should have let me go first,' she complains and storms off back outside.

'What animal has two legs?' Charley wonders. 'Is it a bird?

'Well done Charley,' I say. 'Yes, it is.'

'Blackbird?' Mamie asks.

'No, but you are getting close.'

'Robin?'

'No, think of a bigger bird.'

'Goose?'

'No, but it's about that size.'

Lucifer Box has crept back in.

'Turkey, turkey, turkey,' she says. 'I've guessed right, haven't I, Mama?'

'Nearly, nearly: you are nearly right, Lucifer Box.'

'I am right. You've changed your mind. Cheat, cheat, cheat!'

'Ostrich?' Charley asks.

'No, but you are getting very close.'

'L-l-ladybird?' Frank asks.

'Ladybirds are lovely and they do fly like birds but they are insects and have six legs.'

Frank runs around flapping his wings. Alfie follows him but bumps into Sydney. They both cry. Mamie picks the boys up and holds one on each hip.

'You can be my parrots,' she says.

'Carrot,' says Sydney, and we all laugh again.

'Could it be a flightless bird?' Charley asks.

'It may well be.'

'Dodo!' Charley says.

'Yes! Well done! Your big brother is so clever, isn't he, children?'

'Hold your horses, Mrs Catherine Dickens. I wish to take issue with you,' Charles says. He lifts Walter off my lap, pulls me to my feet and stands legs apart, hands on hips, like a policeman.

'Did you or did you not say it was an animal?'

'Yes. Birds count as animals in this game. Don't they Charley?'

'They certainly do.' He looks at Charles and blushes. 'Sorry, Papa,' he adds.

I sit. Charles pulls me up again.

'Not so fast, my dear wife,' he says. 'May I take a minute to remind you of the rules? Animals have to be alive—and when did you last see a dodo fluttering about?' He sticks out his rear end, flaps his hands and waddles around the room to great hilarity. Frank copies him. Alfie slides down from Mamie's hip and joins in. Sydney has fallen asleep on her shoulder.

'Well, they were alive once,' I say, 'and they are definitely neither vegetable nor mineral.'

Charley stands beside me.

'Mother is right,' he says.

'As head of this household, I will adjudicate in this serious matter,' Charles says. 'Unfortunately my wife has broken the rules and must be punished for it.'

'I told you she was a cheat,' Lucifer Box says, 'but no one ever listens to me'. She stamps her foot, turns and runs back out into the garden, despite the heavy rain.

'I'm innocent!' I plead, leaning back and draping my arm

across my forehead like a doomed victim in a melodrama. 'This is a terrible injustice. Please show mercy,' and I hold my hands together as if in prayer.

Charles walks towards me with his face contorted and arms out like Frankenstein's monster. 'You shall be punished,' he says and reaches for my throat.

'Mercy, mercy!' I cry and drop to my knees.

'Mama, Mercy!' Walter pleads, and wriggles in between me and his father.

'We are only playing,' I reassure him. 'Go and see Mamie.'

Charles scratches his chin as if pondering my fate. He raises his forefinger.

'Eureka!' he says. 'A kiss. You shall forfeit a kiss.'

He pushes Charley aside, pulls me up and takes me in his arms.

'This is no punishment at all,' I whisper in his ear.

Saturday, 11 June 1870—Ten past midnight

A CHEERFUL disposition had been difficult to sustain when autumn turned to winter and the date of Kate's next lying-in drew inexorably closer. As her pregnancy developed and fears of a miscarriage grew less, memories of Sydney's birth forced themselves to the forefront of her mind and she became aware that her stomach was distorted again. Kate remembers Charles taking note of her concerns and acting on them as any loving husband would. Doctors were booked to attend, they would administer chloroform to alleviate her suffering and all would be well with both her and the baby.

And all was well. There had been no call for flowers of condolence when Henry was born. Clever, clever, Henry. So advanced, they called him 'Mr Harry'. Their only son to study at university and just last year, Trinity College, Cambridge had awarded him a top scholarship. Kate had flung her arms around him and said how proud she was, but Charles had been less expressive. He had said nothing more than 'capital', and Mr Harry had confided to Kate how disappointed he was, although he had seen tears in his father's eyes later when Charles had eventually confessed to being overwhelmed with pride. Kate suspected it was the fifty pounds prize money more than the academic achievement that had impressed him but she kept that to herself. How sad that they had not celebrated their son's success together.

Kate yawns. She should be in bed but her mind is too agitated for sleep. She stares at the stars. How distant they are but how bright, like her memories. Her husband had become somewhat more considerate, and so Mr Harry was ten months old before her next pregnancy, or 'uninteresting condition', as Charles preferred to call it. Kate feels tired tonight but back then she was weary beyond weary. There was Charles to please with dinner party after dinner party and she had to be on top form for their fourteenth wedding anniversary celebration. And then there were the children. She had let Charley down by having a miscarriage when he turned eleven and he needed a good send off before departing to take up his place at Eton College, so his thirteenth birthday party had to go ahead. Her parents needed her too, so she was obliged to accept their invitations and accompany them to the opera, and continued to do so even when she was so heavily gravid that she could barely squeeze into a seat.

After each boy's birth Charles had commented how much more partial he was to girls and complained that he had no say in the matter, as if she did. Now, with a tally of six sons, Kate is happy to recall that his wish for a third daughter was finally granted.

Dora—dear, sweet Dora. Her doting father named her after a character in the book he was writing. He loved his baby girl and, at that time, he loved Kate too: she is sure of that. After all, he stayed at their Devonshire Terrace home until he knew that both were well, and then left the baby and Kate in the capable hands of her mother and sister Helen while he went with Georgina and the servants and the other children to Broadstairs.

But he had written lovingly to her. Kate does not need to find the letter he wrote the day after Dora's birth. She sees his handwriting through closed eyes and has the key sentences off by heart:

> I will not attempt to tell you, my love, how delighted I have been to receive such good tidings of you, and what relief and happiness we felt last night . . . I thank God most heartily. I think of you all day. Take every care of yourself . . . God bless you my darling. Without you we shall be quite incomplete and a great blank everywhere.

Kate wishes she had not been in such a hurry to fill the blank by joining them all in Broadstairs when Dora was a month old, and then travelling just a few weeks later to Knebworth House and Rockingham Castle to take part in Charles's latest round of amateur theatricals. There were just so many demands: more dinner parties, visitors, an extended family gathering at Christmas, and dancing until the early hours at their New Year party.

Kate leans forward, chin on chest. She hugs herself and rocks to and fro, but there is no comfort in the motion and no escape from the spectre of guilt which has crept up on her again. Kate condemns herself for the exhaustion she had felt after each birth—an exhaustion which made rising from bed in the morning a Herculean task—and for the blinding headaches which had sucked all light and joy from the world. She had been a burden on all her loved ones—her baby, her children and Charles—and a blight on their lives, sapping their spirits with her melancholy and timidity. She was sure that everyone would be better off without her. In a dark world of doubt, that was the only certainty.

If only Dr Wilson had failed to convince Charles that it was essential she should follow in the footsteps of Darwin and Tennyson and receive treatment under his care, miles from London in Malvern. Kate is forced to acknowledge that their decision to send her away set in motion a catastrophic chain of events, and one whose ultimate cost would not be borne by her.

April 1851

'MORE long walks and cold baths today, Madam?' Anne asks as I walk into the cottage in Malvern.

'If you had told me a few weeks ago that being wrapped in sodden sheets, getting chilled to the marrow, having cold compresses applied to my body and being showered with water from a great height would be beneficial, I would not have believed you,' I say, 'but it does appear efficacious in some way.'

'Having a good rest has probably got a lot to do with it as well, if you ask me,' Anne says, and hurries off to answer a knock at the door.

I'm puzzled as to who might be paying me a call but before

Anne has time to announce anyone, our old friend Forster steps into the parlour, all the way from London.

'John, what a pleasant surprise,' I say, and embrace him. He doesn't return my smile and I don't like the look on his face. He passes me a letter without saying a word. It has my name in Charles's hand on the front.

'I'm the bearer of bad news, I'm afraid. You'd better take a seat.' He sits beside me.

More bad news? I start to pant. Is it Charles? While I was away, his father died and yet they insisted that I remain in Worcestershire, for my health. Should I have been more wifely and returned? Had I been by his side I could perhaps have exorcised the ghosts which possessed him following the death. I should have disregarded Dr Wilson's advice and attended the funeral and then been with him for our fifteenth wedding anniversary. What are my headaches compared to the heartache poor Charles has suffered?

'Is it Charles?' I ask. 'Please tell me it's not Charles, John.'

'Read the note, Kate,' he says. 'You must read it.'

If it's not Charles, it must be one of the children. Charley—yes, it's Charley. My sensitive son has suffered as he did when I went to America. But he is fourteen, not four years old now. Mamie then, it must be Mamie. Has caring for the little ones ground her down? Or headstrong Lucifer Box: has she run away from home? Has Walter fallen down the stairs while sleepwalking? Have Frank and Alfie injured each other while play-fighting? Sydney, then—our little Ocean Spectre: has he wandered off in a daydream? Or has some terrible mishap happened to Mr Harry whilst toddling around at home? Or Dora—my sweet baby girl? She certainly gave us a fright a few weeks ago but she recovered and waved goodbye to me with a big smile on her chubby little face. Of course, it might not be any of the children. It could be Georgina or Mother or Father or Mrs Dickens or Fred or Helen or one of my brothers or . . .

'Kate! Kate!' Forster shouts.

It's not like him to raise his voice to me.

'Forgive me if I startled you but this is a matter of some urgency.' He takes the letter out of my hand. 'Shall I read it to you?'

'No,' I say. 'I will read it.' Once he speaks the words I will have no choice but to deal with what they impart.

Forster unfolds the letter and hands it back to me.

'Then I'm afraid you must read it for yourself,' he says. 'I'll leave you alone and have a word with your maid.'

Charles has written many words—enough to impart some news, followed by an explanation and a message of hope. But the words won't stay still. I blink, look away, look back but they still leap about like imps. The paper quivers in my hand. I lay it flat on my lap, pick it back up, bring it to my face, then hold it further off, like a short-sighted old dame who has mislaid her spectacles, but all to no avail. Charles may as well have written in shorthand for all the sense I can make of his characters. I shall have to relent, find Forster and ask him to read it to me.

Anne passes me in the hallway as she heads towards the stairs. She stops and puts a hand on my shoulder. There are tears in her eyes. 'Mr Forster has asked me to pack the trunk so we can be away directly,' she says.

So I'm going away? Where am I going? Home, I suppose, but what awaits me there? Forster comes out of the kitchen and hands me a glass of brandy.

'Drink this, and then we'll be on our way, but Charles did ask me to emphasise that despite what he wrote, you must prepare yourself for the worst,' he says.

'Whatever has happened?' I ask.

'Did you not read it in the letter?'

I hand it to him. 'I can't seem to focus,' I say.

He guides me back into the parlour, sits me down and raises the glass towards my lips.

'Drink it down,' he says and begins to read.

Words, words, words. They bounce off me without making sense until I hear 'suddenly stricken ill' and Dora's name.

SATURDAY, 11 JUNE 1870—TWENTY PAST MIDNIGHT

KATE remembers nothing of the long journey home, apart from praying for the recovery of her precious baby girl. And if this was not to be the Lord's will, Kate prayed that Dora might be spared long enough so she could hold the child in her arms one last time, kiss her peachy cheeks, feel the tickle of her coconut hair, tell her how much she was loved, gaze into her deep blue eyes, smile reassuringly, watch the gentle shutters of her heavy eyelids close, rock her to sleep, whisper goodbye in her perfect little seashell ear and tell her not to be afraid, for her Aunt Mary would be waiting, arms outstretched to receive her in Heaven.

Dora. Charles had named her Dora after David Copperfield's wife. Kate had thought this a lovely idea at the time but now she recalls that the first Mrs Copperfield was a weak and sickly character who had died young. Had Charles cast a dark spell at their baby's christening? Had he doomed Dora Annie Dickens to spend just eight short months on this earth?

Tears now. Nineteen years of tears. If Kate had not over-stretched herself she would have been with Dora, not miles away from her sick baby. For nearly two decades Kate has buried her anger but now she feels a volcano of rage about to erupt.

Abandoning the stars and the garden, she goes back inside the house, and picks up the bundle of Charles's letters that she has treasured for years. She works her way through them all, discarding each of them, one by one, and flinging them to the floor. A love letter? Meaningless! A message of reassurance? Not worth the paper it is written on! An enquiry after her health? A waste of ink! Ah—here is the one she wants. She holds it up to the light.

'Devonshire Terrace, Tuesday Morning, Fifteenth April 1851,' it is headed; and then: 'My Dearest Kate.'

Charles speaks to her clearly and directly. He tells her to read his letter very slowly and carefully, and not race ahead, even if she apprehends bad news, but to start from the beginning.

'Little Dora,' he writes, 'without being in the least pain, is suddenly stricken ill. She doesn't look it; in fact, there is nothing in her appearance to cause concern. You would suppose her quietly asleep. But I am sure she is very ill, and I cannot encourage myself with much hope of her recovery. I do not—why should I say I do, to you my dear!—I do not think her recovery at all likely.'

Charles says he can do nothing for Dora but does not want to leave her alone, and does not think she should be without her mother either. That is why he has asked John Forster to take his message and fetch her from Malvern.

When she arrives, he urges her not to give way to emotion: as he has often said before, with so many children, he and Kate can't expect to be spared the kinds of sorrow that other large families face. And if he has to tell her that their little baby has died, she must do her duty by the others and rise to the moral and emotional challenge of motherhood by staying strong for the sake of the other children.

Kate reads the endorsement she had made on the back at the time—'Written on the day after our little Dora's death'—with her signature beneath those damning words.

Her husband had lied to her. He had filled her with false hope that her child might survive when, in fact, Dora's lifeless little body was already lying in its tiny coffin. He said it was his way of trying to soften the blow but Kate was humiliated by it. He had called on her to do her duty as a mother and yet had treated her as a child, unable to handle the facts. He handled facts effortlessly, of course: he was a master storyteller and, she now realises, a master of deception too. What had he ever told her that was true? The stories he had spun about Maria Beadnell and Ellen Ternan and Kate herself suggested that he could not tell the difference between fact and make believe.

The heat builds up in her chest again. Molten words erupt from her mouth.

'How could you think that I might betray my children?' Kate asks, knowing there will no longer be any risk of repercussions. 'How could you warn me to be composed in front of them—to show myself worthy of their trust, when you had none in me?'

Charles had been contemptuous of her and yet, within two months, he had made her pregnant for the twelfth time, with her seventh son, Edward—'Plorn'. She had tried to accept God's will and focus on the future; now she gives thanks that she had no idea just what that future would hold.

Letters lie scattered all around her. She eases herself onto the floor to gather them up and wonders how she will ever manage to get back on her feet again.

'And, having got me pregnant for the twelfth time, you tried to commit me to a mental asylum,' she screams. 'What kind of marital devotion was that?'

Crawling around on all fours, one hand clutching a candle, the other clutching a bundle of correspondence to her chest, she concedes that Charles would have every reason to have her committed if he could see her now.

'And you accused me of being lazy and incompetent,' she says, 'but we both know that that's not true. Who organised our move to Tavistock House? I did, and you left me to it.'

September 1851

A CLOUD of dust rises as Charles opens the front door to our new home.

Achoo!

'God bless you, Mousey,' he says.

Bang!

The door slams behind us. Damp walls chill my fingers as I feel my way along the long dark corridor. Floorboards creak. Any moment now, Grip the raven will be back from the grave to swoop down upon us with his death-rattle cawing.

'Hello?' Charles shouts.

The echo of his voice reverberates through the empty rooms but remains unanswered.

'Anyone here?' he calls.

There is no response.

'Where in damnation are all the carpenters and plumbers and painters I was promised?'

Clank! Rattle!

Marley's ghost drags his chains along beside me.

My fingertips make out a doorframe, a wooden panel, a handle.

Creak.

Rattle.

Jangle.

Ding.

'Ouch!'

'What have you done now?' Charles asks.

Dim light from the drawing-room windows reveals my foot to be stuck inside a broken birdcage with a cuttlefish bone and little bell tied to its bars.

Charles comes to help me.

'Ow! What the devil?' he says.

A three-legged chair topples off a low table.

Clonk.

'Let's get more light in here before we both break our necks,' he says, rubbing his shin. 'Help me pull down these curtains. We'll need a stepladder to tackle the blinds.'

The curtains slump to the floor, as if exhausted after years of service. More dust clouds our vision. With candles lit and fires in the grates, the rooms had looked cosy enough when Mr and Mrs Stone lived here; now, in their emptiness, they're as cold and cheerless as a deconsecrated church. Huge spiders hang from sooty webs. Dead flies litter the window sills. Grey horsehairs poke through the faded velvet of the sofas.

An upended trunk stands sentry beside the door. It is covered by a dirty shawl. Moths flutter away as I give the shawl a tug. A severed head rolls towards me.

Faded red ribbons spiral as it spins.

Blonde plaits coil across the floor.

Baby-blue eyes stare out from a pretty face. The sight of them breaks my heart. Dora had fair hair and blue eyes.

Charles kicks the little girl's head like a football. It hits the iron fender in front of the fireplace and cracks.

Glass eyes look back at him reproachfully.

'I dread to think what state the kitchen is in,' he says and stomps off down the stairs.

There is a lingering smell of boiled cabbage but, beneath it, the stench of rotten eggs.

The hotplates on the cast-iron stove are greasy and covered with hairs.

Something lurks in the back of the bread oven. I reach in and lift out an ancient loaf.

'Ugh!' I say, and drop it in disgust. It bursts into a mouldy blue cloud.

Something scurries across the floor.

'Rat!' I screech.

'Can't be,' Charles says.

'It is!' I say, as another one darts across the flagstones and disappears behind the pipe beneath the sink.

'This whole place is turning into a nightmare, Charles says. 'I've paid more than one-and-a-half-thousand pounds to lease an eighteen-room wreck with rats everywhere. I let that sister of mine persuade me to employ her hopeless husband and even paid him

£400 in advance to supervise the works. I'll have a few words to say to her when I get home.'

'You can't blame Letitia,' I say. 'I'm sure there's some perfectly straightforward explanation. Austin is well-qualified and usually reliable. That's why Letitia recommended him.'

'My sweet Kate, may I remind you our current lease is about to expire?'

'I'm sure we'll be moving in long before we have to move out of Devonshire Terrace,' I say.

'I'm not. I'm not even sure that Austin will have finished the work here before its forty-five year lease is up! I'll pen him a stiff letter as soon as we get back to Broadstairs.'

True to his word, Charles is at his writing desk the moment we arrive back at the seaside, upbraiding his brother-in-law for letting us down. While he writes, I'm keen to hear how the girls have amused themselves in our absence.

Lucifer Box is full of a shipwreck by the pier.

'A steamer was lost and the sea was full of cattle and sheep,' she says all agog.

'Oh, don't remind me,' Mamie says. 'It was horrific.'

'I'm so glad Walter is back at school. It would have given him nightmares for months,' I say.

'There were hundreds of them floating about on their backs with their hooves in the air,' Lucifer Box says, waving her stiff arms in Mamie's face.

Mamie pushes her away.

'Do stop, Lucifer Box. Mother doesn't want to hear this,' she says.

The sweet girl no doubt thinks that talk of death will remind me of my loss. I squeeze her hand. She cannot know that Dora is never out of my mind.

'What of the passengers and crew?' I ask.

'All saved,' Mamie says.

'Thank Heaven for that,' I say.

'You could hear the moos and baas from the other end of the beach as the poor creatures succumbed to the waves,' Lucifer Box says.

She does a wobbly dance around her sister.

'Moo, moo, baa, baa, blub, blub, blub,' she says and gradually sinks lower and lower until she is lying on her back on the rug with her hands and feet in the air and her petticoats on full display.

Mamie shakes her head.

'It's no joking matter. Think of their suffering. Cook bought a whole carcass for one shilling and sixpence but I won't be able to stomach a mouthful of it,' she says.

Her sister puts on a gruesome grin.

'The sheep looked like they were smiling, and the cows' big brown eyes stared up as if they were still happily chewing the cud in a meadow instead of having their hides stripped off and tallow cut from around their bleeding hearts. What a stink!'

Mamie puts her hands over her ears.

'Stop! Stop! Stop!' she shouts.

Lucifer Box stands in front of Mamie.

'Dead bodies washed up all over the shore.'

She undoes her buttons, takes off her bodice and waves it above her head.

'Skinned alive! Some only half dead. Imagine being skinned alive when you're only half dead!' Lucifer Box says as Charles walks in the door.

All three of us freeze. No one dares take a breath.

Clonk.

Clonk.

Clonk.

Clonk.

His footsteps reverberate around the room. We shudder like stricken sheep.

He looks his younger daughter up and down.

Rain flays the window. Wind rages down the chimney. Tongues of flame flick from the fireplace. Candles gutter. Primordial elements fight for life—and Charles . . . laughs.

We sigh.

'That's quite a pose, Lucifer Box, but I'll skin you alive if you don't cover yourself up this instant,' he says.

Lucifer Box laughs and slips her bodice back on. 'I was telling Mama about a shipwreck, here, this very day,' she says.

'I'll look forward to hearing all about it later but, at the moment, I need your mother's assistance, to ensure we don't all get cast adrift.' He helps me to my feet, escorts me up the stairs to his study, and hands me a letter.

'I've tried to make my point but in a light way, so as not to cause offence,' he says. 'I know you also fear that time is running out, but you may rest assured, my sweet love, that I will not risk putting my family on the streets.'

'I know,' I say. 'I have every faith in you,' but secretly hope he will not let us down.

The black border of the mourning paper reminds me that Dora will not be moving into the new house with us. I cannot prevent a tear welling in my eye and dripping onto the paper. Luckily, Charles does not notice.

The leitmotif of the letter is that there are 'NO WORKMEN ON THE PREMISES', which Charles writes three times, in capital letters, like the chorus of a song. His state of mind is 'bordering on distraction', he says, because the painting season is 'oozing away', his new book is waiting to be born, he has not heard from his brother-in-law and there are 'NO WORKMEN ON THE PREMISES'. 'The very postman becomes my enemy because he brings no letter from you,' Charles says, and adds that he is so distressed that he has torn all his hair out and taken to beating his unoffending family.

It has occurred to him to send in his own plumber to do the drains, he says, but hasn't done so because he doesn't want two sets of plumbers to turn up. 'Where are you? When are you coming home? Where is the man who is to do the work?' he entreats. 'O rescue me from my present condition. Come up to the scratch, I entreat and implore you!'

He adds, as a postscript, 'NO WORKMEN ON THE PREMISES: Ha! Ha! Ha! (I am laughing demoniacally.)

'What do you think?' he asks me.

'Perfect,' I say. 'Forthright but as amusing as ever, notwithstanding your frustration and our other troubles.'

Charles frowns at the mention of 'other troubles' because work on Tavistock House is meant to distract me from the death of my baby.

'No doubt your wit will elicit a favourable response,' I say and force a smile.

SATURDAY, 11TH JUNE 1870—12.35 AM

'OFF you went to London,' Kate says, 'back to your magazine, leaving me to take care of the girls, and to grieve, and to write to the older boys at school, and to grieve, and be aware of the younger ones' suffering under Georgina's strict regime back at Devonshire Terrace, and grieve, and run the house, and grieve, and pray we'd all have somewhere to live before the winter, and grieve, and fear I was pregnant, and grieve, and grieve, and grieve.'

Kate sets the candle on the table. She crawls back into the armchair with her armful of letters and starts to sort through them.

'You claimed to feel Dora's loss as keenly as I, but it didn't take much to restore your spirits did it, Charles?' Her husband cannot deny it, for Kate holds the proof in her hand.

Office of Household Words, Thursday Eleventh September 1851

My Dearest Kate.

I have had a perfectly tremendous day with Henry Austin. He thought it best to go over the whole place in detail with only me, and to make plans and statements of all the alterations (which he did with infinite trouble) and to make his own estimate, and see Cubitt himself tomorrow. He proposes to offer him a month to do it in, and says it should be well done within a week of that time. We shall get a broad notion of the expence (I hope) before I leave for Broadstairs tomorrow.—I quake, I must say.

You can hardly imagine, even in the midst of the dirt and desolation, the effect upon the house of the windows being open and the dirty blinds gone! Of the bow in the drawing room, and of the general air of the room, I cannot speak in terms of sufficient praise. I almost begin to doubt whether the back room on the second floor which we once intended for Mamey and Katey, will not be the best room for us. It is half as large again as the front one,—with an outside place on the top of the drawing room bow, just like that outside the Devonshire Terrace nursery, to which I have ordered the wirework to be fitted. You shall decide.

I think it will be best for you in a week or so, to come up with me for a few hours and choose the papering.

He adds that Georgina's room will need to be made as comfortable as possible, with any little extras that can be ingeniously got into it: a larger washing stand, a table with ample writing materials and a selection of books including Nathaniel Hawthorne's *The Scarlet Letter*, published only the year before, and Sydney Smith's humorous *Elementary Sketches of Moral Philosophy*, which had also only just come out.

She had followed his instructions precisely. Kate always followed his instructions precisely. The slightest lapse, however unintentional, would bring forth his wrath and she had to protect the children. It was her life's work to keep Charles happy and, notwithstanding his constant fear of overspending, he was always happy to enjoy the fruits of his prodigality.

October 1851

CHARLES seems in good humour so I risk asking for a report on Tavistock House and if we are still on course to take up residence next month.

'I'd suspected that we were falling behind, and at a most triumphant pace. But yesterday we rather recovered, so have no fear, my Dear,' he says, and tries to swing me round as he used to but fails even to raise me off the ground. This does not seem to lower his spirits but does rather dampen mine.

'The thing is, the painters kept mislaying their brushes and wouldn't stop whistling, and the carpenters seemed to spend all their time looking sideways, down long pieces of wood, to judge their straightness, without then doing anything, but there was progress elsewhere. The kitchen walls have been white-limed, the water closet is looking almost civilised, and the bathroom is turning from abstract concept into reality.'

'That's all very encouraging,' I say. 'And how are the bedrooms progressing?'

'I found the young paper-hanger looking hard at the servants' room, at the top of the house, as if he meant to get round to it one of these days.'

'And the drawing-room?'

'No hope there whatsoever. They keep putting up reams of

blank paper on the walls, and then pulling them off again, which looks like insanity. No progress in the study, either, but the staircase is painted. And I came across Irish labourers howling with laughter in the schoolroom.'

'Is that a good sign?' I ask.

'I really don't know,' he says. 'I saw nothing to set them off and nothing to stop them, but the whole pack fell silent when they saw me, as if I was their headmaster brandishing a cane to beat them into shape.'

'Ah, to be sure, that's a good one!' I laugh and he runs out of the room and returns with a walking stick.

'You are a very naughty girl, to laugh in that way, like the Irishmen do, and to make fun of them,' he says. 'Bend over and raise your skirts, that I may punish you.'

'No! No! I am a very good girl,' I say, and lift my skirts, but only to facilitate my escape.

He chases me round the furniture. I take refuge behind the armchair and dodge left and right as he reaches out to hook me with the walking stick handle.

'I give in,' I say, grab the end of the stick and pull him towards me.

He pecks me on the forehead.

'I'll deal with you later, young Lady, but I'll be keeping a close eye on you in the meantime. I've spent all day watching the foreman,' he says.

'Doesn't he mind?' I ask.

'It makes him uneasy but he's so sweet tempered that he tries not to show it. To see me hovering gloomily through the premises all day must be quite a trial for him but I have the idea that more work is done when I flit, bat-like, through the rooms, than when there is no one looking on.'

'Try not to intimidate the poor man,' I say, then fear I may have gone too far. Charles does not like taking instruction. Fortunately, he laughs.

'He jumps when I appear in doorways and drifts away to other parts of the house, and then swoons with confusion when he encounters me again!'

Charles flaps his hand in front of his face like a maiden stricken with the vapours and collapses onto the sofa. I fetch the bellows from the grate and puff air into his face.

'Fresh air! Fresh air!' he cries, leaping up, and chases me again. I'm as joyful as a jack-in-the-box to be released from my prison and remember what it's like to have fun again. He raises the walking stick above his head like a wizard's wand and brings it down hard on the back of the sofa. 'I'll get you, my Girl, and I'll give you a good spanking!' He raises the stick once again, ready to give the sofa another whack.

I laugh and say, 'Take care you don't split the cushions.' But I'm too late. The stick snaps in half and with a loud *crack* the magic spell is broken.

A heavy hand compresses the spring inside me, shuts the lid of my box and forces me back down into my darkness.

Shame on me! I have no right to be happy when my baby lies cold in her grave. Dora will never toddle about, splash in the sea, build sandcastles on the beach, ride on her brothers' shoulders, steal her sisters' dollies, wear a ribbon in her hair, pull the cat's tail, tip custard on her head, or lick the spoon when I mix her first birthday cake.

'I'd better check on dinner,' I say, wiping away a tear.

Charles takes his watch from his waistcoat pocket, checks the time, frowns and holds it to his ear.

'Yes, it's nearly time,' he says and gives the watch a tap. 'Make sure it's not late. I'm ravenous.'

SATURDAY, 11TH JUNE 1870—12:45 AM

SHE had made her way upstairs slowly, sat at her husband's writing desk and looked out over the grey sea, wishing she could write away her feelings in the way Charles did. Kate longed to feel the cold waters close over her head, to sink far beneath the waves and rest on the seabed. Sleep would find her there and she would be at peace with her little daughter, rocking together as the tide flowed to and fro over them and the moon waxed and waned.

'What did you do?' Kate asks. 'Did you sit with me? Hold my hand? Put your arms around me? Cry with me? Buy me red roses? No—you left me, didn't you? I had to grieve for my baby with a paint brush in my hand, because you were busy with your amateur theatricals.'

She picks up another letter, written in November 1851 after a production at Clifton's Victoria Rooms, the largest and most fashionable venue in town for concerts, lectures, readings and theatrical performances. Charles, she notes, is in raptures:

> We had a noble night. The room (which is the largest but one in England) was crammed in every part. The effect from thirteen to fourteen hundred people, all well dressed, and all seated in one unbroken chamber, except that the floor rose high towards the end of the hall, was most splendid; and we never played to a better audience. The enthusiasm was prodigious; the place delightful for speaking in; no end of gas; another hall for a dressing room; an immense stage; and every possible convenience. We were all thoroughly pleased, I think, with the whole thing, and it was a very great and striking success.

'Good for you,' she says: 'another triumph. You were free to swan off without a care in the world because you trusted me to deal with everything back at home. Later you made a bonfire of my letters, Charles, in an attempt to rewrite our history but, praise the Lord, you could not stop me from keeping yours, and your own words provide ample proof of how competent I was.'

> My Dearest Kate.
>
> I have just received your second letter, and am quite delighted to find that all is going on so vigorously, and that you are in such a methodical, business-like, and energetic state . . .
>
> I am continually thinking of the House in the midst of all the bustle, but I trust it with such confidence to you that I am quite at my ease about it.

'"Quite at ease about it"?' Kate growls. 'I bet you were. "Methodical, business-like and energetic." Not lazy and incompetent, then.

'Were you equally supportive? Did you love me, comfort me, honour and keep me, in sickness and in health; and, forsaking all others, keep thee only unto me, so long as we both did live? Did you even lighten my load when you came back from Clifton? No, for there was *Household Words* to edit, books to write and all those fallen women you needed to pick up.

I'll tell you something for nothing, Charles: women don't fall—

men push them. You knew you'd pushed me too far. That's why you bought the roses wasn't it?'

December 1851

'THESE are for you,' Charles says. He holds out a bouquet of red roses.

I glance up, say, 'Thank you', and continue writing out the menu for the next in the long line of dinner parties designed to show off our new home to all and sundry.

'I thought you loved roses,' he says.

'I did,' I say. 'Beef or mutton?' He's still holding out the bouquet. His arms must be starting to ache but I show him no mercy.

'I defer to you in all matters culinary,' he says. 'Shall I ask Anne to fetch a vase?'

'I defer to you in all matters floral,' I say and smile sweetly at him.

'Kate!' he says taking the menu from my hand and placing the bouquet on my lap where the damp stalks will surely stain my skirt. 'I've just had a first-rate idea!' My discordant tone has prompted one of his leaps of the imagination, and he's delighted with himself.

I take a single stem from the bouquet, drop the rest on the floor and brush the drips off my skirt.

'You must write a cookery book!' he says, and claps his hands as if applauding his brilliance.

I sniff the flower, as he would a pinch of snuff, and say nothing. Recognising with a jolt that I probably deserve a little recognition, he sets his first-rate idea aside for a moment and throws me a bone.

'Your dinner parties are unparalleled!' he says, hoping that a word of flattery will be sufficient and that he can now return to his first-rate idea. But I don't let him.

'Unparalleled? Do you really think so, Charles? I thought they were merely methodical and business-like, and perhaps a little inept, like everything else that I attempt.'

'They are the very best in all of London,' he says, 'and that is why the very best of London will want to read your secrets.'

I pick the leaves off the rose and scatter them across the floor.

'I could get Bradbury and Evans to publish it for you,' he says as he picks up the leaves.

'If you haven't fallen out with them. You seem to be in the habit of falling out with your publishers,' I say.

He reaches out for my hand but grasps the denuded rose stalk. One of its thorns draws blood.

'If you didn't want to use your own name you could take a pseudonym,' he says, sucking his wound.

'I suppose you already have one in mind?' I say, aware that his scheme is calcifying even as he speaks.

'You gave such an excellent performance as Lady Maria Clutterbuck in our recent theatricals, my Love, I rather thought you might like to make use of that name.' He has already incorporated the name in a collection called *The Widow's Mite* so, if I agree, all credit will accrue to him.

I don't think I can extract much more from him today. He has praised my dinner parties and now my dramatic performances. What else is there left? 'Well, perhaps it might be of value if I shared some of my recipes,' I allow myself to concede, and look down at the roses in a noncommittal way.

'And I shall write a Preface for you,' he says and reaches for my hand again.

'Won't that rather give the game away, Charles?' I ask, withdrawing my hand and making for the door, 'on top of my using a name that you have trademarked?'

'Then choose a name that is more to your liking, and I shall be anonymous,' he says following in my wake.

'Boz, The Inimitable, Charles, John, Huffam, Dickens, and now Anonymous: that will be quite a novelty,' I say and breeze out without holding the door for him to follow.

SATURDAY, 11TH JUNE 1870—12:55 AM

KATE still feels proud that *What Shall We Have For Dinner?* by 'Lady Maria Clutterbuck', was well-received and that it was reprinted several times, in spite of efforts to belittle it. Some suggested it had really been written by Charles; others that Mrs

Dickens was undoubtedly the author as the rich meals explained why she was so fat.

Charles's Preface, attributed to 'Lord Clutterbuck', made it clear that a wife needed to make an effort to keep her husband happy, that good food was the key to marital harmony, and that a thoughtfully prepared dinner could keep a husband's affection firmly at home when there were competing attractions in gentlemen's clubs.

Kate had provided Charles with good food but apparently this was not the key to their marital harmony. She had borne him ten children and given him her undying love, dedication, admiration and self-sacrifice, but all this had evidently also been insufficient. He had success. He had fame. He had money. And he lived in a mansion. But Kate knows she could not give him what he now yearned for. For that, he looked back to his first love, Maria Beadnell, her mother-in-law's favourite.

April 1855

'COME in and take a seat, my dear,' I say. 'Tea is on its way.' Maria Beadnell—now Mrs Henry Winter—looks around the room.

'Is Charles not here?' she asks.

'He appreciates how very kind you are to call but I'm afraid he will not be able to join us today.'

'What a shame. Or rather, what a disappointment. I mean, neither a shame nor a disappointment: after all, it is you that I have come to see,' she says.

She slowly lowers herself into an armchair, looks deflated, then pops back up on her feet.

'Not that I would not wish to see Charles, if he could spare the time, but I understand he's very busy—very, very busy—what with writing and travelling and amateur dramatics and consorting with celebrated friends and his various charitable works, such as helping Miss Burdett-Coutts to save fallen women, which is an admirable cause, seeing how easy it is to fall these days—even for respectable women—especially when they lack more onerous occupations such as yours, Mrs Dickens, and your arranging of dinner parties such as the marvellous one that my husband and I had the good fortune to attend recently, and your turning of your expertise in the kitchen into the writing of a cookery book deserving universal praise rather than injurious carping of the kind that Carlyle's wife hurled at you when complaining that your desserts were "overloaded", which I found to be far from the truth—'

'Well, I am very pleased to make time to see you again,' I say, breaking in on a monologue that seems to have no end. 'I was glad to make your acquaintance at our dinner party, having heard so much about you over the years, and to meet your husband.'

I am about to ask her what she wants with me when she sits back down and continues from where she left off.

'Oh, I know you are busy too,' she says, 'what with your ten children.' She stops and grips the arms of her chair, no doubt hoping that she will thereby be saved from floating away on the torrent of hot air blowing from her mouth. 'Nine—I meant, nine children. I should not have included your third daughter. Poor little Dora. What a tragedy. But Charles said he thought you conducted yourself with admirable composure and that your loss had been character-building, and that you would not have wished to call little Dora back although, as he says, it is always possible for you, with his help, to commune with the spirit world and speak to the child if you wished to call on her emanation to show itself, whereas in my case, I have suffered troubles that cannot be eased in a session of table-turning, though nothing in comparison with a dead baby, of course, but . . .'

Her words stab me as if she has pulled a hat pin from her bonnet and plunged it into my heart. That Charles has confided his most intimate thoughts about our baby daughter's death to this chatterbox—that he may have suggested that losing Dora had done me good and that I would not wish to restore her to life—renders me speechless.

Seeing the look on my face, Maria drops her reticule, spilling coins, keys and a comb onto the floor. Her bending down to retrieve them affords me a few moments of respite from her infernal babbling and allows me to find my own voice.

'I'm most sorry to hear you've been troubled, but pray do not concern yourself about our affairs,' I say to pre-empt any further elaboration by her on this or any other subject.

'I must confess—unless perhaps you already know this from

Charles?—no, I'm sure he would not think that his present relationship with me . . . not that there is a "present relationship" to speak of but, if there was, I'm sure he would not think it of sufficient significance to mention it to you. Or has he? It was just some foolishness, nothing more than a vain attempt to turn back the clock and roll back the years and set back the timepiece to our younger days.'

Maria extracts her handkerchief from her sleeve and mops her brow. She is far from the fire but her face is flushed.

'I'm sure we all hanker after our childhoods but time marches on,' I say, wishing the minutes to tick by at a greater pace and put an end to this interminable encounter.

Maria wraps her handkerchief round and round her hand like a bandage. 'To be open and candid, and entirely without deception, and without wanting to cause any upset, not that there is any reason for upset, there has been correspondence between your husband and myself,' she says.

'Charles writes many letters,' I say quickly, wondering what on earth he could have said to disturb her so. Anne bringing in refreshments provides a welcome distraction.

My unwelcome guest takes a biscuit and consumes it.

Then another.

'Do have some cake,' I say.

'I shouldn't,' she says, but reaches for the biggest slice.

With cake in one hand and spoon in the other, she stirs sugar into her tea. The handkerchief on her hand unravels and falls into her cup. She glances up. I look away, to save her embarrassment.

'You were speaking of correspondence?' I say. She puts her spoon down on the saucer, crams some cake in her mouth and covers the teacup with her hand.

'Words of affection were exchanged which should not have been resurrected from those long-gone days and . . .' she says, and gives a nervous cough, causing her to spit out cake crumbs.

'Old friends may remain affectionate,' I reassure her quickly, in an attempt to forestall anything more she may wish to add.

'. . . but Charles imagined himself "exactly nineteen" and I told him, "Three- or four-and-twenty years have vanished like a dream" as indeed they did . . .'

'Reminiscences of happy times can bring solace in later life,' I say, hoping again to stem her flow.

'. . . but although Charles assured me that the letters were "between ourselves alone" and that he was acting "in perfect innocence and good faith", as I'm sure he was—as indeed was I—nevertheless I wanted to put your mind at rest on this matter, always assuming that dear Charles has alluded to it, which he may not have done, in which case it doesn't matter, or shouldn't matter, for there is no matter pertaining to it . . .'

Not wanting to offend her by insisting that Charles clearly wishes to forget she ever existed, I offer her more cake.

'I do apologise, dear Mrs Dickens, for I fear my tongue has run away with me—as it is wont to!' She grins and takes another slice. She tries to sip her tea but the soggy brown handkerchief plops onto her skirt and sits there like a toad on a lily pad. She screams, flaps her hands and drops her cake. The toad tumbles onto the floor. I ring for Anne.

'Shall I bring more refreshments, Madam?' Anne asks, picking up the tea-stained handkerchief and lumps of sodden cake.

'No, thank you, Anne; I think we're all done—unless you cared for another slice, my dear?

'I couldn't,' says Maria. 'You have already been more than generous and overloaded me beyond my capacity—I mean . . . deliciously so, for I loved every bite and hope I was able to keep pace with you and your own hearty appetite, but I must be going, and please, Mrs Dickens, be assured of my apologies and think nothing of what I have told you, for our warmth for each other was long, long ago, and Charles meant nothing by suggesting that we meet here in secret when you were out . . .'

'You may be certain, Maria, that I will hide this conversation in the furthest recesses of my mind,' I say, and call for Anne to let her out whilst attempting not to wonder why my husband would invite an old love to visit him when I was away.

'I'm sure a tryst was as far from his intention as it was from mine . . .' Mrs Winter confides to me, as Anne sees her to the door.

SATURDAY, 11TH JUNE 1870—1:10 AM

POOR plump Maria. Kate wonders what might have happened had she retained her girlish face and figure. Kate also wonders what might have happened had she herself kept her girlish face and figure.

Kate picks up the candle that Matilda has left for her in the hallway. The flickering flame casts an eerie glow as she regards herself in the looking glass on the wall. The critics of her recipes were right: she has grown portly and her face has lost its once-fine contours. Poor Charles had wanted to forget he was getting older and had searched for his youth in Maria Beadnell, only to find that she had become the unlovely Mrs Henry Winter and a reflection of his own wife's loss of bloom.

Maria's words had unsettled Kate, and now she had questions for Charles, but her slippery husband always had the answers he needed to get himself off the hook. How innocent she had been to believe that he would tell her the truth.

April 1855

'I'M sorry to disturb you my dear,' I say, opening the study door cautiously, but Charles is nowhere to be seen.

One of the long curtains twitches; he is hiding behind it.

'Has she gone? he asks.

'She has gone, yes, but she left something behind.'

'She did?' he says, emerging into the room. 'What could she have left? She won't come back for it will she?'

'No, it's a trail of destruction,' I say.

He looks down. 'Oh, Kate: I'm sorry I ever offered to renew her acquaintanceship,' he says.

I concentrate on a droopy ringlet and twiddle it round my finger in a vain attempt to make it spring back into curl.

'May I ask you why you did?'

He turns away from me and looks back to the window, with his hands clasped behind his back.

'Unfinished business from years ago, and fear of time running out, I suppose,' he says. 'She broke my heart—or, rather, her parents did when they sent her to a finishing school abroad.'

'But you waited?'

'I lived in hope that she would return with her feelings for me undiminished, but it was not the case. She treated me cruelly.'

He rocks backwards and forwards, pivoting from toe to heel.

I sit on the window seat in front of him, spread out my skirt and squeeze my hands together to pump the words out of my mouth.

'You would have married her?'

He shrugs.

'I wanted to but—but that was then. I was Charley's age. I had more purpose and energy than he has but I was just as naive.'

'Charley thinks he's very grown up.'

'As did I. Only this morning I told him that when I was his age, I was teaching myself shorthand, a very difficult art, and walking miles every day to practise it in the courts of law. He seemed to think I must have been one of the most unaccountable of youths.'

'You are inimitable and Charley does have many tender qualities,' I say.

'Inherited from you,' Charles says, sweetly.

Encouraged, I stand beside him and follow his gaze into the garden. Birds flock around Anne as she scatters cake crumbs on the grass. If I don't ask him now I never will.

'Are you regretful?'

A jackdaw lands and feasts on the cake, scaring off the tits and sparrows.

'Regretful?' Charles asks.

Another jackdaw arrives but the first one holds its ground. The pair flutter around in circles, squawking and complaining, their plumage clashing.

Charles turns to me, puts his hand on my chin and gently tilts my face towards his.

Tears pool inside my eyelids. I look down and pretend to study the patterns on the turkey rug as they fall.

'Of whom you married,' I say, trying to keep my voice steady, but it sounds as tremulous as Walter's when he wakes from a nightmare.

Charles laughs.

'So that is what this is all about,' he says. 'What on earth has Maria been saying?'

'That you've been corresponding,' I say.

'Yes?'

He tips his head to one side and holds his palms open, as if appealing for more evidence.

'Affectionately,' I add, sounding rather foolish.

Charles smiles at me. 'I write hundreds of letters. Should I not be affectionate to an old friend?' he asks.

'Exactly what I told her,' I say and smile back at him, glad he has not taken offence. Buoyed, I venture the more serious matter.

'But she said you invited her to visit you here when you were sure I would not be at home . . .'

He pauses, nods his head slowly and takes my hand.

'Of course I did. I wanted to spare you from having to listen to her prattle. She rarely drew breath at our dinner party, as you'll recall, and I didn't want to put you through that again. I do hope you don't suspect my motives, Kate?'

'No, no, certainly not. Maria mentioned a tryst but I knew she must have misunderstood,' I say.

'I made it absolutely plain that I was acting in perfect innocence and good faith,' he says.

'Of course you were. I don't doubt you.'

So he was thinking of me all the time. I clasp his hand in mine. What sort of a wife would I be to mistrust my husband?

Tears fall.

Charles puts his arm around my shoulders.

'What is it, Kate? Pray tell me so I may put your mind at rest.'

Words won't come. My mouth opens and shuts.

'Kate, Kate, Kate,' he says and squeezes me to him.

'Dora,' I say and sob. 'She said . . . she said you thought that losing Dora had done me good.'

'That is the problem with sharing words with a scatterbrain,' he says. 'Look at me, Kate. I merely meant to convey that losing our precious baby girl had made us appreciate our many blessings.'

I tuck my face into Charles's shoulder and his scent fills my nostrils. A deep inhalation of him inflates my courage.

'And we would not call her back if we could?'

'She is at peace in heaven: why would we call her back to this world of suffering?' he asks.

'I know, I know, and it is selfish of me, but I would give my life to bring my baby back.'

Charles wipes the tears from my cheeks.

'I'm sure you would,' he says and embraces me with both arms. 'The loss of our child is a pain to be borne every day of our lives.'

'I should never have left her,' I say.

'I left her too,' he says, 'to give a speech. They waited for me to finish before telling me. Maria broke my heart when I was twenty-one but it shattered into a thousand pieces when Dora died. I had so longed for her.'

He releases me and wipes his eyes with a handkerchief.

'My heart broke too,' I say and pull him back towards me.

'But you did not become cold to those you love,' he says and turns away. 'What sort of father am I when I protect myself from my children's growing independence by becoming distant from them in retaliation? It is hateful of me. As they mature, I become the child.'

I reach out for him as he paces to the window.

'We all love you, Charles, and I know you try your best to be a good father,' I say. 'And you will never be old in my eyes.'

'Bless you, my sweet Kate,' he says. 'I love you too.' He takes my hand. 'Shall we go upstairs for a moment?'

SATURDAY, 11TH JUNE 1870—1.20 AM

HOW happy Kate had been to hear Charles speak words of reassurance and to be able to believe him. They had been intimate that day, not just physically but also in the opening up of their hearts. Kate asks herself if it was the last time that they had been so close. Charles had even said he loved her. Had he ever said it again? She cannot be sure but thinks not. Her stubby candle gutters.

She had relished his ridiculing of Maria Winter as a scatterbrain of no possible interest to him, but she had not relished the cruelty he had shown her. He had avoided her in life but not in fiction, using her as the model for pretty little Flora Casby, in *Little Dorrit*, whom he had made silly, old and fat when she became Mrs Finching in later life. Middle-aged Maria, with her loose tongue, had evidently taught Charles a lesson. He would be more circumspect in future in his quest for eternal youth.

The wick in her candlestick fizzles and drowns. She does not care. There is comfort in darkness. She reaches out to put it down on the hall table but misjudges the distance, and bangs it against the side. Hot wax spills onto her hand and, in pain, she drops it onto the tiled floor.

'Is that you, Madam?' Matilda shouts down from the landing.

'Yes, Matilda!' Kate shouts back. 'The candle you left me went out and I dropped it.'

'I'll bring mine down and assist you,' Matilda says.

Kate is glad of the offer. Her knees are so stiff that they refuse to bend and her back is so stiff that it refuses to straighten.

Matilda patters down the staircase with her own candle, links arms with Kate and helps her upstairs to her bedroom.

'I'll get you tucked in and then go back down to clear up the wax,' she says. 'This overnight jug needs topping up with hot water,' she adds, lifting the jug from the washstand.

'No need, my Dear,' Kate says as she opens the windows. 'A cold-water wash will suffice this evening. It's like a furnace in here.'

'If you're sure, Madam.'

'Very sure. I'm sorry I disturbed you, Matilda. Goodnight, Dear.'

'I couldn't rest until I knew you was settled, Ma'am. Sleep well.'

Matilda lights a candle for Kate and leaves.

The tepid water is refreshing on her face. The towel is soft. Kate lifts her heavy breasts, sponges underneath each of them where the sweaty skin is sore, and pats herself dry. She holds onto the washstand and squats to sponge around the inflammation at the tops of her legs where they chafe each other. These days an egg dangles between them as she walks. Kate squeezes out the sponge, presses it against the bulge and forces it gently back inside her. She is more comfortable now but knows it will not last. Her stomach sags onto her thighs as she sits on the edge of the bed. She swivels round slowly, slips under the sheet, throws off the blanket and lies on her back, determined to sleep.

After a moment she turns onto her left side and her breasts flop together like empty bellows. She waits, then turns to the right. Her breasts flop across the other way. Is this how Charles pictures her? In a moment of revelation, Kate is rocked by the realisation that Charles will never think of her again. She takes a handkerchief from beneath her pillow and holds it to her eyes as tears well up. How she wishes for sleep to claim her. She flaps the sheet to fan herself but it does nothing to cool her mind. She waggles herself up, plumps the pillows to support her back and sits upright. What a foolish young woman she had been to believe that marrying for love ensured a couple stayed in love. That last summer they had spent together as husband and wife in his new house in the Kent countryside, Charles had been proud to show off Gad's Hill Place to Hans Christian Andersen, but not even the master of fairy tales had been able to ensure that they lived happily ever after.

June 1857

'HE'S here!' Charles says, as he marches into the morning room.

I put down my embroidery. It takes me many squints to thread a needle these days, so I take care to pull enough grey silk through its eye, and then push the needle back into the fabric to secure it.

'Hans Christian Andersen?' I say. 'I can't believe it. Here at last —after nine years of promising to come and not making it?'

'His English isn't much improved. *Mahy deyah frend, Deckens*,' he says in mockery of the Danishman.

'Charles!' I say, but laugh with him.

'Don't concern yourself, my Sweet. He has been shown to his room and I will take care not to wound his feelings. I have even gone so far as to praise his linguistic abilities in our correspondence,' he says.

'You are incorrigible!'

'I'm "The Inimitable"!'

'You most certainly are. Did he say how long he plans to stay?'

'About ten days—a fortnight at the most—but I will take him on trips around London: the theatre, the Houses of Parliament, the British Museum, Westminster Abbey, all that sort of thing. He won't want for amusement.'

'I've planned to serve all his favourite dishes.'

'Oh,' says Charles, looking squeamish. 'Then we'll be having fish for breakfast, fish for lunch and fish for dinner: you know what they're like in Copenhagen. I'd better treat him to meals at the Garrick Club or we'll all have grown gills by the time he leaves,' Charles says. He pouts like a salmon and leaps around the room.

I laugh so much my stomach aches.

'I've told Plorn he can come down from the nursery for five

minutes to meet his favourite author at dinner. He will worry that we're eating the Little Mermaid. We must have read it at least ten times this morning,' I say.

'It's a shame the other boys won't be back from school before he leaves, but nine children might prove too much for an old bachelor's constitution. They sometimes prove too much for mine!'

'Look out, Hans Christian! It's a leaping salmon!' I call, and throw Charles a cushion from the sofa beside me. Charles throws it back to me, and we laugh.

'Hurra! Well caught, Mrs Deck-ens!' he cries. 'We will make a feesher-mayn of you yet.'

'I think it may be a little late in the day for that,' I say.

'Nonsense!' he says, now back in his own voice. 'Move aside, Hans Christian. This is a woman of many talents. Some may be well hidden but I am the man to uncover them.' He lifts my skirts and throws them over his head, like a photographer about to open the shutter.

I jerk my skirts back and smooth them down, in parody of an affronted maiden.

'Behave yourself, Charles! Mr Andersen is blushing.'

'I'm blushing as well,' he says, making to grab my bosom.

I slap his hand away, fold my arms across my chest, and make a show of hurrying to the door.

'You will never escape my advances,' he says and chases me out of the room.

I shriek and run straight into Georgina, who is dragging Plorn across the hallway.

'Catherine!' she says, affronted. 'Pray remind me, dear Sister, just how old you are?'

She does not wait for an answer.

'Is this the sort of example you wish to set your son?'

I hang my head like a naughty schoolgirl but wink at Plorn. He laughs, but Georgina is not amused.

'Come on, Young Man. It is high time you got some fresh air and exercise,' she says.

'Must I, Mama?' he asks.

Before I can answer, his aunt pushes him out of the front door and pulls it shut.

'It would seem you must,' I say.

DINNER is a stilted affair. Georgina is obviously still offended by the sight of my frolicking earlier and refuses to smile. Charley, Mamie and Lucifer Box do not recall being spellbound by Mr Andersen during our summers in Broadstairs when they were little and cannot muster any special affection for his books now they are older. I want at least someone round the table to be enthusiastic about his *Fairy Tales, Told for Children.*

The only possible candidate is Walter Young Skull. He would put our guest at his ease. They have so much in common. Walter is an avid reader, with a vivid imagination, and wants to follow in his father's footsteps and become a writer. It's such a shame that Charles will not hear of it and insists on his serving in the Army on the other side of the world. He says it will make a man of our sensitive sixteen-year-old. He has already enrolled him at the Royal Military Academy in Woolwich and Walter, thanks to the good offices of Angela Burdett-Coutts, has been granted a cadetship in the East India Company's Bengal Army, and will now depart for India in a month's time. I fear for how he will manage, not least with many of the natives in open rebellion, but I do not wish to distract myself with such troublesome thoughts and so concentrate instead on our guest.

We struggle to understand Mr Andersen's mangled English, then struggle to understand his mangled French and Italian when I suggest we change language.

Charles rolls his eyes at me. I raise my eyebrows back at him.

'He can't even pronounce the name of his own book,' he whispers. 'Why can't he speak English? They manage it in India. They manage it in Ceylon and the Cape Colony. Why cannot they manage it in Denmark?

Charles does his best to lighten the atmosphere but even the past master of successful dinner parties struggles to elicit any response. Mr Andersen's regard for his literary idol has left him dumbstruck and he shows no interest in the rest of us. When he does decide to string together a few words, they are gibberish.

Fortunately, the fried whitings in shrimp sauce seem to please our guest and he smiles when a shimmering salmon is served. This king of the fish lies on a seaweed bed of watercress, lapped by waves of lettuce, freshly picked from our kitchen garden this morning.

Charles looks at me and says, 'More seafood! How original!' He grins and reprises his aquatic pout.

I take a sip of wine to drown my giggles but launch into a coughing fit. Charley hands me my napkin. Mr Andersen does not notice. He concentrates on tackling his salmon, perhaps afraid it might leap off his plate and race back to the ocean.

We hurry to eat our food to spare our guest further awkwardness. Silence falls. I am gradually overcome by an itching sensation that extends from my toes to my head and have to fight the urge to scratch myself.

I cannot think of anything to say.

Charley is the last to finish eating and carelessly drops his knife onto his cleared plate. We jump like startled cats.

'I do apologise,' he says.

Georgina tuts.

Poor Charley reddens.

Mr Andersen looks as stern as a judge for a moment, but then picks up his own knife and lets it drop onto his plate. The sound hangs in the air. Georgina looks discomfited. Mamie turns to Lucifer Box. Charley turns to me. I glance at Charles to gauge his response.

Charles claps his hands in appreciation.

'Capital, capital! Good man,' he says, ever our master of ceremonies.

Mr Andersen smiles proudly.

We all laugh like audience members at the most amusing play we have ever had the good fortune to attend. Spurred on by his triumph, Mr Andersen picks up his knife and drops it again. We honour him with an encore but he is obviously working towards a standing ovation for he now picks up his fork and drops that too. We would like him to know that to drop a fork as well as a knife is astonishingly funny but, try as we may, we cannot sustain the same level of hilarity, and our laughter subsides.

'Well done, Mr Andersen.' I say, having failed to calculate that praise might encourage him. He reaches for his spoon. 'Take care,' I call out in desperation. 'You'll need that spoon for your greengage tartlet.'

The door flies open. Plorn runs in. I have never been so grateful for a child's interruption in my entire life.

'Mr Anders Son,' he shouts and rushes at our startled guest.

'I'm so sorry,' I say. 'This is our youngest: Plorn. He has been waiting all day.' Plorn's nursemaid appears, as flustered as a feather duster.

Mr Andersen comes to life as if we are minor characters and the main protagonist in his story has arrived.

'Plorn, thot is a fina oldah Danish nom and it is only givin to maagical childron,' he says and lifts our little boy onto his lap.

'What did he say?' Plorn asks me.

'Mr Andersen says you are a magical child, but I have always known that,' I say.

Plorn stares up at the long thin face and large nose. 'Are you a giant Mr Punch?' he asks.

Everyone, with the exception of Georgina, smiles at this rather accurate description of our guest.

'Manners!' my sister shouts. 'Back to the nursery with you.'

The nursemaid steps forward to carry out her instruction but Plorn protests.

Mr Andersen lifts him onto his shoulders and says Plorn has grown into a great big giant and he will tell him tales which can only be heard by those with enormous ears.

I don't think the magical boy understands a word but it matters not a jot. Mr Andersen gets up and strides out of the room, and Plorn, carried aloft, waves down at us from on high as the nursemaid trots after them.

Charles shuts the door behind them. The communal sigh of relief is so forceful that the candles flicker. Greengage tartlets have never tasted so good.

I AM grateful to Mr Andersen for getting Plorn off to sleep but, in the morning, there are raised voices on the landing as I make my way downstairs to check on preparations for breakfast.

'I'm sorry, but I am neither equipped nor willing to oblige,' Charley says.

Something is said about customs in Denmark.

I retrace my steps. Mr Andersen towers over my son on the landing, brandishing a cut-throat razor.

'Whatever is amiss?' I ask and step between them.

'He insists I shave him,' Charley says.

'Ja' Mr Andersen says and waves the blade up and down each side of my face. I stand very still.

‘Fetch your father,’ I say, moving only my eyes and mouth like a ventriloquist’s dummy. ‘He’s in his dressing room.’

Fearful I am about to die, I utter the immortal words, ‘Did you sleep well?’

He waggles the razor from side to side like a menacing metronome and shakes his head in perfect synchronisation.

‘No,’ he says and makes an odd miaowing sound.

My failure to grasp his meaning provokes my razor-wielding household guest to step forward. Rather than slitting my throat, he leans towards me, licks my face, purrs in my ear and indicates his bedroom door.

With the remnants of my wits I gather that Charles’s cat, Bob, had miaowed outside Mr Andersen’s room the previous evening and that the felonious feline had foolishly been granted admittance. He had then proceeded to extinguish all Mr Andersen’s candles, a trick he’d devised some years ago to gain Charles’s attention by preventing him from writing late into the night. Having reprised this performance, he curled up on his companion’s pillow, repeatedly expressing his pleasure by licking his partner’s unbewhiskered face.

‘What’s all this, my dear fellow?’ Charles calls as he approaches with Charley, in time for them to witness Mr Andersen attempting to drag me by the hand into his bedroom.

Our strange visitor lets go of my hand, retreats into the room, scoops the cat up from his bed and returns with it in his arms, as if he’s produced the defence’s star witness. Bob is as delighted as ever to see his master, and leaps onto Charles’s shoulder. Charles tickles him under his chin. Encouraged, Mr Andersen steps forward and strokes Bob’s back. Likewise encouraged, the cat leaps onto his head and settles there like a black-and-white turban. The two men walk off as if all is just as it should be and our guests always wear cats on their heads in the morning.

Charley and I follow them down the stairs and catch a whiff of kedgeree outside the dining room. Bob sticks his nose in the air, jumps down and follows the aroma. Charles shoos him away as we take our seats at the table.

‘I do apologise for that cat,’ he says to our visitor, ‘and for that little misunderstanding with my son. I’ll make a regular appointment for you at the barbers in Rochester.’

Mr Andersen nods. He cannot speak because his mouth is full

of kedgeree but he has not forgotten his feline friend and shares with him a forkful of fish.

'Take care or he'll want to come and live with you in Denmark,' Charles says.

Mr Andersen swallows. 'It wood be 'im on the platt in somm Dansk veelages,' he says and laughs.

Charles rushes round, snatches up his cat and leaves me to entertain our guest, who seems oblivious to the affront he has caused.

'Kom, kat! Kit-ty, Kit-ty, Kit-ty!' Mr Andersen calls after them.

CHARLES spares us Mr Andersen's company at dinner and any risk of Bob becoming an addition to the bill of fare by making arrangements to dine with him at the Garrick. We are all grateful for a fish-free meal and for the company of my Aunt Helen. We gather in the music room. I play the piano and she sings exquisitely for our entertainment.

Rather later than expected, Charles arrives home. He is distraught. Mr Andersen has wandered off and become lost in London. Searching has been to no avail so we are resolved to wait up and pray for his safe return.

Long after we would usually retire he hobbles in, sits and pulls off his boots. He turns the boots upside down and onto the floor tumble a watch, some coins, a train timetable, a pocket book, a pair of scissors, a penknife and two small books. He rubs his feet, looks up, gazes from face to face and seems bemused to see so many wide eyes and open mouths.

'Feeird pick pocots,' he says. We are all struck dumb. 'Oliver Twist, Fagin,' he adds in full and final explanation, and walks out in his stockinged feet.

THERE is no disturbance on the landing next morning but also no sign of Mr Andersen at breakfast.

Georgina bashes the head of a boiled egg with her spoon and says, 'Plorn is of the misguided opinion that magical boys are exempt from house rules.'

'At least that lunatic didn't expect you to shave him and come at you with a cut-throat razor when you refused,' Charley says, and stabs his fork into a sausage.

'He's a bony bore,' Lucifer Box says and takes a big bite of toast.

Mamie, generous as ever, says, 'He can't help being boring,' and passes the pot of honey to her sister.

'He has amused us in very many ways,' I say, but then fear that I have been uncharitable as our laughter has largely been at Mr Andersen's expense.

Charles reminds us that he is a friend and a guest in our house and that it is therefore incumbent upon all of us to do whatever is needed to make him feel at home. He frowns at each of us in turn.

We study our plates in silence.

Bob wanders in.

'And that includes you,' Charles says. 'You are required for serving up on the platts of Dansk veelages.' He raises his knife menacingly but drops it on his plate, laughs, picks it up and drops it again. Then he pulls off his boots, empties them of imaginary valuables, jumps up, and dances around the table.

'Here kit-ty, kit-ty, kit-ty,' he chants.

How we laugh.

Charles stops cavorting, catches his breath and puts on his boots.

'What's that noise?' I ask. It sounds as if Bob is wailing but he's under the table, searching for scraps.

'It seems to be coming from the garden,' Charles says.

We gather by the window and are treated to the spectacle of Mr Andersen lying prostrate on the lawn, with one long arm stretched up above his head and the other stretched out sideways. Fearing he is injured or stricken with a sudden malady, we run out to assist him.

We form a circle around him like a clock face, and note that his arms seem to be indicating the time as three p.m. I kneel and take his minute hand.

'Whatever is it?' I ask.

He lifts his head and wails like a banshee. Tears stream down his face. 'Are you in pain?' I ask.

'Ja,' he says.

'Where?'

'Eeen my 'art.'

'It's his heart, Charles. Send for the doctor,' I shout.

'No, doctor. 'Art brokon, baahd revu,' he says, and sits up.

I stand with my hands on my hips, unable to believe a grown man would react so violently to such a thing.

Charles raises his hands palms up, as if I'd aimed a pistol at his friend.

'Leave him to me,' he says. He helps Mr Andersen up and walks him across the lawn to the dry soil at the edge of the path.

'He picks up a stick and writes in the sand. 'There is the review,' he says, and uses the toe of his boot to rub out the words. 'And there: it's gone and forgotten in a flash. I never take the trouble to read reviews and suggest you don't also. They mean nothing.'

Mr Andersen throws his arms around Charles and hugs him, but evidently finds this an insufficient gesture because, despite my husband's protests, he then lifts his host right off his feet, spins him around and throws him to the ground in a whoop of joy. Charles sits cross-legged and looks round at us with narrowed eyes.

We all turn away and hurry back to the house, commending Charles loudly for having saved the day.

ANGELA Burdett-Coutts hosts a party in Mr Andersen's honour. I am a little apprehensive, but we agree to attend and, on arrival, make the necessary introductions.

Our hostess is a singular woman and does not make one feel inferior, despite her own flawless appearance. She allows all her guests to gather and mingle for half an hour, then orders the dinner gong to be struck. Gentlemen line up ready to escort the ladies in to dine. Charles stands at the head of the procession and smiles at our hostess, who stands alongside him at the head of the female line. He sticks out his elbow, ready to link arms with her. She glides across the floor towards him but a gigantic Mr Punch leaps in front of her, rushes ahead, grabs Charles and drags him into the dining room as if he is a reluctant Judy.

The face of our hostess betrays not a flicker of the surprise she must be feeling. Serene as a yacht in full sail, she adjusts her course and reaches out to take another gentleman's arm. I am full of admiration for her, but fear that my patience for him will not survive to the end of his ten-day stay with us. We are, after all, not yet half way through and I am already starting to pull out my hair.

FRANK, Alfie, Sydney (our 'Ocean Spectre') and Mr Harry return from France for the school holidays. Our guest is still in situ. Charles is too busy to take him on any more excursions. He is working with Wilkie Collins on a play called *The Frozen Deep*, in preparation for a performance before the Queen.

Mr Andersen becomes a Pied Piper and leads the children on expeditions through the woods. They return with arms full of leaves and twigs and spend hours fashioning them into supernatural nosegays. Georgina complains about the mess in the nursery but to my mind it is a small price to pay for keeping the younger ones entertained. Wilkie Collins is not entertained when the Pied Piper commandeers his hat, decorates it with a daisy chain and offers it back to him like a crown at a coronation. To please the children, however, he takes it and wears it with good grace.

The nursery becomes a phantasmagoria as paper is cut into scenes from fairy tales and displayed on the walls. Frank and Alfie compete to produce the most imaginative designs. There is much snatching of scissors and occasional acts of sabotage as unguarded mermaids lose their tails or have their long golden locks, and sometimes their whole heads, shorn off. Mr Harry, a precocious eight-year-old, prefers not to engage in flights of fairy fancy and questions the existence of mermaids and therefore the value of employing them as wall decoration. Ocean Spectre Sydney, although two years his senior, has no such qualms. His big blue eyes gaze in wonderment as the nursery transforms into a grotto.

'Can you hear the waves, Mama?' he asks, looking around the walls.

'Don't be ridiculous: it's just pieces of paper,' Mr Harry says as he scrunches up offcuts.

'Using your imagination is not ridiculous, Harry,' I say. 'Try closing your eyes and see if you can picture being at the seaside.'

'I forst met yor mudda at Broadsteers befor yew boorn,' Mr Andersen says. He holds up an intricate storm-at-sea silhouette.

Harry looks at him as if he's an imbecile.

'Are you attempting to communicate that you met my mother at Broadstairs before I was born?' he asks.

'Ja, Broadsteers. I hellp you if too 'aard,' Mr Andersen says and hands him a sheet of paper and a pair of scissors.

Mr Harry slams them down on the table.

'It is not that I find it difficult—I just don't see the point,' he says.

'D-d-d-do try H-H-Harry old man,' Frank says. 'You can't d-d-d-do any worse than Alfie.' He picks up his brother's outline of the Ugly Duckling, dangles it in Alfie's face and says, 'Quack, quack'.

Alfie says, 'Quack away ugly d-d-d-duckling,' mimicking his brother's stammer and snatches back his handiwork. Unfortunately, this does not improve the duckling's looks or ability to quack as his bill is thereby amputated and falls to the floor.

Plorn picks up the sliver of yellow-painted paper and hands it back to his big brother.

'No cry. Mr Anders Son can mend,' he says.

Saturday, 11th June 1870—1:45 am

KATE now recalls Hans Christian Andersen with fondness, in spite of her misgivings at the time, and the embarrassing scene at the Royal Performance of *The Frozen Deep*, when he was so moved by Charles's death scene that he cried out loud. Queen Victoria was not amused and focused on the performance on stage rather than the one-man-show in the audience. When they arrived home Mr Andersen was aggrieved that Her Majesty had barely acknowledged his presence at the event.

He shed more tears when the time came for his long-anticipated departure, which had lengthened far beyond its planned extent. Apart from Plorn, we all struggled to appear downcast. We watched and the little boy waved until Mr Andersen's cab had turned the corner. Then we all cheered and followed Charles up to the newly-vacated guest room where he wrote on the mirror, 'Hans Andersen slept in this room for five weeks—which seemed to the family AGES!'

Plorn was the only one who did not applaud. 'Why did he have to go?' he asked.

He'd asked the same question a week later when Walter left for India.

At the time, Kate had no inkling that a little while after, she would also be sent away against her will, and that Plorn would again ask why someone he cared for had had to go.

No one dared give the little boy the true answer back then, but there is nothing stopping her now. She throws off her sheet, gets out of bed, stands as upright as she can manage and tilts up her chin.

'Your father drove me away because he had fallen in love with little Ellen Ternan,' she says, and trudges across the room to the commode. She sits on her throne and relieves herself loudly.

Kate feels strong enough to want to lay Ellen's ghost to rest, but how? Charles kept his mistress so secret that she was barely ever more than a phantom. There's nothing to grapple with, nothing to challenge. Kate recalls the flesh-and-blood young woman she met in Manchester when she took a journey that would change the course of her life and that of so many others forever, but knows it is the ghost within herself that she must exorcise.

August 1857

CHARLES springs up onto the Manchester train like a man half his age. I hobble along the platform, leaning on a walking stick like a woman twice my age. With each step, the pain that has been plaguing me shoots down the back of my leg. I'm starting to regret my decision to travel, but I have never missed a performance of a Wilkie Collins's play and I'm intrigued to see what Charles's professional actresses make of the parts our girls have played.

I'm hauled aboard as Mamie and Lucifer Box pull from inside the carriage and Charley pushes from outside. Georgina has already taken a seat at the far end of our compartment and begun reading a new book on household management. Charles stands back as I slump into my seat by the window next to the door.

'Now we are all present and correct, I'll go and check on the other members of our esteemed theatrical company,' he says. He crosses his arms, raises one foot and dances the hornpipe across our carriage. The others hum the tune and clap along, and he deftly avoids stepping on their toes. A salute signals the end of his performance. He flings open the carriage door, takes a bow, leaps out and strides off.

I watch all the back-slapping, hand-shaking and embracing as he guides his friends and their wives into the carriages he has reserved for members of *The Frozen Deep* cast.

'All aboard! All aboard!' he shouts and waves his arms as if he's the guard. He probably wishes he had a flag and a whistle.

'Such high spirits,' I say to Charley.

'Yes, father is certainly in his element, but how are you, Mama?' he asks and sits beside me.

'The pain subsides when I'm still,' I say.

He takes my hand. 'I'm glad to hear it but you do look tired. Are you still struggling to sleep?' he asks.

'I spend much of my nights praying for Walter's safety. The news from India is not good. There is much talk of unrest,' I say.

Charley shakes his head. 'He should never have gone,' he says. 'He begged Father to let him stay, right up until the moment the gangplank was raised.'

The thought of my beautiful boy's anguish is too much to bear. Charley hands me his handkerchief.

'Your father has admitted to suffering some self-doubt about his decision, and as you know, that is not at all like him,' I say, dabbing my eyes.

'He should have listened to you but what is done is done, and we must trust that my little brother will give a good account of himself and make Father proud,' he says.

'He does not need to risk getting slaughtered to make me proud. The Indians are behaving ungratefully but Our Lord beseeched us to turn the other cheek,' I say.

Georgina snaps her book shut. 'For Heaven's sake, Catherine,' she says. 'Those mutinous little natives must be taught a lesson. When all is said and done they're barely more than savages. Charles says he'd slaughter the lot of them. He always knows best and may I remind you that questioning his judgement is tantamount to disloyalty on *your* part.'

Charley puts his arm around my shoulders and opens his mouth to speak. I put my finger to his lips. I do not wish him to quarrel with my sister for, like Charles, she is not one who easily forgives any who gainsay her.

Lucifer Box tuts and frowns at her aunt.

'Try not to distress yourself, Mama. I'm sure Walter won't be sent straight into the fray.' She reaches across to pat me on the knee.

Mamie nods. She looks as if she is about to agree but sees the look on Georgina's face and busies herself with the picnic hamper that Cook has prepared to sustain us on our long journey.

The whistle blows and I am reminded of another child lost on a train journey long ago. The door swings open. Charles staggers in, just as he does in the last scene of the play. He had exited in the role of its jovial actor-manager and returns as its tragic leading man.

He snatches a pork pie from Mamie's hand.

'Spare a morsel for a starving man who has survived the Arctic wastes,' he says. He sits at the far end of the compartment on the opposite side to me and gobbles like a glutton. We leave Euston Station in an outpouring of smoke.

Charles stands and brushes crumbs from his lap.

'Swap seats, young Man,' he says to Charley.

Charley does as his father bids.

Charles offers me his half-eaten pie. I shake my head.

'Why so glum?' he asks but already knows the answer. 'Won't my little mouse take a tiny bite, to please her bewhiskered husband?' he asks, and preens his moustache with his fingertips.

Everyone laughs.

He breaks off a small piece of pastry and pops it in my mouth. 'That's my girl,' he says, and hands me the rest. 'Eat up and think of an anagram for a nine-letter word. We shall play Conundrum. You always enjoy that.'

His good humour is as infectious as his bad moods. I choose a word and tell them the letters. Everyone starts guessing but they get nowhere near to finding it out.

'We will have to enlist the help of everyone in the other compartments,' Charles says.

'And how exactly do you plan to do that?' I ask.

He picks up my walking stick. 'We'll write a message, spear it on the end of the stick and poke it out of the window for our neighbours to grab. Collins is never without an umbrella so he can use that in turn to communicate with those further down the train.'

'Ingenious idea!' I say.

'Are you sure that's allowed in the rules?' Georgina asks.

'I make the rules,' Charles says. He finds a pencil and paper in his bag, writes down the nine letters, impales the paper onto my walking stick and opens the window. The rush of smoky air sends the ribbons on my bonnet cavorting around my face. Charles sticks his head out of the window and holds the stick in both hands like a fishing rod.

'Collins!' he shouts and taps the side of the next compartment.

'Charles? What is it?' his friend shouts back.

'Grab the paper off the end. We're playing Conundrum,' he bellows. 'Use your umbrella to send it further down and pass the answer back here when you've got it.'

A windswept Charles closes the window. He runs his fingers through his hair and coughs.

'Roll up! Roll up! The circus is in town,' he cries. He points the stick at me. 'Behold the Queen of Conundrum and of my heart,' he says.

Everyone applauds, apart from Georgina, who has gone back to reading her book. Now that the game has been shared I wish I had chosen a different word but my thoughts are interrupted by a tap on the window.

'Your reign is about to come to an end,' Charles says. He reaches out and grabs the paper. Shock flashes across his face but he slaps on a smile and laughs. He laughs a second time. 'That's a clue,' he says to the others. They stare back blankly. 'I'm surrounded by dunces. I laughed and laughed again, did I not? "Laughters" is the answer! My Kate is as clever as ever.'

'You've taken so long over it, I'd quite forgotten what I thought of,' I say and look at Charley.

'Picnic time,' he says, rubbing his hands together.

Mamie opens the hamper.

'I could eat a horse,' Lucifer Box says, riffling through the contents and holding them up for the others to choose.

'Me too,' says Charley. 'I'll have a hardboiled egg.'

Georgina puts down her book.

'Are you sure "laughters" is a proper word, Charles?'

Before he can answer she looks at me.

'It wasn't by any chance "slaughter", was it?' she asks.

My heart is derailed but the train trundles on as if it hasn't heard her. The wheels keep their steady rhythm along the tracks.

Everyone stares.

'Slaughter?' I say.

'Yes, as in your son getting slaughtered in India,' Georgina says. 'I seem to remember you discussing it with Charley earlier.'

'No,' Charles says. 'You were thinking of that little porker in the pie, weren't you, my Dear?' He squeals like a stuck pig.

The children laugh.

Georgina remains stony-faced.

The train lets off steam in a hiss.

No one hears my sigh of relief.

I am even more relieved to arrive at the Great Western Hotel, where I discover that Charles has taken twenty-three rooms to accommodate the theatrical company, along with private dining and sitting rooms. Supper of more pies along with tarts, beef, cold fowls and jellies is washed down with copious amounts of beer and punch. It is good to see such a happy throng, but Walter is the spectre at the feast and I am glad when Charles finally leaves them to it and escorts me up the grand staircase to our rooms.

The clock strikes twelve. We lie side by side under the white sheet as if interred in a family mausoleum and listen to the sounds of merriment, which show no signs of abating. Charles puts on his dressing gown and goes downstairs to ask them to pipe down.

There is more disturbance. The revellers sing salacious songs as they pass along the corridor and bid each other fond farewells before slamming their bedroom doors. Charles seems able to close his ears to all this. Almost as soon as his head is back on the pillow, he starts to snore. I lie awake a while longer, but finally succumb to nightmares in which Walter tries to rescue piglets from a naked Charles, who fires a musket whilst Bob the cat sits on his head like a turban and Hans Christian Andersen shouts that the emperor isn't wearing any clothes.

BREAKFAST is rather a subdued affair. Charles has set off early for the theatre, without eating anything. Many of the others prefer an extra hour in bed and those who have made the effort to appear express regret for their overindulgence last night. The pain in my back and leg is not so bad today and exercise may do it good so I decide to walk to the theatre.

I'm glad of Charley's arm to support me as we are jostled in the crowds who have come for an art exhibition. The new Manchester Free Trade Hall, with its neo-classical arches, is as impressive as any of the London theatres. In a spirit of reconciliation I smile at Georgina.

'It's a beautiful building,' I say as we enter an auditorium that is filled with colour.

My sister returns a withering smile. 'I'm glad you think so. You realise it was built on the site of the Peterloo massacre.'

The ornate ceiling I was admiring now seems oppressively ostentatious. Pain shoots down my leg. I lean more heavily on Charley's arm.

Charles greets us from the front of the stage.

'Ah, here are the amateurs,' he says. 'Come on up and meet Mrs Ternan and her two daughters—the professionals who'll be taking on your roles.'

Lucifer Box is first up the steps. 'We were good enough for Her Majesty the Queen and Prince Albert at the Royal Command Performance last month,' she says.

'Now, now,' says Charles. 'That was a much smaller venue, which made it easier for the audience to hear you. We need this big theatre to raise as much money as we can for my dear friend Douglas Jerrold's widow, and your voice will get lost.'

Mrs Ternan coughs, raises a handkerchief to her mouth and coughs again more loudly. This attracts everyone's attention. I take her hand, then let it go—and sneeze. Mother and daughters must have doused themselves in lavender oil, so overpowering is the scent billowing off them. She smiles as if I am an old friend rather than the wife of her new employer. She is taller than me and slender, but looks older. Decades of treading the boards and travelling the country in all weathers have obviously taken their toll. The deep lines on her face form a road map of all the long journeys she has made.

'I'm delighted to make your acquaintance,' she says in a voice that could easily be heard in the back row. 'May I present my second daughter, Maria, and my youngest, Ellen?' She gestures with one arm so widely that I have to take a step back to avoid being knocked off the stage. Charley reaches out to steady me. 'We call her Nelly,' she says in a stage whisper, as if trusting me with a confidence meant for the whole audience to share.

'Nelly will be playing your part, Lucifer Box,' Charles says.

Despite her smile, I know she is disappointed at being replaced. Ellen is quite similar in height to Lucifer Box but, with her thin lips and small eyes, is plainer than our pretty daughter and her face is powdered and rouged so thickly, it's as if she's wearing a mask.

'I'm sure you will give a magnificent performance, Ellen,' I say, but remain unconvinced that there was any need to employ professionals. Lucifer Box and Mamie could both have learnt to project their voices to the back of even this vast auditorium. My sisters, Georgina and Helen, never had a problem making themselves heard and nor had Charley; at least, not from the stage.

'My three daughters were almost born in the limelight,' Mrs Ternan says. 'Fanny was a child prodigy and is too much in demand with professional companies to be with us here. Nelly was only three when she gave her first performance—and that was fifteen years ago.'

'Then Ellen is the same age as our Lucifer Box—Katey,' I say. 'Is Mr Ternan not part of your talented troupe?'

'My beloved husband sadly departed this world many years ago,' Mrs Ternan says. She dabs her dry eyes with her handkerchief.

Charles pats the diminutive Ellen on her head. She smiles up at him. He winks at her like a doting father.

'Nelly must have been an infant phenomenon!' he says.

'That's what you used to call Charley,' Lucifer Box says. Her big brother blushes and moves to stand behind me.

'Shall we take our seats, Charles? I ask.

'A good idea,' Mrs Ternan says. 'Sit anywhere that pleases you: you'll be able to hear us whether you're next to the Pit or right up at the back of the Gods.'

'I don't doubt it,' I say but stand my ground and look at Charles.

'Yes, please do: we were about to begin our final rehearsal,' he says.

I lead the cast-off cast into the front row of the stalls. We are all keenly aware of our new and much diminished position as mere members of the audience. Charles, however, and his men friends have retained their roles and Charley has had a last-minute reprieve.

It is an unsettling experience watching strangers perform instead of my sisters and my girls. Having helped everyone learn their lines and seen the play so many times, I know most of it off by heart. Ellen's big sister Maria stutters. She has taken Mamie's part and I am able to prompt her. Mrs Ternan peers down through the footlights in search of the disembodied voice. She does not look grateful.

'Thank you so much, whoever you are,' she says, 'but I'm sure Maria would have recovered, if she had been given the time to do so.'

'I was happy to help,' I retort.

'Ah, I thought it might be you, Mrs Dickens. You are evidently possessed of a very good memory but being lit up on stage is quite a different matter from sitting in the shadows,' Mrs Ternan informs me.

'I am well aware, my Dear Mrs Ternan, having performed with my husband many times over the years and always received very favourable reviews,' I say.

'Ladies, ladies,' Charles intervenes. 'We are with professionals, now, and it is time to concentrate on the current performance rather than harking back to our days as amateurs. Please proceed, Maria. If you falter again I will feed you your line.'

'Bravo! Well said, Charles,' says Mrs Ternan, 'but there won't be any more hiccups. My daughters are always word perfect.'

Mamie takes my shaking hands in hers. I remind myself of my Christian duty to be charitable. It cannot have been easy for Mrs Ternan to bring up three daughters alone and she must have worked very hard to protect them from being treated as women of ill repute, as so many professional actresses are. Nevertheless, much as I try to remain impartial, I cannot help but conclude that Maria and Ellen are not greatly endowed with talent. Charles must be well aware that their performances are inferior to those given by Mamie and Lucifer Box in everything except volume.

SATURDAY, 11TH JUNE 1870—2:00 AM

CHARLES was elated about the vast sum raised for the widowed Mrs Jerrold and even more about the rapturous applause which had followed his performance. He boasted to friends of his ability to make an audience of two thousand weep, along with the stage hands, the carpenters and even members of the cast. Kate congratulated her husband warmly but the Ternans eclipsed her with a display a hundredfold more effusive, crying crocodile tears and throwing themselves at his feet like worshipers before a deity. Kate breathed a sigh of relief at the thought that their association with the overly-theatrical family had been brief and was now at an end. 'If only that had been the case,' she says.

Sweat stings her eyes. It trickles down between her pendulous breasts. She clambers off the commode and makes her way to the window. The light breeze blows gently onto her clammy skin. It brings a little relief but no respite from memories.

Within ten days Charles was on the road to Doncaster with Wilkie Collins. Ostensibly they were going to carry out research for an article they were planning to write for Charles's magazine. At the time Kate had no idea that the Ternans were performing there. She does not blame herself for her lack of suspicion: the two men were fresh from a successful collaboration on the play and Charles was always travelling, so there was nothing new about his being absent. What was new was the paucity of letters from him while he was away but, even then, Kate had not fretted. He would be back in a fortnight and she would hear all about his exploits then. She always enjoyed listening to her husband's anecdotes and watching him act out scenes from his journeys, playing all the characters he encountered. These private performances were a joy she cherished.

But there was no joy when Charles returned from Doncaster.

September 1857

'READ "Ugly Duckling" again, Mama,' Plorn says.

The front door slams.

'Papa!' shouts Plorn and we jump up excitedly, run to the landing and hurry down the stairs so we can greet the Hero of the Hour.

Charles's portmanteau has been abandoned in the hallway.

He is not in the drawing room.

'Charles? Where are you, my Dearest?' I call out.

He answers from the dining room. I hurry in with my arms outstretched. Little Plorn follows me.

'Papa! Present?' Plorn shouts, then coughs and sneezes, and runs to Charles, ready to be swung onto his father's shoulders and taken on their customary treasure hunt for his new toy.

Charles ignores him, narrows his eyes and glowers at me.

'Have you not taught him to use a handkerchief?'

I pass mine to Plorn and tell him to blow his nose.

'This place is a pigsty! How many times have I told you that chairs must be tucked under tables at all times?' Charles asks. 'And the boys are back at school so you cannot lay the blame at their door this time!'

I hurry to remedy the situation and wonder what on earth could have caused this outburst. Publishing deadlines, household expenses, begging letters, unrepaid loans and my numerous shortcomings are the usual sources of his ill humour, but he has just returned from what should have been a pleasant trip with his friend.

Plorn stops jumping up and down to attract his father's attention and his head droops like a dying daffodil. As he plods across the room towards me, the sun shining through the window catches his golden brown curls.

'Look Papa—me helping Mama,' he says and tries to push a heavy chair back under the table. It topples onto its side.

'Stupid, lazy, useless! Just like your mother and brothers!' Charles rages. 'I never wanted you but she couldn't stop having one baby after another.' He shoves his son aside and sets the chair straight.

Plorn falls to the floor and bursts into tears. I kneel down and put my arms around him. Mamie and Lucifer Box appear in the doorway. Their eyes dart between the three of us. I take my little boy's hand in mine, pull him to his feet and lead him towards his big sisters.

'Take him back up to the nursery,' I say quietly.

Charles turns. His eyes target the girls like an assassin taking aim.

'I'll be up to inspect your rooms later and woe betide the pair of you if I find untidy drawers and crumbs on the carpets again,' he says.

'He's really on the rampage this time,' Lucifer Box mutters. 'It's a blessing Frank is at school or he'd be forcing the poor boy to read all of Hamlet's soliloquies out loud again to make him stop stammering. Welcome home, Father,' she says in a loud, cheerful voice and leads the other two quickly out of the line of fire. This incenses Charles all the more.

'Some welcome this is! I turn my back for a few days and look what happens. The whole place goes to wrack and ruin.'

He turns slowly on the spot, his gaze surveying the room like a lighthouse beam.

‘That picture is not hanging straight!’ he shouts and points his finger at the offending frame above the fireplace.

I hurry to put it right but Charles marches ahead of me.

‘I’ll do it, Dearest. Don’t let it vex you,’ I say.

‘Things shouldn’t have got into this state in the first place.’ He frowns at the calm seascape showing the sunny sands at Broadstairs and concentrates on aligning the frame perfectly with the mantelpiece.

‘Just what have you been doing these past two weeks?’

‘Plorn caught Georgina’s cold so I have been ministering to both of them day and night,’ I say. ‘I would have written to tell you but I did not have your address.’

‘Does a married man forfeit his right to a modicum of privacy? I trusted you would be able to cope while I was slaving away to earn our living,’ he says.

‘You have always in the past written to tell me of your progress and never sought privacy before, Charles. Has something happened to unsettle you, my Dear?’ I reach out to caress his shoulder and soothe his woes.

He writhes as if I have struck him, brushes my hand off his jacket and exits the room.

‘I’m going upstairs to rest and I do not wish to be disturbed,’ he shouts back at me.

‘Very well,’ I say, as I scurry along behind him. ‘I’ll bring you some refreshments a little later. Perhaps a little toasted cheese?’

‘Please do not trouble yourself on my account, ma’am—you never have before.’ He picks up his portmanteau and climbs the staircase.

His words knock the air out of me. I clutch the banister and try to take stock. What should I do now? I must reassure Plorn and the girls that all is well. I am not at all sure that it is, but I haul myself slowly up.

SATURDAY, 11TH JUNE 1870—2:15 AM

THE glass feels cool as Kate rests her forehead against the window pane. Unseen dogs bark at imaginary intruders. Owls hoot. Horses’ hooves and coach wheels clatter past on the cobbled street. Heedless of all else, two tomcats on the pavement exchange ungodly wails, like the newly born babies of demons. Three floors above them, a window is thrown open. There's a shout. A slosh of water. The sodden felines yowl and bolt, watched by a curious fox. Way above them, the higgledy-piggledy skyline of rooftops and spires is silhouetted by moonlight, as if Hans Christian Andersen has cut it out to stick upon the nursery wall.

But there are no children now: all the boys were sent to boarding school in Boulogne when they were six or seven or eight years of age. After that, most were packed off to the colonies—two to India, two to Australia, and Ocean Spectre Sydney went to sea. Kate cries for the sons she never saw again, cries for little Dora, cries for Charles too, now he has gone forever, and cries for herself, for not having had the courage to stand her ground and insist on keeping her children close by.

Absence hangs from her like a wet cloak. Charles's absences from home had become more and more frequent. Kate does not want to relive all the pain but knows there will be no going forward until she has gone back. She must face the past now if she is to secure peace of mind in the future.

September 1857

SHOULD I write to Wilkie Collins and enquire whether he can tell me what ails Charles? No. I must not put him in so delicate a position; and even were I to do so, Wilkie, no doubt, would keep his counsel, out of loyalty to his friend.

Perhaps there are financial difficulties I know nothing of. That would account for this prolonged ill-humour. It is surely my duty to discover the source of his distress that I may alleviate it.

I fetch the ledger from the dresser and run my finger down the columns. Each has been neatly subtotalled by Georgina. Turning the pages one by one, all appears in order. The usual cash payments for household expenses are itemised chronologically.

I am about to close the book when, right at the bottom of the page, I observe an entry detailing a cheque made payable to Mr Buckstone at the Haymarket in the sum of fifty pounds. Fifty pounds! I cannot fathom why my husband would be paying a theatre manager such a large amount. Would Georgina know? Even if she does, I could not abase myself by asking my little sister to explain my husband's spending. The supercilious look on her face would be more than I could endure. No, I must confront Charles—yet in a manner that does not further inflame his current antipathy towards me.

I knock softly at his study door. Ordinarily, he would call out, 'Is that you, Kate, my dear?' but this time there is no response. My courage falters. I turn to leave, yet summon my strength to return and rap once more, a little louder than before.

'What?' Charles shouts.

'It is only I, my Dear. May I come in?'

I open the door just a crack.

'If you must,' he replies gruffly.

Charles sits at his desk, clad in one of his colourful new waistcoats, embroidered with a peacock feather design.

'What is it?' he asks, without looking up from the letter he is writing.

'Forgive my intrusion, but I fear something may be amiss,' I say.

His nib scratches busily across the paper.

'I was wondering if any unexpected expenses might have been bothering you . . . '

He blots the ink.

'. . . for it is clear that something grievous is troubling you . . .'

'Only repeated interruptions when I am trying to compose a letter to my sub-editor,' he says and resumes writing.

'And nothing else?' I ask as I approach him.

'You, ma'am, are troubling me at this moment,' he says.

'Charles,' I say, stepping around the side of his desk. I long to stand behind him and rest my hands upon his shoulders, but he sits as stiff as a tailor's dummy, so I restrain myself and instead lean lightly on the back of his chair. Glancing over his shoulder I read: *I am going to take the riddle into the country this morning . . . So let the riddle and the riddler go their own wild way, and no harm come of it!*

Charles snatches up the sheet of paper and shoves his chair backwards. One of its legs lands on my toes. I yelp. He rises. I extract my injured foot and try to limp away, but the hem of my dress has snagged and, as I move, it tears.

'That will teach you not to snoop,' he snarls. Folding the letter with deliberate care, he seals it, puts it in his pocket and walks out.

The front door slams. I dither in the hallway. *Riddle, riddler, riddle, riddler, riddle, riddler.* Wherever I look those words appear. *Riddle, riddler, riddle, riddler, riddle, riddler.* What never-ending parlour game is this? *Riddle, riddler, riddle, riddler, riddle, riddler.* I must puzzle my way out.

Lucifer Box comes in from the front garden, carrying the last of the summer's roses.

'I see Father is off again,' she says and sniffs the blooms. 'I don't suppose he's bothered to tell you where he's going or when he'll be back?'

'Oh, he's just going out to post a letter,' I say with a smile.

She picks off a petal infected with blight.

'He'll probably make it last a week,' she says and drops the petal on the floor.

I laugh. 'Ha-ha.' It sounds hollow even to my own ears. 'And then I think he may be planning to take a ride in the carriage.'

'At least we will be afforded a little peace while he is gone. I suspect you can offer no idea why he's behaving like a mad man?'

'You know your father: there is always something to vex him, but his good humour will return, as it always does, given time and understanding.'

I hobble across the hallway to pick up the discarded petal. Pain stabs me in the back as I try to straighten. I cry out. My daughter drops the flowers and rushes over to me.

'You're getting too old to endure his petulance, Mother,' she says. 'He must learn to comport himself with more maturity, and stop behaving like a love-sick whippersnapper.'

'Lucifer Box! Show some respect for your father,' I say.

She steps behind me and rubs my back.

'I'll respect him when he respects you,' she says. 'It's bad enough that his attentions stray to other women—but to consort with an actress!'

'Lucifer Box, that is a disgraceful thing to say. You should be ashamed of yourself.' But Lucifer Box is not ashamed, and fifty pounds to a theatre manager weighs heavy on my mind.

'Think back, Mother. You remember how he looked at her in Manchester? He was scarcely home five minutes before he set off for Doncaster. We all knew that was the Ternans' next engagement.'

'I didn't'.

'You are too trusting and always see the best in everyone but some of us lack your innocence.'

'Please tell me you're not suggesting your father had an improper liaison with Mrs Ternan.'

Lucifer Box laughs outright in my face.

'No, Mother, that is not what I am suggesting,' she says.

I try but cannot grasp her meaning. I feel as if I'm playing Conundrum and can see all the letters of the anagram but cannot turn them into a word that means anything.

She looks me in the eye. 'Do I really have to spell it out for you?' she asks.

I bite my lip and nod.

She goes into her father's study and returns with the third edition of Charles's periodical *Household Words*.

'Have you not read "The Lazy Tour of Two Idle Apprentices"?' she asks. 'It's his account of his trip with Wilkie Collins. They went to Doncaster races and stayed at the Angel Hotel. Father is Francis Goodchild, and Mr Collins, Thomas Idle. Listen.' And Lucifer Box reads out a passage:

> Mr Goodchild would appear to have been by no means free from lunacy himself at 't'races, though not of the prevalent kind. He is suspected by Mr. Idle to have fallen into a dreadful state concerning a pair of little lilac gloves and a little bonnet that he saw there.
>
> Mr Idle asserts, that he did afterwards repeat at the Angel, with an appearance of being lunatically seized, some rhapsody to the following effect: 'O little lilac gloves! And O winning little bonnet, making in conjunction with her golden hair quite a Glory in the sunlight round the pretty head, why anything in the world but you and me! Why may not this day's running . . . be prolonged through an everlasting autumn sunshine, without a sunset!

Lucifer Box whispers in my ear. 'It's the story of Father falling in love with Ellen Ternan. Dear, sweet, innocent little Nelly.'

'Never! It's not possible. She's the same age as you,' I say, shaking my head in disbelief.

'Exactly! She's in search of a father.'

'But he's not in search of a daughter.'

'That's right, Mother: he's not in search of a daughter. Having daughters makes him feel aged. He wants youth, and thinks that possessing her will restore his own, although it will probably send the old fool to an early grave.'

My leg hurts, my back hurts, my toes hurt but these are nothing to the pain in my heart. I heave myself across to the hall chair and perch on the edge of it. I rock to and fro in my agony.

'I cannot believe this of your father. He has laboured tirelessly to improve the lot of fallen women.'

'He would say that her lot has improved considerably under his patronage and who could argue against that?'

The front door swings open. Charles does not acknowledge our presence. He dashes past me and takes the stairs two at a time.

'Rushing off for a ride?' Lucifer Box shouts after him and laughs.

I hold my breath and wait for her father to charge back down to punish her insolence but he cannot even be bothered to do that.

Lucifer Box pulls off my shoes. The toenails on one foot are bloody. She picks up the discarded nosegay.

'These were for you, Mama,' she says.

Their scent is sweet. 'Your father gave me roses when Dora died,' I say. My tears form dewdrops on the red petals.

'Come, let's put them in water before they wilt and then we'll set about bathing your foot and mending that rent in your skirt.'

'I caught it under my chair,' I say.

'Of course you did,' she says, 'and I suppose you trapped your own toes under it too.'

She kisses my damp cheek.

SATURDAY, 11TH JUNE 1870—2:25 AM

DARK clouds glide past the moon. A halo of white light hovers over the spire of the church. Kate believes God has sent her a sign not to think of this world but the next. Adultery is a cardinal sin but she loved him and loves him still. She puts her hands together, closes her eyes and prays that Charles may be received in Heaven.

Kate sees now that she had been a complacent, naive wife. She had believed that security in a marriage grows stronger over time.

Now she knows better, she must re-examine her life in the cold, hard light of the moon. Hindsight will help her bring Charles to his Day of Judgement. He had protested his innocence and insisted that Ellen, too, was beyond reproach, but if he had in fact sinned in straying from the vows of marriage, and she can find it within herself to forgive him, then surely Our Lord will take mercy on his soul.

So, who was *the riddle* that Charles, *the riddler*, had taken for a carriage ride that morning long ago if it was not Ellen Ternan?

He had paid fifty pounds to Buckstone at the Haymarket Theatre but was it to employ his little actress?

The evidence against him piles up: the unexplained absences, his failure to write home, the change in his attitude towards her and their children.

She finds Charles guilty as charged.

Kate's bed is empty but it does not beckon her, for this is not a night for repose. She sees their divided bedroom in Tavistock House. The thought of it still shocks her: time has not diminished that pain. Only a man who wants to erase his wife could be so cruel as to block her out of the room he sleeps in. And why would a man want to cut himself off in this way? Because there is another woman, waiting for him in the wings—that's why.

October 1857

THE carriage pulls up outside Tavistock House. I pray our return to London will herald a fresh start and allow us to put our recent troubles behind us and become a happy family once again. We need that greatly.

Dear Anne opens the door and looks at the children.

'Welcome home, Mrs Dickens, and you Master Charles, and Miss Mary, and Miss Catherine and young Master Edward,' she says.

'My name is Plorn,' my youngest says, scowling at her, 'and the others are Charley, Mamie and Lucifer Box.'

'Anne is calling you by your Christian names, and she is right to do so,' I say. 'Take your bags up to your rooms and unpack before your father arrives.'

Anne looks at my bag. 'I'll get yours taken up directly,' she says, 'but won't you take a little refreshment first?'

'Thank you, Anne,' I say. 'Tea would be most welcome. I'll take it in the drawing room. Bring two cups and you can tell me all the news.'

'Very kind of you, Ma'am but I must get on,' she says.

'Nonsense. I insist.' I try to catch her eye, but she hurries away with her gaze cast down.

There is no sign that the house has been shut up all summer. Anne has removed the dust covers, lit a fire in the hearth and made sure all is spick and span, despite being married and having her own home to take care of now.

There is comfort in familiar surroundings. The gas lamps are not lighted but the mirrors that Charles and I chose and positioned so carefully reflect what little light there is on this dull autumn day.

The story of our life together is depicted on the walls. A portrait of my handsome young writer husband, with the wavy brown hair I so admired when we first met, hangs beside me as I once was—a slender young woman with golden brown ringlets framing a pretty face. There are Charley, Mamie, Lucifer Box and baby Walter in the Maclise painting I took across America all those years ago. If only we could be frozen in time as our portraits are, Walter would not now be on the other side of the world.

The grand pianoforte reminds me of singsongs with the children, and with their Uncle Fred and Aunt Helen, and Forster, and Maclise and the Macreadys. Its black woodwork is so well polished, it shines like a sheet of obsidian. My hand glides along the edge of the lid as I study the framed photographs of us that rest upon it, taken not only in this country but all over the Continent too, with our ever-increasing brood.

Oh! And here is a new one, in a delightful silver frame, positioned directly above middle C. I pick it up to look at it more closely. It shows the amateur cast of *The Frozen Deep* in the sunny Gad's Hill Place garden, just a few short weeks ago. How reassuring that Charles has taken the trouble to get it displayed and ready for our return. He looks relaxed, leaning back on the grass, centre front of the picture, surrounded by his family and friends.

'You have so much to lose,' I warn the man in the frame, but he gazes on past me, regardless. Anne comes in with a tray. 'Beg pardon, Madam?' she says, steadying the tray and minding the tea. 'What is it I have? I didn't quite catch.'

'Nothing,' I say. 'I was just admiring this photograph.'

'Oh, that one! Yes, the master brought it to show the original cast to the family of actresses he was auditioning here,' she says.

I replace the frame on the pianoforte lid.

'What did you make of them?' I ask, taking a seat on the sofa.

'I wasn't needed, Ma'am. I would willingly have tidied up but he said they were professionals, so used to all kinds of places, and dust sheets would be the least of their worries.'

Anne sets the tea things out on the table beside me.

'It was thoughtful of him to have framed it to welcome us home,' I say.

'Oh no, I did that while you were away in Manchester. Shall I pour?' she asks but looks at the teapot.

'Yes, please,' I say.

My maid sits beside me and stares at the tea leaves in her cup like a gypsy about to tell my fortune.

'Is anything amiss, Anne?' I ask.

'I'm quite well, Madam,' she says to the milk jug.

'And your husband?'

'Up and down as ever.' She takes a letter from her apron pocket and waves away a fly with it.

'You've certainly been busy getting this place ready for us.'

Her face reddens.

'Yes. That is certainly the case,' she says.

'You must say if it's all getting too much. I'll gladly speak to Mr Dickens on your behalf.'

She stirs her tea. 'Please say nothing to the master. I would hate for him to think as I had spoken out of turn.'

I take her hand. 'As you wish, but I hope you know you can confide in me? We have been through so much together over the years.'

'I do know that, Madam, but, truth be told, I need this job more than ever, my husband's health being what it is.'

She looks at me for the first time today. There are tears in her eyes.

'I'm so sorry, Madam.' She hands me the letter and scurries out of the room without stopping to clear the tea things away. I ought to change and make myself presentable for Charles, should he choose to grace us with his presence tonight, but Anne is clearly agitated, and so the letter she has just passed to me must receive my immediate attention.

Gad's Hill Place, Sunday Eleventh October 1857

My Dear Anne

I want some little changes made in the arrangements of my dressing room and the Bathroom. And as I would rather not have them talked about by comparative strangers, I shall be much obliged to you, my old friend, if you will see them completed before you leave Tavistock House.

I wish to make the Bathroom my washing-room also. It will be therefore necessary to carry into the Bathroom, to remain there, the two washing-stands from my Dressing Room. Then, to get rid altogether of the chest of drawers in the Dressing-Room. I want the recess of the doorway between the Dressing-Room and Mrs. Dickens's room fitted with plain white shelves, and closed in with a plain light deal door painted white. Rudkin can do this—or Lillie, being in the house, can do it if he likes. The sooner it is done, the better.

My wardrobe will then stand where the chest of Drawers stands now, and a small iron bedstead will go behind the door, with its side against the wall, as you enter the Dressing-Room; its head towards the stairs, and its foot towards the window. I have ordered the bedstead and bedding, and they will be sent to Tavistock House to you. The chest of drawers shall come down here, when the van comes down to bring our luggage home at the end of the month.

They all send their love.

Ever Faithfully Yours

Charles Dickens

Who is the 'Charles Dickens' who wrote this? Surely it cannot be my husband and bedfellow of twenty-one years?

In truth, Charles has always flirted with adoring maidens. There was that sweet little minx he carried screaming into the sea, despite my protestations. I remember that her silk dress was ruined and that he laughed when I suggested he should pay to replace it. None of his dalliances was ever of any consequence to him. All disposable; all replaceable. They grew up and married and he moved on to the next pretty young thing. His infatuation with Ellen Ternan will surely follow the same pattern.

I put the letter in my pocket. Let it be the end of the matter.

And yet . . . building a barricade in our bedroom to separate those whom God has joined together? I will not believe he has done such a thing until I see it with my own eyes.

UPSTAIRS, all appears as it should be. The new door and shelves do not look out of place. No one would ever know there had ever been an opening into his dressing-room. It is uncanny.

But, did not Charles convert the old schoolroom into a theatre? Perhaps he has made our bedroom into our new stage set. Yes, I am sure of it: he will come home full of enthusiasm for a new play he has written with Collins, and hand me my lines. We will act together as we used to.

A tap on the shelves dispels this idea. They are solid wood.

I must not become hysterical. This is our home—the home I am entitled to live in. The home I helped to design and decorate. A happy home. Brimming with love for each other and our children and our friends. A home full of fun—theatricals, parlour games, music, laughter, singing, dancing, fine wines, and good food—all the food that became recipes in my book. A house full of all we have brought to it. So I must be in the wrong room.

But no. There is our bed, with the curtains we chose to match the pretty wallpaper we both admired.

Am I hallucinating? Did Anne drip laudanum into my tea? Has our chest of drawers danced across to the other side of the room? Has our wardrobe grown legs and walked off?

No. There is no letter and there never was. Nor is there a rift. I will wake up shortly with Charles beside me and he will smile at me the way he used to, and run his fingers through my hair, the way he used to, and this nightmare will be at an end.

I stand by the shelves and hope to wake. The clock ticks but nothing changes so I make my way out of the bedroom to discover what lies on the other side of the wall.

The door from the landing is still here but dread stops me at the threshold. I'm little Walter in Italy, worrying that Fearsome Fred is going to make him walk the plank into the shark-infested seas. I must take courage and cross.

A new bed blocks off the dividing door. It is a single bed. Someone has made it up with fresh bedding. It is not of my choosing.

A storm engulfs me. Wind blows my breath away. Rain lashes my cheeks. The deck tilts beneath my feet. I am flung overboard. I am hit by wave after wave after wave. Drowning. Down. Down. Down. Grasp the washstand. Sea sick. Bowl fills with bile. Night falls.

'MADAM! *Madam!*'

Anne's voice is far away.

'Please wake now.'

Slap, slap, slap on my hand.

A light *slap* on my cheek.

My maid nose to nose with me.

'What did you do with the letter?' she asks.

'Pocket,' I say.

'Thank heaven,' she says. 'Can you stand?'

I'm not sure but nod anyway.

'Let's get you up, then.'

Half way up, my strength fails me. There is the ceiling above me again.

'Give yourself time,' Anne says and takes my arm. 'No rush.'

We pause. 'Ready? Try again. Up we go. Let's get you back to your bedroom.'

So, there's a 'my' bedroom now.

We both avert our gaze as we pass the new bed and wobble out onto the landing, like a pair of skittles. Charles almost bowls us over.

'What is the meaning of this?' he asks.

'The mistress has been taken ill,' Anne says.

'What was she doing in my bedroom?' he asks, as if I have ceased to exist.

'I went to call Madam down for lunch and found her insensible on the floor,' Anne says, trying to manoeuvre me around him.

'In my room?'

'Yes, sir.'

He smells of fresh autumn air, heathland and saddle soap but underneath there is a hint of a floral fragrance. Lavender. My stomach heaves.

'Might you assist me, Sir? We need to put her to bed and Miss Hogarth is busy with the accounts. Can you take her other arm?'

'She can walk if she wants to, although it's a wonder you managed to haul her up at all without a winch.' He laughs at his own joke, then shouts at me, 'You need to stop this playacting!' as if I'm an imbecile.

'I'll be back directly I have made Mrs Dickens comfortable in her own bed,' Anne says.

'No need, Anne,' says Charles. 'I'm not going to spend the night under the same roof as that pathetic lump. I'll walk to Gad's Hill.'

Insult upon insult has rendered me senseless but I need to respond, if only to reassert my self-respect. But what can I say? I don't have the verbal imagination that comes to him when he is enraged with me. I find myself trying to placate him, instead, because it is what I do best, and I hate myself for it.

'I know you think nothing of long walks, Dear, but thirty miles? Why fatigue yourself on my account? Stay the night. I have no wish to vex you and I shall remain in my room, I promise.'

He spits his reply back in my face. 'I shall take pleasure in every step on the road that takes me further from you.'

He enters his new bedroom and slams the door shut. The key clicks in the lock.

Anne looks aghast.

'I feel rather pleased I was sick in his basin now,' I say.

'Don't blame you, Ma'am,' she says, as we hobble along together, arm in arm, ''cept it will be me as has to clean it up.'

MAMIE and Lucifer Box tiptoe in.

'She looks pale,' Mamie whispers.

'That's because she's asleep,' her sister whispers back.

'I was just resting my eyes,' I say.

Mamie takes my hand and asks, 'Are you quite well, Mother dear?'

'If she was well she wouldn't be lying down in the middle of the afternoon,' says Lucifer Box. She walks to the other side of the bed.

'I needed a little rest. The journey took it out of me,' I say and smile.

'You've travelled to and fro without any ill-effects before and Anne said you were sick. We're not to have another little brother, are we?'

'Lucifer Box!' Mamie shakes her head. 'Please forgive her impertinence, Mother.'

But her sister is not to be silenced.

'I can imagine that pushing Father to the edge of sanity,' she says. 'You know he's had enough of his existing children so he certainly won't be wanting any more.'

'I'm sorry, Mother,' Mamie squirms. 'Lucifer Box is showing off. Lucifer Box, stop being cruel to Mama.'

'I'm not being cruel,' she replies. 'He's the cruel one. You've heard him shouting and screaming. He's never been this bad before.'

'Your father is not himself at the moment,' I say, without wanting to elaborate, but Lucifer Box does that for me.

'No, he's not, because he's besotted with you-know-who.'

'Who?' Mamie asks.

She looks from me to her sister and back again.

'Who?'

I glance up at the new partition.

My daughters follow my gaze.

'What on earth has he done now?' Lucifer Box says. She stomps off to the end of the room and taps on the new shelves. 'This is just the limit,' she says. 'I assume his bed is on the other side?

Mamie gasps.

I cannot deny it.

'The very limit. You cannot endure any more, Mother.'

Mamie looks away and rubs her hands together as if trying to wash them clean.

'It's nothing important,' I say and manage to get to my feet. 'These things happen. Now, I suggest we all go downstairs and have a drink of brandy to lift our spirits.'

'Just you, Mother: not us. We must not always resort to drink to dull the pain—must we, Mamie?' says Lucifer Box, rather too pointedly.

I'm horrified to see Mamie's hands start to shake.

'Maybe just a small glass?' she pleads.

I have been so preoccupied with my own pain that I have entirely failed to register Mamie's suffering and her manner of relieving it.

'I'm sure that a cup of tea will be sufficient to calm your nerves,

Mamie,' Lucifer Box insists. 'The Queen is said to have drunk copious amounts to ease her worries about the Crimean War.'

'And what about the domestic war, Mama? What is going to happen with us?'

'I don't know, Mamie, my Dear, but I will do my best to take care of everyone, and pray that God will give me the strength to face whatever is to come,' I say.

I put one arm around each daughter and we walk together along the landing. When we reach the top of the staircase, we hear a sob. It is Plorn, curled up on the bottom step. We make our way down to him.

'Whatever is the matter?' I ask.

He sobs louder.

'There, there: do not take on so,' I say, and pat his back.

One sister pulls him up, the other dries his eyes with a cloth.

'Pay no heed to what Aunt Georgina told you,' Mamie says. 'She can be beastly.'

I sit on a step and hug Plorn to me.

'What's all this about?' I ask.

'I wanted you,' he says.

'I was having a little rest—' I cannot bring myself to say in 'my' bedroom, so add 'upstairs' instead.

'Anne told me.'

'So why the tears?'

'I wanted you.'

'You could have come up.'

'She said no.'

'Anne?'

'No: *her*.'

'Aunt Georgina?'

He nods.

'I expect she wanted me to have a nice sleep,' I say.

'Didn't.' He gulps and shudders at the sound of Georgina's footsteps on the flagstones.

The girls hurry away into the dining room. Plorn clings to me.

My sister stands over us, threateningly.

Plorn sniffs. He wipes his nose on his sleeve.

'How many times has your father told you to use your handkerchief?' Georgina asks.

He flinches and turns his head away.

'He's upset about not being permitted to see me,' I say.

'I thought it for the best,' she says. 'Anne said you were overwrought, and that young man needs to learn to do as he's told, without causing a scene.'

'I'm sure you meant well, Sister, but I'd ask you not to stop any of my children coming to me, particularly when they are distressed,' I say.

'I didn't stop him.' She pulls Plorn out of my arms and wags her finger at him. 'You must not tell lies or you will burn in Hell.'

He shakes her off and runs away shouting, 'You liar, not me!'

The front door opens. Charley looks from me to my sister. He puts down his briefcase and rushes over. Mamie and Lucifer Box peer round the dining room door.

Charley sits beside me on the stairs. 'What the devil?' he asks.

'I need to find Plorn,' I say.

'I'll fetch him,' Mamie says.

'I hope you had a nice quiet day at the bank, Charley,' Lucifer Box says. 'Father has blocked off his dressing room and plans to sleep there alone, without Mama. Mama collapsed. Aunt Georgina wouldn't let Plorn see her. She said he had better get used to his mother not being around.'

I stand up. 'How dare you say such a wicked thing, Georgina? You know I would never leave my children.'

My sister sneers and says, 'You may not have much choice.' She tosses her head and walks off.

'Well done, Mama! It's good to see you stand up for yourself,' Lucifer Box says.

'That's quite enough from you,' Charley says, 'but one thing is clear: we none of us can permit this intolerable situation to go on. Enough is enough.' He rests his hands on my shaking shoulders.

SATURDAY, 11TH JUNE 1870—2:50 AM

KATE paces up and down. She tries to be impartial. Was Ellen Ternan the only explanation for Charles's choosing to sleep apart from her after twenty-one years of sharing their matrimonial bed?

She didn't snore. Charles did, but she never complained. In truth, it was comforting to hear him next to her in the small hours.

They shared the sheet and blankets equally. He never accused her of hogging the counterpane.

Their mattress didn't bow in the middle. She didn't roll over onto him—except when he wanted her to.

Or was she physically too hot for him? No, Charles always felt the cold and insisted the warming pan was run over the sheet before they retired.

She often heard Charles get out of bed to use the commode during the night but, when it was her turn, she always crept quietly across the room and never disturbed him.

When he suffered nightmares, a frequent affliction of his, Kate took pleasure in soothing him back to sleep, just as she did their children. She wrapped her arms around him, whispered he was safe, brushed her lips against his clammy forehead and repeated 'you have my heart' until his breathing slowed and deepened. Why would he wish to forgo this, and suffer alone in the next room?

Kate stops pacing. By process of elimination, she is left with Ellen Ternan as the only answer.

Charles is guilty as charged.

She sighs, gets into bed and wishes she could sleep, but her mind has become as unbalanced as the scales of justice on which piles up the evidence of his guilt. She must try to find something to redress the balance. Perhaps what he had told her about buying jewellery was true? Her spirits had revived that April as the sun shone brighter, longer and warmer but it was a cruel spring nonetheless.

April 1858

'THERE'S a package just delivered, Madam,' says the housemaid.

I finish my line of knitting and stick the needles into the ball of wool.

'For me?'

'No, for the master but the jeweller's boy said it was wanted urgently.' She hands me a square parcel wrapped up in plain brown paper, and takes her leave.

Tomorrow will be our wedding anniversary. Dare I hope that Charles has ordered a special memento to mark it? I rest the parcel on the flat of my hand and try to gauge its weight. Not too light but not particularly heavy either. The package is too big for a ring. A necklace perhaps? A brooch? Whatever it contains, it is surely a symbol that my dear husband has come to his senses at last. My prayers have been answered. Purgatory is at an end. Praise the Lord. Hallelujah!

A little shake will do no harm. Hmmm—not the rattle and slide of a necklace.

A turquoise brooch to match my engagement ring, perhaps? Turquoises are supposed to bring good fortune and keep away evil spirits, but my old stones seem to have lost their efficacy.

Emeralds overcome misfortune and fortify the spirit. Goodness knows how low my spirits have sunk of late. Could Charles have chosen emeralds to help me recover my sense of joy? My eyelids are heavy shutters. It is an effort to force them open, but the thought of emeralds helps to relieve the weight.

The package is addressed to *C.J.H. Dickens Esquire, Gad's Hill Place, Higham.* I should leave it on the hall table for him. I know that that is the correct thing to do but my rebellious fingers cannot resist the temptation to untie the twine, which I let drop to the floor. I will just take a peep inside, and then wrap it up again so no one will ever know my guilty secret. This small deceit is forgivable, I tell myself, because it will spare me another day of distress. With my peace of mind restored, I will sleep better tonight and, in the morning, when Charles toasts our twenty-two years of marriage and presents his gift, I shall employ my acting skills to appear surprised. I shall not need to act delighted because exhilaration will be truly mine.

Waxed paper crackles in protest at being stripped off. Velvet as soft as a horse's muzzle caresses my finger tips as I lift out the beautiful presentation box. The lid resists attempts to prise it open like an obstinate oyster. Pearls. There may be pearls inside—purity, wisdom, spiritual transformation.

But no—gold! A gold bracelet gleams out at me like spring sunshine, set off by the perfect foil of a midnight blue lining. It encircles my wrist. A snug fit but not so tight as to leave a red ring. It catches the light as I raise my arm and twist my wrist to admire it. With reluctance I tug it off. 'Until tomorrow,' I say and raise it to my lips for a parting kiss. An inscription inside the band catches my eye. It will say, 'Darling Kate, 2nd April 1858', of course. What else could it say? Oh, my loving husband: inconsistent, tempestuous but ultimately thoughtful.

I can't quite make out the words so I take the bracelet to the window and read the message: 'affectionately yours CD'. Well, it's not quite what I'd hoped for but it's close enough. I expel my sorrows in a long, long sigh. Hope expands as my lungs reinflate.

Bob is curled up on the window seat. I stroke him and break the good news. He purrs. He's happy for me too. But as I give the bracelet a quarter turn, I notice another word: 'Nelly.' The full inscription reads 'Nelly affectionately yours CD'.

The bangle slips out of my fingers and hits the floor. Bob pounces on it, loses interest, and tangles himself in the twine.

Wood pigeons coo in the garden, dogs bark at passersby, hyacinths scent the room, breakfast crockery is clattered away, servants chatter as if nothing is amiss, and the sun still shines through the window. How can this be, when my whole world has come to an end?

'I'm home, Georgy!' Charles shouts. 'Going to work in my study. Get tea brought in.'

Time to take action. I untangle Bob from the twine, releasing him to leap on my ball of wool and roll around with it on the floor. The comforter I was knitting to give Charles tomorrow starts to unravel. Hey-ho: Bob may as well have his fun.

I smooth the wrapping paper flat on the table and place the box back on top of it. I can imagine the bracelet burning a hole in the carpet, so diabolical is it, but cannot bear to pick it up. Not wishing to be contaminated, I spear it with a knitting needle and deposit it in its silk-lined casket. The lid snaps shut. It is shrouded in brown paper tied with cat-frayed twine.

Am I ready? Yes. I have nothing to lose now. Bob follows me out of the room, then senses trouble and runs upstairs.

Anyone who wishes to enter The Inimitable's inner sanctum must be sure to knock first. I'm tempted to throw open the door but years of training cannot be wholly overcome in an instant. I hammer at the door with a clenched fist.

'Tea at last. Come in,' Charles says.

He turns in his chair and smiles. His face falls when he sees it is me.

I smile back sweetly as if I hadn't noticed the change in his countenance.

'I've brought your package, my Dear,' I say and hold it out for him to see.

He looks up and drops his pen. Ink splatters his newest peacock waistcoat but he pays it no heed. Mesmerised, his eyes widen as if I'm about to fire a cannon at his head.

'Nothing to say?' I ask.

The world-famous wordsmith is lost for words.

Charles shudders as if I have just walked on his grave.

'Where did you get that?' he asks.

'It was delivered just after breakfast this morning,' I say. 'While you were out. Again.'

'Here?' he asks.

'Yes. Apparently you wanted it as a matter of urgency? I suspect it might have something to do with our wedding anniversary tomorrow. Twenty-two years! Shall I open it now?' I tease the twine with the tips of my fingers.

Charles jumps up and snatches the package from me.

'It's nothing of consequence,' he says, but clasps it with both hands.

'Why the urgency then?'

'The jeweller must have misunderstood.'

'Oh, so it's jewellery?'

'I thought you said so?'

'I didn't but the maid did mention that the jeweller's boy brought it.'

'You can't trust anyone to do as they're bid these days.' He bangs the box down on his desk.

'What was supposed to happen?' I ask, and sit in his chair.

'It was to be delivered to my office. It's a business matter.' He sweeps his thinning hair across the top of his head.

'How interesting,' I say, and tap my fingers on the box as if practising scales on the piano, 'but when do matters of business take the form of love tokens?'

'Gifts often smooth the way in commerce but I cannot expect you to know about such things.' He's trying to put me in my place, but I no longer have a place.

'You're quite right, my Dear.' I get to my feet and pick up the parcel. 'Enlighten me.' I take a step towards him. 'I so long to be enlightened. What did you purchase?' Another step closer. 'For whom?' Another step. 'And what are you smoothing the way for?'

He grabs for the packet, knocking it from my hands, but I catch it.

He turns his back on me and walks away.

'These matters do not concern you,' he says.

I creep up and tap him on the shoulder. He starts, turns and looks at me as if I am a stranger accosting him in the street.

'But I am concerned, Charles. Very concerned—and with good reason,' I say with only the width of the box between us.

There is a tap at the door. The maid enters with the tea things.

'I do apologise, Madam, I didn't know you were here. I'll fetch another cup,' she says.

'Please do not trouble yourself. Mrs Dickens was just leaving,' Charles says.

'Actually, I think I'll stay a little longer and take some tea with my husband, but don't bother with another cup. We can share, can't we, Charles, like we used to when younger?'

Wispy hair has flopped back to reveal his bald pate. Struck dumb again, Charles is only able to manage a jerky nod as he mops the perspiration that has broken out in the furrows of his middle-aged brow.

'Very well,' says the maid looking from one of us to the other. 'Thank you, Sir. Thank you, Madam.' She hurries from the room.

'I must get back to work,' Charles says and returns to his desk.

'Work does not seem to have been a priority since you met the Ternans,' I say.

His face blanches at the mention of their name.

'That family, like others, required my assistance,' he says.

That is a jibe at my parents but I will not be sidetracked.

'Would you have the goodness to assist me by revealing what you purchased. Was it for them?' I ask.

'Of course not,' he says.

He picks up his pen. It waggles as if keen to get on and write me out of his story.

I hand him the parcel. 'Unwrap it, Charles, or I will,' I say.

One glance in my direction convinces him I am in earnest.

He makes a show of struggling to untie the twine.

'A Gordian Knot,' he says.

'Use scissors,' I say.

'I don't have any in here. Perhaps you could fetch me some from the kitchen?'

I yank open his desk drawer. It bangs his knees. He yelps. I extract a letter opener. The twine resists being severed by one pass of the blade. Sawing like a surgeon, however, does the trick.

Charles peels back the paper fold by fold, picks up the box and tilts it towards me as he opens the lid to reveal the contents.

'There you are. A trinket. Pretty but worthless.' He snaps the box shut and starts to re-wrap it.

'Not gold then?' I say, and hold out my hand. 'Let me take a closer look.'

'For the love of heaven, Catherine, there is nothing more to see.' He fumbles in his hurry to re-tie the twine.

My hand hovers, as I wait for him to hand it to me.

'There is nothing to be gained by pursuing this course of action, Kate, my darling.'

'Oh, I'm *Kate your darling* again now, am I? You haven't called me that since you met Ellen Ternan, or should I call her "Nelly" as you do?'

He passes the box to me and rests his head in his hands.

'You know, don't you?'

'Only because I prayed that it was a present for me.' My voice cracks. I squeeze my eyes shut to try and dam the tears.

'It means nothing. I often give such things to people who perform for me.'

'But you said it was not for the Ternans, Charles. You lied to me.'

He shakes his head.

'That's true. It was not for the family,' he says.

'Indeed it wasn't,' I say. 'It was just for one of them: the one who performs for you. Especially for you. Your Nelly—*affectionately*. Happy Anniversary for tomorrow, Charles! What an April Fool I am.'

I turn from my husband of twenty-two years minus one day and leave the room.

SATURDAY, 11TH JUNE 1870—3:10 AM

GUILTY as charged, Charles. Guilty as charged.

You always gave freely of your time and energy but your generosity would never extend to purchasing gold jewellery for a young actress unless you were certain your investment would pay handsome dividends.

Kate blinks in her twilight world. Have vultures flown into the room to pick the flesh off her husband's reputation now he is dead or is it just the curtains blowing in the summer breeze? Is someone whispering 'actress, actress' or is it just the hiss of a gaslight in the street?

A diminutive Mr Pickwick stands on her bedside table. He points a finger at the portrait of Charles hanging from a chain on the wall. 'Tut tut, tut tut,' says the pendulum clock in the hall. Mamie's first doll is tight-lipped but her eyebrows are raised. Frank and Alfie's favourite tin soldiers stand to attention on the mantelpiece, seeming to nudge and wink at each other. Snippets of conversations float in through the window. Everyone is gossiping about her husband but, not to worry, he has found a sure-fire way to quell the rumours.

The Lord may forgive him for what he asked of her but Kate is not sure she can.

April 1858

'DON'T go, Mother. Don't go!' Lucifer Box is in tears.

'There, there, Lucifer Box. Don't take on so. I have no option. Do you want to see me cast out without a penny?' I ask. 'I don't want to end up in Queer Street.'

She throws my arm off her shoulders and stamps her foot—a petulant little girl again.

I try to take her hand but she is too distraught to let me. 'I have shed many tears,' I tell her, 'and begged your father not to make me do this, but he will not relent.'

'But it's too much to ask. How can you be expected to face that woman, knowing what we know?'

She stomps off towards the door. 'Is he home? I'm going to tell him what I think of him.'

I grab her arm.

'Do not, my Dear. It will only make matters worse.'

'What can be worse than this humiliation upon humiliation?'

'Your father will blame me for confiding in you and I'll have to go regardless. Do you want to do something useful? Help me choose what to wear.'

We go through my wardrobe. There are many choices. One gown, desperate to avoid selection, drops off its hook. We settle on silk. It is neither too ostentatious nor too plain. Charles used to love me in blue. He said it matched my beautiful eyes. I will wear my jet necklace as a subtle signal that I am mourning my situation. Ellen may choose to show off her gold bracelet. I select two of mine—one for each wrist.

Lucifer Box puts extra pins in my hair and ties my bonnet with a perfect bow.

'There now. You're as neat as a new pin,' she says.

'I feel like a blunt old pin, discarded at the bottom of the needlework box,' I say.

'Oh Mama, let me accompany you. I'll show them what pins are good for!'

'Thank you, my Dear, but I don't want you to face your father's wrath. But if you would pray for me . . . ?'

'I'll pray that the Ternans all drop down dead. Don't let them get the better of you.'

My cloak billows out behind me in the breeze as the cabman helps me up the steps. If only I could fly up in the air like a kite and never come down. My daughter waves me a sorrowful goodbye, as if I'm off to join Walter to put down the Indian rebels, and I suppose, in a way, I am about to do battle.

GREEN fields and market gardens have been replaced with rank grass and builders' rubble in this new suburb of Islington. The carriage jolts and threatens to tip me out of my seat, as it navigates a precarious course along unmade roads.

'Park Cottage' in Northampton Park sounds like a rural idyll but as we pass brick fields between the Balls Pond Road and the North London Railway line, I suspect it is all just castles in the air. In the cattle market, grizzled farmers prod and poke doomed cows. They moo in regret at having outlived their usefulness, now that their calving years have passed.

'We have arrived, Madam,' the cabman calls.

The mean-looking house has been tacked onto the end of a terrace. Its facade is covered in Roman stucco but this is no sunny Mediterranean home. It faces north.

I huff and puff and almost trip up the steps. There are only four but they feel like forty. With gaping mouth I thrash around, heaving for breath, like a freshly landed fish. Mrs Ternan finds me slumped over her railings. This is not the dignified entrance I had planned.

'Oh, my word! My dear Mrs Dickens! Fanny! Maria! Nelly!' she cries.

They help me into a sitting room so small that it can barely accommodate their four voluminous gowns along with my more up-to-date daywear.

Mrs Ternan guides me into a threadbare armchair.

'Fetch our guest a drink of water,' she says and sets about slapping my cheeks.

Fanny obeys. Ellen fans me with her handkerchief, which stinks of lavender. Maria waves a bottle of smelling salts under my nose. The fumes make me gasp. The women's faces blur. They fade into the distance. I'm dying. Charles will be glad to have me gone.

'My darling wife died peacefully in the arms of her dearest friends,' he will say.

I shall rest in peace with Dora in my arms once again, but what of my other children? With Charles increasingly distant, they need me now more than ever.

Fanny tips water into my panting mouth. I choke on it, splutter, and cough it out in a spray that drenches everyone.

Something bubbles up inside me. Please God, don't let me vomit. Not here. Not today. Please leave me a shred of dignity, following the horror show of my entrance.

My mouth opens. Oh no! No, no, no, no . . .

Out comes a belch and a laugh. A belch and a laugh!

I have tortured myself day and night with what might happen at this charade, but not once have I envisioned this show-stopping performance.

I laugh at the ridiculous nature of my situation—having to sit with a mother who parades her daughters before all comers. I laugh at my husband—his absences, his pathetic excuses, his tirades, his silences, his new waistcoats, even the newly-grown moustache intended to conceal the tell-tale lines of age around his middle-aged mouth. I even cry with laughter over my husband's bracelet bungle and his single bed in a separate room. I laugh because the man I love is besotted with one of this woman's daughters and I have no idea what else to do.

'I do apologise,' I say, dabbing my eyes, mouth and dress with my handkerchief. 'The prospect of our meeting appears to have overcome me.'

'No need to apologise, my dear Mrs Dickens,' the mother says, brushing off the splattered water. 'I threw on this silly old gown in the knowledge that you would not wish me to stand on ceremony meeting an old friend such as yourself.'

She's embracing the role Charles has assigned her, but I'm not going to play along.

'You are too kind, particularly as I have only once before enjoyed the pleasure of your company, but I believe my husband has more than made up for my neglect?' So polite, so apologetic, such an innocent enquiry that she can't take offence at.

'Oh yes, Manchester. Mr Dickens has certainly become a guardian angel and a most generous benefactor since then. Hasn't he girls?' she says.

They sit up and nod in unison like well-trained circus ponies.

'Not that we need support, of course,' Mrs Ternan adds.

'I'm glad to hear that. Where are you playing at present?' I ask, as a true friend would.

She sighs. 'We have decided to take a rest between roles,' she says.

'You have certainly earned a rest after all those decades touring the country,' I say, oozing compassion. 'But what about you, Fanny? It must be most trying to have your promising career put on hold for a season. I understand you were quite the child prodigy.'

'Fanny is concentrating on her singing at present. She is blessed with the voice of an angel,' Mrs Ternan says.

'An angel, how wonderful. Are you concentrating on your singing too, Maria, or is it more your acting skills that audiences cry out for?' Lucifer Box would be proud of me.

She shakes her head and opens her mouth as if about to explain.

'Maria is resting too,' her mother says.

'Well Nelly, and what dizzying heights have you moved on to, after the part you played with my husband at the Free Trade Hall?'

'Perhaps you three would like to fetch our guest some tea?' Mrs Ternan says.

They nod and leave with a swish of their costumes.

Mrs Ternan reaches across to the dresser for a scrapbook and passes it to me.

'Reviews of our performances. All glowing,' she says.

Their lives are told in playbills and newspaper articles. Mrs Ternan, carried on stage as a baby, does the same with her daughters. *Theatrical Babe-in-Arms Steals Show!* As soon as they walk they work. *The Sweetest Little Darling Daughters!* Two-and-half-years touring America. *Sisters' State-to-State Success!* Not so many playbills on their return, though. She looks shorter, stouter, more middle-aged.

So does her husband. Bald too. Mr Ternan risks everything to become an actor manager. *Mr. Ternan Takes on Two Theatres!* They make a loss. He is taken ill. Their baby son dies. Mr Ternan dies. *The Terrible Tragedy of the Ternans.* The four women continue to tour. *Plucky Actress Family Soldiers On Alone.* Their names slip to the bottom of playbills. *Other Members of the Cast Include . . . Also featuring . . . .*

I know something of this life. I've acted with my family, toured America, lost a baby. I'm now in danger of losing my husband so I too face an insecure future.

'I'm so sorry about your husband and your baby boy,' I say, and I am. 'I lost my little Dora at eight months.'

'I don't think a mother ever recovers from the loss of her child and Thomas was my only son,' she says. For once she is speaking to me rather than to an imaginary audience.

'I fear I may lose Walter too. He's fighting in India,' I say.

'At least I have my daughters close at hand,' she says.

'That must be a great relief,' I agree, 'although there are different perils for girls.'

She doesn't answer. I must push the point home.

'I have heard talk—'

'There are always those only too willing to besmirch the good name of working women, however above reproach they may be,' she says, trying to recover her customary timbre of voice.

'Both our families have much to lose,' I say and hand back her scrapbook.

She hugs it to her chest.

'I have very little left,' she whispers, dropping the bravado.'

'But your good name?'

'Good names do not pay the rent or put food on the table.'

Well, that's honest of her. I suddenly find it in my heart to pity them.

The girls bring in the tea.

Maria hands me a cup and saucer. Her cuffs are frayed. Fanny turns to place the teapot on the table. The back of her dress is darned. Ellen sits. She crosses her legs and swings her foot restlessly. Her shoe is down-at-heel.

I pull off my gold bracelets and hand them to her sisters.

'Now you have one each,' I say.

I slip off my jet necklace and place it round Mrs Ternan's neck.

'In memory of Thomas,' I say, and make my way out of the silent room.

Saturday, 11th June 1870—3:35 am

AFTER a shaky start, it seemed to Kate that the visit had resulted in some mutual understanding. Having shown she bore them no ill-will, she would no doubt now be treated by the Ternans with compassion, and Charles would be grateful to her for helping save his reputation, despite her tears and trepidation. Perhaps he had been right all the time in insisting on the meeting. She knew it was right to forgive him, as she always had done, for that was the Christian way. But would the Lord forgive Charles for what he did next?

What was it Lucifer Box had said about her being too trusting and seeing the best in everyone, as if these were vices to be overcome?

When Charles called her into his study the next day, she found him pacing up and down with his hands behind his back, muttering in the way he did when trying to resolve a situation with his fictional characters. She imagined he was going to thank her for visiting the Ternans and trying to find the right words. Not every wife would have shown them such understanding and kindness.

Kate had been proud of herself—and pride is ever followed by a fall. Always hopeful, she little anticipated what would happen next. She blows at the candle, extinguishing the flame. Today all hope is extinguished. Charles is dead and she is truly alone in the darkness.

April 1858

'SO, you visited Mrs Ternan and her daughters yesterday?' Charles asks.

Lucifer Box must have confirmed that I had carried out his wishes when they breakfasted together this morning. Charles could have asked me himself, were he not now in the habit of walking out whenever I enter a room.

'As you requested, my Dear,' I say, taking a seat.

He sits on the other side of his desk, picks up a ruler and seems to beat out time to a tune I cannot hear.

'There were gifts?'

Tap, tap, tap, tap . . .

Dear old Mrs Ternan must have made a point of contacting Charles to inform him of my generosity.

'I thought it would be charitable and show goodwill.' Another smile goes unreciprocated. Obviously displays of charity and goodwill were not what Charles required of me.

'You made an almighty fuss when I bought a gift for the Ternans and yet when you wish to do the same, you grant yourself every freedom. What a hateful hypocrite you are. On top of which, you offend me by giving them gifts that I meant for you, showing me that you neither value them nor honour my kindness in bestowing them upon you.'

Tap Tap Tap Tap Tap . . .

I'll have to raise my voice to make myself heard above the ruler's crescendo.

'I'm sorry, Charles! I did not mean to upset you and I treasure everything you have ever given me, truly I do—'

Tap Tap Tap Tap Tap . . .

'—but I have been blessed with so much and the poor dears have so little that I was moved to share my good fortune! Just as you were moved to share yours with Ellen!'

'Don't shout at me and do not utter that innocent young woman's name! She asks nothing of me!' he barks.

Charles stands, dashes the ruler to his desk and leans across to stare at me with bulging bloodshot eyes. Pearls of spittle sparkle on his beard.

'Never have you appreciated the efforts I make, every day of my life, for you and your children and your family. I remember how high and mighty you all were when we first met. Personal friends of Sir Walter Scott, too grand for a poor Marshalsea boy. You won't rest until you see me back there. Perhaps you'll let me share a cell with your father. Remind me who baled him out of the debtors' prison?'

Rage on, Charles, rage on. There is nothing new here and nothing to be gained by interrupting. Instead I'll let my head droop in apparent contrition. Being supine usually placates him—makes him feel in charge.

'You may well hang your head in shame after the spectacle you made of yourself!'

I jump like a startled cat. Such betrayal! He cannot be quoting Mrs Ternan, for she had tears in her eyes as I left. I want to lash out. I want to say, 'Did I make a spectacle of myself, Charles? How terrible!' But sarcasm will not save me and heaven only knows what he will do if I provoke him. Instead, I offer up a silent prayer for sweet Jesus to come to my aid. He sends my sister, Mary.

'Breathe, Kate, breathe. Release your grip on the chair. Hands in lap. Head up. Look him in the eye. Calm countenance. Speak softly,' says her voice in my head.

'I admit my nerves threatened to overwhelm me but I regained my composure,' I say.

Honesty will prevail, won't it Mary?

Bang

His fist hits the desk.

'Don't bother to deny it!' he says. 'You made a spectacle of yourself.'

I want to shout back, 'It's your fault! You forced me to go! You put me in that intolerable situation!' but the thought of Mary makes me restrain myself.

'I'm at your side, dear Sister,' she tells me. 'Calm yourself.'

'Has anyone said I behaved in such a way as to embarrass you, Charles?' I enquire, solicitously, marvelling at my own self-control.

'You were hysterical—panting, choking on water, spitting, belching, braying like a madwoman!'

Would Fanny or Maria portray me thus? No: they slipped the bracelets onto their wrists and squeezed my hands in thanks.

'You are unwell. You need help—medical help. Nelly is concerned for your sanity.'

Oh, so it's Nelly who's concerned for me? Of course she is. I have underestimated the sweet little viper's flair for theatrics. I must contain my scorn. Hold my breath. Tighten my stomach. Cross my legs. Clench my fists and not laugh out loud at the notion that Nelly has anything but contempt for me.

'I need my husband, not a doctor,' I say and reach to take his hand.

He pulls it away as if I wish to claw him.

'You will be examined,' he says.

The earth quakes. My head shakes in an involuntary denial.

'Shaking, strangulated speech: you obviously belong in Bedlam.'

'Control yourself, Kate. Still body. Tranquil mind. Soothing voice,' Mary whispers, but I am not my saintly sister.

'I belong in Bedlam? For baulking at being forced to visit your mistress? What sane woman would relish such a command?' I shout.

'Mistress! Another symptom of your insane jealousy. First it was Augusta De la Rue, now it's Nelly Ternan.'

'I will not submit to an examination,' I say and march to the door.

'Then you will be confined to your room until you do.'

This stab in the back brings me to a standstill.

'You mean to imprison me?' I see myself trapped in the distorted reflection of the brass door plate.

'Don't be so melodramatic, you halfwit. You would still host our dinner parties.'

One foot turns, the other foot follows, inch by inch. I'm a baby taking precarious first steps in a new reality.

My parents' portraits on the walls urge me to say 'no'.

My reflection in the window shakes her head.

Mary's ghost says 'no, no, no'.

'I will do no such thing,' I say to this stranger who is masquerading as my husband.

'Then there is no point in keeping you in London. You will reside here at Gad's Hill Place.'

Banished. I'm to be banished. What an effort it is to wend my way to the sofa. What a relief to sit down.

'Compose yourself before you answer,' Mary says.

'How kind of you to banish me here. And the children?' I ask as if we are discussing a family outing.

'They would remain with me of course, with their wellbeing entrusted to the capable hands of Georgina.'

Of course. Of course. No question. They are his property. We are mere goods and chattels, to be disposed of according to his whim.

'No, in that case.'

He strolls up and down in front of me, appealing with his hands as if he's giving one of his readings to an unappreciative audience.

'You would see them when you came back to town to accompany me on visits to friends—important to preserve the appearance of family unity. You could even stay there sometimes. We could exchange houses.'

He's as smooth as the velvet cushion I am resting on for support.

Mary whispers, 'Don't live a lie,' in my ear.

'I will not live a lie,' I say.

Charles pauses dramatically, then paces as he does when acting out the scene in *Oliver Twist* where Bill Sikes murders Nancy.

'Then you must go and live abroad,' Bill growls. 'Alone.'

Nancy cringes.

'You cannot ship me out like a convict,' she pleads.

Bill steps back.

'You don't need to be shipped anywhere. Just agree to see a doctor. That is all you have to do. It's entirely your choice—' he says.

Nancy shakes her head.

'—just as it was your choice to go off to Malvern, to seek a treatment for your headaches, and leave little Dora to die alone.' Bill's voice snarls.

Nancy, bludgeoned by Bill's cruelty, staggers towards the door. She throws it open and crashes into Georgina who is eavesdropping in the hallway. I hold out my arms to her: I am in dire need of a living sister's embrace. Georgina will support me through this trial. Georgina will hold my hand during the doctors' examination. Georgina will not let them lie. Georgina will stop Charles from committing me to an asylum.

Georgina pushes me away.

'You shouldn't argue with Charles, Kate. He is a man of genius.'

'You cannot believe that I am insane?'

'It is not for me to say, but I know that Charles has your best interests at heart. After all, he's paying professionals to give you a diagnosis so you may be cured.'

'He means to have me locked away.' Now I truly am a frightened mouse.

'The doctors are on their way,' she says and heads off, no doubt to attend to more important matters such as turning all the teacups in the crockery cabinet so their handles line up, like soldiers saluting on parade. Georgina values order above all else.

In my bedroom I seek solace but can find none. Charles has summoned the doctors. Charles will pay the doctors. The doctors will agree with Charles. I will be locked up. I will rot, as unwanted wives customarily do.

The stench of Bedlam stings my nostrils. The screams of madwomen strike my ears. Shackles bite my wrists. Rats scuttle up my legs. I am a quivering maniac in a carnival of deformities. I am purged, bled and blistered.

Heavy footsteps pound on the stairs: Georgina's—and others. They are coming for me.

There is a knock at the door.

'Pray, Kate, pray.'

Two doctors come in. They question me, goad me, challenge me. I do my best to answer truthfully but struggle to believe my own account of how Charles has treated me and the children. It sounds too outrageous to be credible.

And in truth, isn't it Charles who has taken leave of his senses? He has never been in control of himself. He has always suffered from melancholy and fits of temper, but now rages like a madman. He, however, remains free and admired; I, by contrast, am diagnosed to be a hysterical woman. It doesn't matter what I say: doctors will dismiss it as a symptom of my malady.

But what of my children? Walter is already fighting for his life. He does not need bad news from home. And Charley cannot rely on his father's support. My girls need me. And what will their other brothers think when they return from school to find me consigned to a lunatic asylum? And what of six-year-old Plorn? Is he to be left to the mercies of a stern aunt and a father who never wanted him?

'That will be all, Mrs Dickens. We are obliged to you for your cooperation,' one of the doctors says.

'And now what happens to me?' I ask.

'We will send our findings and our recommendations to Mr Dickens in due course,' says the second doctor, as he packs away his stethoscope.

'Will you say I'm insane?' I should have kept quiet. Asking if I'm insane may be twisted into an admission that I've said I think I am.

'Our opinion will form part of a written report. In the meantime try not to distress yourself unduly.' Doctor Number One is slightly more reassuring than his partner.

SATURDAY, 11TH JUNE 1870—3.45 AM

HAD the doctors pronounced her insane, would Charles have immediately discarded her along with all the other detritus of their marriage: the broken chairs, the rickety cradle, the moth-eaten blankets, the half-bald dolls and the broken toys that had been locked away in the attic?

Evidence. What evidence is there either for or against him? She throws back the sheet, gets up and makes her way downstairs in the darkness. As she walks, her nightdress clings to her sweaty legs, like a frightened child. She passes the parlour window and draws the curtain aside to light the room, but dawn is still half an hour off. She feels along the mantelpiece for the tinderbox. The lid is stiff. It gives and the flint flies out onto the floor. Kate sighs and feels around with her bare feet to recover it. She finds it and picks it up. Strike one fails. Strike two is no better. She perseveres and is rewarded with enough of a spark to ignite the kindling in the base of the box and, using that, she lights a candle.

Now she is able to open the top drawer of her writing desk and read articles she has set aside, written by Charles. She finds the one that was published on his return from meeting Ellen in Doncaster. Kate had found his words chilling back then.

> She was . . . a weak, credulous, incapable, helpless nothing.
>
> . . . She was not worth hating; he felt nothing but contempt for her. But she had long been in the way, and he had long been weary.
>
> . . . When . . . the rising sun flamed into the sombre room, she heard it hailed with, 'Another day and not dead? Die!'

His words are just as chilling now, but would Charles really have left her to die in Bedlam? She will never know. Only the Lord can see into his soul. Only He can decide what her husband's fate will be.

Her fate had been sealed the day that Charles met Ellen Ternan, and Kate was now to discover just how ruthless he could be. There was no cause for celebration after that, not even on her forty-third birthday.

May 1858

WHAT A contrast between last year's birthday and this one. A year ago Charles delighted in welcoming me to Gad's Hill Place—our new home in the Kent countryside—by throwing a surprise party. There is no party this year. No gift. Not even a birthday greeting. He throws me nothing but a withering look.

He says one thing only: 'I'll stay at the office to give you an opportunity to pack in peace.'

He can be magnanimous now. Always the author, with the power of creation and damnation, he hasn't allowed the unplanned twist in his plot to throw his narrative off course. When real-life doctors refused to pronounce the protagonist insane he simply consigned her to a sub-plot.

Mother busies herself folding gowns into trunks, wrapping ornaments in newspaper and swaddling pictures in blankets.

'What about this?' she asks and holds up a portrait of Charles as a young man.

'Yes,' I say. 'He gave me that to mark our engagement.'

'You'd never know it's the same man. This one is clean shaven with a full head of brown hair and a handsome youthful face whereas . . . '

'Yes, mother. I'm well aware of the changes in my husband, just as he is well aware of the changes in me.'

'Very well, very well. I'm only trying to help.'

She throws the portrait in a trunk and covers it with a teacloth.

'Here's a lovely one of you. He can say what he likes. I think my little Hen is as beautiful now as ever.'

'I may as well take it. If I leave it, Charles will only turn my face to the wall.'

She wraps up the girl who used to be me and places her gently in the trunk.

'That Nelly might be young, slender and pretty now but give her twelve babies in twenty-two years and then we'll see how she fares.'

'Charles would never dream of having a child out of wedlock! Besides, her looks may fade and her waist may widen but she is twenty-seven years his junior and so will remain forever young in his eyes.'

Mother slams down the lid of the trunk and secures the straps.

'Marriage vows are intended to stop husbands swapping their wives for pretty young women as soon as they can afford one.'

She takes my hand and pulls me up off the bed.

'Let's get away from here. I've never liked it.'

But I don't want to get up. I want to lie down and sleep and never awaken.

'I am heartbroken, absolutely heartbroken,' Charles would say, 'but my dearest wife Kate died peacefully at home with her mother at her side. That is my only consolation.'

He would omit to mention that Ellen Ternan was on the doorstep before my corpse was cold.

'Dear Mother, please give me a moment,' I say.

'There is no sense in lingering, Kate. The Brighton train leaves at four o'clock and time and tide wait for no man.'

'I need to compose myself before saying goodbye to Georgina . . . and my children.'

'Of course, of course. Take all the time you need, Hen. Lie on the bed for a wee while. We can catch a later train but please do not think of saying goodbye to Georgina. I for one will never speak to her again.'

'Mother, Mother, you know she's always loved Charles and she can't abide change. Even if she could, what choice does she have?

You cannot afford to keep her and Charles would cut her off without a penny if she left with me.'

'Two wrongs don't make a right,' she says.

'To err is human, to forgive divine,' I say.

'Still, the road to Hell is paved with good intentions,' she replies.

'And actions speak louder than words,' I counter, and we both laugh.

'You've always been far too forgiving if you ask me,' she says.

I don't answer.

'But what do I know?' she asks.

I say nothing.

'But you're right, Hen. Least said, soonest mended. I'll go and arrange for your trunks to be brought down.'

I don't really want to take anything but I don't want to leave anything behind either, least of all my children. I have the portrait of Charley, Mamie, Lucifer Box and Walter which accompanied us to America, so it will accompany me on my solo journey to an unknown destination. I don't want a likeness of them. I want to hold all of them in my arms again, kiss their cheeks as they try to wriggle away, run my fingers through their hair, talk about their hopes and fears and let them know that all I want is for them to be happy.

How many times have we slept together, his arm over mine, my leg over his, basking in our shared body heat? How often have I lain awake, comforted by his soft breath on my face? How often have we laughed and how often cried together? How many times have I brought him broth, mopped his fevered brow, bandaged his gouty feet, and creamed his bloody haemorrhoids? Will Ellen nurse him as I have?

But how can I walk away? I would rather rip the wallpaper off the walls, throw the rugs on the fire, smash the mirrors and the vases, and break up the furniture than bequeath it all to my husband's plaything. Let her have one hundred gold bangles, she will never have the memories that I treasure.

I take off my gold locket, prise it open and stroke the lock of Dora's hair.

Perhaps he will one day tire of Ellen and come to appreciate our more mature sensibilities? Perhaps he will think more fondly of what we shared?—the decades of lovemaking, of homemaking, of children born, of travels, of friendships, of the selfless support I always gave him.

Just last summer we were happy here. Hans Christian Andersen's visit may not have been a resounding success but there was croquet on the lawn and dinner with friends. The boys home for the holidays playing cricket with the villagers. Charles strutting around like the lord of the manor, a part he had coveted since he first set eyes on the house as a young lad, walking past with his father. Mr Dickens had said that if Charles were to be very persevering and work very hard, he might one day live there—and the die was cast.

For the moment, separation is the lesser of the other evils on offer, so I must take my leave.

There is a whiff of claret on Mamie's breath as she leans forward to kiss my cheek. She sways and catches my nose instead.

'Ooops,' she says and giggles. 'Sorry, Mama—I'm a little woozy this afternoon. Have a nice time in Blighton!'

My poor child staggers off towards the stairs. What will become of her? What can I do to save my sweet daughter when I cannot save even myself?

Lucifer Box throws her arms around me.

'Wish I could come with you,' she says, 'but I'll be straight round as soon as you're settled back in London.' She glares at Georgina who has opened the trunks to check what I'm taking.

'You seem to have emptied half the kitchen,' she says.

'Charles said I might take my favourite pots and pans,' I say.

'You don't have to answer to her,' Mother says.

Plorn skulks in the corner. He sucks his thumb and stares at the floor. My arms reach out for him. I breathe in my baby boy as he burrows into my chest. This is too much. Charles asks too much of me. How can he wrench a mother from her son?

'Don't go Mama,' Plorn pleads.

I don't want to go! Your father is forcing me out! He has fallen in love with someone the same age as one of your sisters! A stage strumpet! A lightskirt! He bought her a bracelet and stopped sleeping with me, tried to consign me to Bedlam, hoped to lock me up here, or in London, or send me overseas! I want to shout these truths, but that will not help my son. I must quell his fears, tell him he will be well cared for and loved—but I cannot say what I do not believe.

‘Be brave,’ is all I can manage.

His little body vibrates in tune with mine.

Georgina puts down her inventory and yanks Plorn away from me.

‘Please take care of him!’ I shout above his screams.

‘Come along.’ Mother leads me away from my child.

He kicks out at Georgina.

‘I hope you’re proud of yourself,’ Mother says.

Georgina reaches out.

‘Please Mama,’ she pleads.

‘Call yourself a sister?’

‘But Mama . . . ’

‘You lost your mother when Plorn lost his,’ she says. ‘I am no longer your flesh and blood.’

Mother tries to pull me towards the door but I have no power of locomotion. Lucifer Box shunts me out.

‘You’re not safe here, Mama. He’ll stop at nothing to get what he wants and to hell with the rest of us.’

She takes a piece of card from her apron pocket. She has painted a picture of the garden and stuck a dried flower to it.

‘I pressed a rosebud from the flower bed for your birthday,’ she says.

Our tears dissolve the watercolours.

Mother shuts the door behind us. I will be forever haunted by Plorn’s muffled cries of ‘Mumma, I want my Mumma.’ Mumma wants him too.

I’m at the end of the line. My engine is about to explode. Shall I smash windows? Scream? Kick the door down? Prostrate myself on the grass like Hans Christian Andersen? The gardener was told to plant more lavender in the front garden. The first of the new bushes resists my tugging but I yank up the second by its roots, toss it aside and grab a third. This one is far more acquiescent but a fourth puts up more of a fight.

‘Don’t struggle! Give up! Give in! You *will* be uprooted!’ I shout.

‘Kate, Kate, the servants! Come along now, come along,’ says Mother.

‘I told you she was mad,’ I can hear Charles say.

The lavender admits defeat. It flies through the air and lands with a *clomp* against the front door. Georgina appears. She stands hands on hips. Plorn pushes past her. Lucifer Box follows him and picks up the plant.

'Get back inside this instant!' Georgina shouts.

'Well done, Mama!' my daughter says and throws the lavender to Plorn. He tosses it back towards her. Georgina tries to intercept but it hits her in the face and showers her with soil and twigs and seed. Mother takes my arm and we walk away to the sound of my children's laughter.

BRIGHTON is no Broadstairs or Genoa. My children are not with me. They don't laugh or skim stones or throw pebbles in the sea. There are no sandcastles, no paddles, no pirates, no picnics. Seagulls still squabble and screech out at the injustice of having to fight for their food but Walter is not here to say, 'Feed birds, Mama'. Walter is a soldier fighting for the Empire on the other side of the world whilst I fight for my empire nearer home.

Sea air does not help me sleep any better than I did at home. I creep out, so as not to disturb Mama and, without Georgina to admonish me for risking my shoes getting scuffed and my dress getting dirty, I walk on the seashore as dawn breaks. Little surges of white water break at my feet and rattle the pebbles as they draw back, as the sea tries to shush away my sorrows. Early morning sun lights the horizon and paints a rosy highway across the waves but I am stranded on the shore. Low tide has etched a pattern of intertwined branches on the sand like a page from a fairytale. As the tide turns, water erases the edge of the enchanted forest.

I step into the sea and turquoise water licks around my toes. Tomorrow raging grey waves may grind pebbles into sand. Charles, despite a myriad of humours, is always Charles. But without my husband who am I? Miss Catherine Hogarth? No—I have been Mrs Charles Dickens longer than I was that optimistic, trusting, naive, young virgin. I am a mother of nine living, one dead and two unborn children. There is no going back now but how do I go forward on my own? God joined us together 'until death us do part'.

SATURDAY, 11TH JUNE 1870—4:00 AM

BEREFT. That's how she was. That's how she is. Brighton was a rehearsal—a bereavement with no body. Just the corpse of a marriage washed up on the shore. Charles could surely not have foreseen how she would suffer or he would never have sent her away. Would he? He could never have been so heartless. Could he? Kate can just about grasp the idea of one love ending and another beginning but there must be a residue of feeling left over. Mustn't there? A drop of water left in the dried-up well. A memory at least of the love that's lost. How can love be denied? Once felt, surely it lives on, never to be wholly forgotten? She still loves Charles, which brings her back to the same old question: did Charles ever love her and, if he did, how could he have treated her so cruelly?

Control, control, control. Mary had warned her. Charles could not live without it. He had to build up piles of money, surround himself with a golden wall—an impenetrable fortress no one could breach. But the walls were crumbling now. Wealth could not stop the passage of time. Fear forced her husband to look for a way to rejuvenate his ageing body and revive his flagging spirits. That way was Ellen, his fountain of youth.

'You were right to be frightened, Charles,' Kate says. 'Twelve years was all the life left to you.' She wonders how much longer she will live. Brighton had been the death of one Mrs Dickens but the birth of another who didn't know her fight for survival had only just begun.

May 1858

NIGHT after night of restless turmoil.

Another blinding headache.

Our blowsy Brighton landlady, Mrs Parsons, catches me standing sentinel by the front window as she arranges the tables for breakfast.

'Expecting another visit from that Mr Smith, are you, Ducks? We gets lots of Mr Smiths here. And Mrs Smiths!'

'He's my solicitor,' I say, not taking my eyes off the garden path.'

'We get a lot of soliciting, here, Dear.' She claps her hands as if applauding a Punch and Judy show being played out on her premises. 'But I wouldn't lose any sleep over your husband's shenanigans. They all get bored with their little tarts eventually. You mark my words. I've seen it all over the years. Never with someone famous like Mr Dickens, though,' she says. 'He's quite the talk of the town.'

'I trust you've not indulged in idle gossip about my private affairs,' I say, having overheard her doing just that many times during our stay.

'Of course not, Ducks. Soul of discretion, me. My father's cousin's friend was a footman at the Royal Pavilion. The stories he tells of goings-on there would make your hair curl, I can tell you that for nothing, but all three of them were shocked to hear that the great author is no better than he should be, despite all his airs and graces.'

She gives a snort, and I'm not sure whether it is an attempt to clear her catarrh or a sign of contempt.

'Shall I make a start on your breakfast or wait for your mother?' she asks.

'Just a coffee for me please.' My breath mists the window as I speak.

'I won't argue. Waste of good food with you throwing it back up all the time,' she says, in an obvious allusion to the guilty secret I've taken a great deal of trouble to conceal.

I feel as if she's rammed her fat fingers down my throat. I should know by now that gluttony may fill my stomach but not the hole in my heart, and purging does not flush away pain.

Through the condensation on the glass, an outline of my lawyer appears at the garden gate. I wipe it clear to bring him into full focus. He looks grim. My stomach churns.

Mrs Parsons shows him in and brings my coffee. She loiters in the doorway, no doubt keen to hear all about Mr Punch's latest assault.

'Don't let us keep you, Mrs Parsons,' he says.

She blows her nose into her apron.

'You'll have to excuse me. I must get on,' she says.

Mother joins us. Our landlady is right behind her as if vying for the last seat in the house.

'Good morning Mrs Hogarth. The usual for you?'

Mother nods. 'And a coffee for Mr Smith, if you'd be so kind.'

'Certainly, Ducks.'

'And do shut the door on your way out,' my mother adds.

I put my finger to my lips to remind Mama that our landlady is sure to be eavesdropping on the far side of the door.

'Good morning, Mr Smith. I haven't had a wink of sleep all night. Catherine, her sister Helen and my husband are all exhausted too and I'm sure you are equally weary of all the to-ing and fro-ing. Did Mr Hogarth's letter put an end to all my son-in-law's nonsense?' Mother asks.

'It may assist if we remind ourselves of what we submitted to Mr Dickens's solicitor, Mr Ouvry, on Mr Hogarth's behalf, before I go on to elucidate his client's response?'

'Very well,' Mother says, 'if you have to prolong the agony.'

Mr Smith takes a letter from his briefcase, clears his throat and reads. 'Your husband said:

> I can have no difficulty or hesitation in assuring you that the report that I or my wife or daughter have at any time stated or insinuated that any impropriety of conduct had taken place between my Daughter Georgiana and her Brother-in-Law Mr. Charles Dickens is totally unfounded.
>
> It is of course a matter of grief to us that after the unfortunate differences which have arisen between my daughter Mrs. Charles Dickens and her husband, my daughter Georgiana should remain with his family, but while we regret what we regard as a mistaken sense of duty, we have never for one instant imputed to her any improper motive for so doing.'

'Exactly right,' my mother responds. 'Georgina—*not* Georgiana—is misguided in choosing to stay under Mr Dickens's roof and I have been at pains to point this out to her on more than one occasion, but she is stubborn and will not hear. As different as chalk and cheese from Catherine and Helen—or her brothers, come to that. In a world of her own, most of the time. Never could look anyone in the eye—but she was never one to disobey, I'll say that for her. Give her a rule and she'd stick by it through thick and thin. That's why she gets on so well with Charles: he can always be relied upon to lay down the law for her. She never wanted anything new: she always screamed the house down when I insisted that she'd outgrown her frocks. Many's the time when she was little that—'

'Mama, we must not presume too greatly on Mr Smith's time, so may I suggest we turn our efforts to trying to resolve the matter at hand?' I say and pat her hand. She doesn't draw breath.

'—and we never for one moment suggested that Georgina or any of our children would ever behave in an unbecoming manner, unlike my son-in-law and that little Ellen Ternan trollop—and she no more than a slip of a girl and he a married man twice her age who ought to be horsewhipped for the way he's treated my little Hen, here. In fact, horsewhipping would be too good for him, if you ask me. If I had my way, I'd have him hung, drawn and quartered!'

'Mother, I think Mr Smith is aware of your views on Charles's shortcomings as a husband,' I say.

Mother picks up a napkin and strangles it.

'All I was saying—' she begins again, but Mr Smith manages to forestall her.

'Unfortunately, Madam, Mr Dickens's solicitor has informed me that his client requires that you and Miss Helen Hogarth put your signatures to this document which the eminent Mr Ouvry and Mr Dickens have taken the trouble to draft for you,' he says, passing her a sheet of foolscap which he has taken from his briefcase.

'The cheek of the man!' shouts Mother. 'Not satisfied with torturing his wife, now he wants to punish us as well.'

'I believe that Mr Hogarth's letter proved unacceptable because it repeated the accusation about Miss Georgina Hogarth's being in an immoral relationship with Mr Dickens before then denying it,' Mr Smith says as if he is speaking to a slow-witted child. 'Had the reader not read to the end of the sentence, the accusation would have stood. The issue at law has to do with sequence.'

Mother looks overheated and ready to burst. She fans herself with the document and takes a deep breath. It does nothing to calm her demeanour. The more she tries to steady her hand, the faster the paper flutters. I take it from her.

'Please will you read it out to us, Mr Smith?' I ask.

He sighs. 'Indeed. Mr Dickens wants your mother and sister to agree that "in reference to the differences which have resulted in the separation of Mr. and Mrs. Charles Dickens, certain statements have been circulated that such differences were occasioned by circumstances deeply affecting the moral character of Mr. Dickens."'

He clears his throat and continues. 'He requires your mother and your sister to declare solemnly that they now disbelieve such statements. They will sign, also, that they both know that such statements are not believed by Mrs. Dickens and that they pledge themselves "on all occasions to contradict them as entirely destitute of foundation."'

'So Charles accepts that I don't believe the rumours about Georgina?' I ask.

'I believe that to be so. In fact, Mr Ouvry asked me to point out to you that Mr Dickens is aware of your tender feelings towards him and does not wish to cause you any unnecessary suffering,' Mr Smith says.

It is all I can do to stop myself leaping up and dancing a jig around the dining table.

'You see, Mama, despite everything, Charles does still care for me,' I say.

Mother rolls her eyes.

'Kate, Kate: it's a matter of divide and rule.'

'But he wants to spare my suffering,' I say, less sure now, but hoping that saying the words will make it so.

She groans.

'There's none so blind as them as will not see,' she says, 'and I'll sign that pack of lies over my dead body. They're trying to make me and Helen confess that we slandered him, when we've done nothing of the sort, so he can get us caught up in another round of legal tangles. The truth is, he doesn't want anyone to know what he's been up to with that little actress: that's the fact of the matter, but truth will out!'

'There may be something in what you say regarding Mr Dickens's motives, Mrs Hogarth,' acknowledges Mr Smith. 'He may also be concerned that a scandal will affect ticket sales when he embarks on his next reading tour, which is imminent, I believe. That would explain why he is quite so insistent on tying up all possible loose ends quickly.'

'He can insist until he's black and blue, and blue in the face, and purple with rage, and green around the gills, but he won't make liars out of me and my daughters!' Mother says. 'Take him to court, Catherine. Shame him in public. That's what I say. He's got more to lose than we have.'

'Bankrupting Charles would not benefit anyone, Mother, and

no matter what he does to me, I could never do that to him. Besides, his shame would reflect on me, no matter how much his readers sympathised with me as the injured party.'

'Mrs Hogarth,' says the solicitor, 'I must warn you, if you do not sign, there will be grave consequences for your daughter. Mr Dickens has stated that he will reply to your non-compliance, and that of Miss Helen, by in turn not signing the separation agreement. Mrs Dickens may well end up with no home and no income.'

'That's how much he cares about you, Kate. Blackmail, that's what this is. Blackmail—no other word for it. He should be locked up, like his father before him. I am weary of holding my tongue whilst gentlemen of fortune torment their wives and escape all blame! Tell Mr High and Mighty Charles Dickens Esquire he cannot buy my silence!'

Mother shouts loud enough to ensure that Mrs Parsons catches every word as she listens in the wings.

'No one can force you to sign against your will, and Angela Burdett-Coutts has offered me a place with her, so please shush,' I say and indicate the door.

'Walls have ears,' says Mother, 'and also noses, and the Parson's Nose may as well sniff out what we're saying along with everyone else!'

Our landlady clatters in with a tea tray right on cue.

Mr Smith stands.

'Very well, Mrs Hogarth, Mrs Dickens: I have my instructions. I'll leave you to your breakfast and let Mr Dickens's solicitor know of your response,' Mr Smith says. 'No need to see me out.'

Mrs Parsons watches him go, and shakes her head.

'Deary, deary me, such goings on,' she says, picking up the statement to make room for mother's plate of bacon and eggs. Her eyes take a quick tour of the paper. 'I couldn't help but catch a few words you was sayin', what with you all hammering on. Ellen Ternan is the woman, or should I say "girl" in question? Obviously likes 'em young, your Mr Dickens, as many do as shouldn't. He wouldn't be the first to have two on the go but he needs to be careful: counts as incest with a sister-in-law, you know.'

She wipes the document against her grease-stained apron and hands it to my mother.

'I wouldn't sign it neither,' she says.

Saturday, 11th June 1870—4:10 AM

KATE feels terribly sorry for her father. The penniless young reporter he had taken under his wing was now breaking one daughter's heart, threatening to ruin the reputation of another, and calling the third a liar—in public—as well as making mischief for their mother, who didn't think she could be bought, but who was purchased as easily as a bun in a baker's shop. Charles knew how to bargain. He knew that Mrs Hogarth loved her family and would wish to spare them heartache, and took this as a vulnerability he could exploit. It was rumoured that he would never let anything or anyone stand in his way and it didn't take long for him to prove it.

June 1858

'WELL, this is certainly no Tavistock House or Gad's Hill Place,' my youngest sister Helen says to our mother as I show them round the house Charles has leased for me in Gloucester Crescent, now they have signed his statement.

'How the mighty have fallen,' says Mama as we reach the kitchen. 'How dare he fob you off with four hundred a year and a carriage, when he squanders that much on claret?'

Helen unpacks two saucepans from one of the trunks and passes them to our mother, who bangs them down on the kitchen table like a cook who's just been given notice. I don't dare mention that he's now withdrawn the offer of a carriage, to punish me for refusing to sign the latest draft of his separation agreement.

'At least he's paid for the lease on this house,' I say, hoping to calm her.

Bang! Bang!

The colander and sieve are next called into service to amplify her feelings. I don't think I'll let her loose on my crockery.

'He'd be able to afford a lot better if he wasn't forking out for that little actress to live in the lap of luxury—and I've heard tell that he's paying for her sister to study singing in Florence, with the mother as chaperone. He never offered to send you and me to

Italy, did he, Helen? And that wretched Fanny sings like a half-strangled cat, compared with you.'

The baking tray in which I used to make Charles his favourite Welsh rarebits hurtles across the table like a sled. It collides with a cake tin and they both pitch onto the flagstones. The tin clatters, in lament at being about to be consigned to a lonely existence at the back of a dark cupboard. A few months back, I had filled it with creamy butter, fresh eggs, pure white sugar and finely milled flour and baked an Ugly Duckling cake in it for Plorn's sixth birthday. I can still see the delight on his little face.

'But at least Charles has agreed that Charley may live here with me. That's a blessing,' I say.

'Agreed? He could not prevent it. Now Charley is of age, he can live where he likes. The rest would do likewise if they could. It's only natural.'

My favourite mixing bowl is quaking in her arms, fearing it is about to be shattered.

'Charles says they may visit whenever they wish,' I say and rescue the bowl from her clutches.

'When will you get it into your head that what Charles says and what Charles does are two totally different kettles of fish? You should go to court and show him up for what he is—an adulterous hypocrite! That will wipe the smile off his smug face.'

If my mother doesn't stop, my head will explode. I ask my sister to intercede.

'She's right, though,' Helen says. 'It all stinks worse than the Thames. He has forced us to keep quiet about Nelly while he—'

'Helen and I will have to leave you to it, Dear,' says Mother, hastily. 'We must keep an eye on your father. I've no idea what he's doing. Come along, Helen.'

'—while he takes to the press to tell all!' Helen shouts, refusing to be hushed by our mother. She stabs a carving knife into a chopping board.

'The press?' I ask.

'Trust you to let the cat out of the bag after we agreed to spare her,' Mother says.

'Spare me? From what?'

Mother takes a newspaper from her apron pocket and hands it to me.

'Got any brandy?' she asks, as I start to read.

The Times
7th June 1858

Some domestic trouble of mine, of long-standing, on which I will make no further remark than that it claims to be respected, as being of a sacredly private nature, has lately been brought to an arrangement, which involves no anger or ill-will of any kind, and the whole origin, progress, and surrounding circumstances of which have been, throughout, within the knowledge of my children. It is amicably composed and its details have now but to be forgotten by those concerned in it.

By some means, arising out of wickedness, or out of folly, or out of inconceivable wild chance, or out of all three, this trouble has been made the occasion of misrepresentations, most grossly false, most monstrous, and most cruel—involving, not only me, but innocent persons dear to my heart, and innocent persons of whom I have no knowledge, if, indeed, they have any existence — and so widely spread, that I doubt if one reader in a thousand will peruse these lines, by whom some touch of the breath of these slanders will not have passed, like an unwholesome air.

Those who know me and my nature, need no assurance under my hand that such calumnies are as irreconcilable with me, as they are, in their frantic incoherence, with one another. But, there is a great multitude who know me through my writings, and who do not know me otherwise; and I cannot bear that one of them should be left in doubt, or hazard of doubt through my poorly shrinking from taking the unusual means to which I now resort, of circulating the Truth.

I most solemnly declare, then—and this I do, both in my own name and in my wife's name—that all the lately whispered rumours touching the trouble at which I have glanced, are abominably false. And that whosoever repeats one of them after this denial, will lie as wilfully and foully as it is possible for any false witness to lie, before Heaven and earth.

'Mama?' Charley shouts from the hallway. I drop the newspaper and cannot trust myself to speak.

'In here with me and your Aunt Helen,' Mother says.

I lift the lid on a trunk and busy myself with sorting through tablecloths and tea towels as he enters.

'I've come to help do more unpacking,' he says, smiling at

everyone. His face falls as he notices the newspaper lying on the floor. He bends to pick it up. I beat him to it.

'*The Times*?' he asks.

'Yes. Shall I put the kettle on for tea?'

'Good idea,' says Helen.

'So you've seen it too,' he says, and puts his arms around me. 'I'm so sorry, Mother.'

Kindness opens the tap to my tears.

'He's telling the world that the Ternan girl has nothing to do with our separation and that I'm happy to be parted from my husband and children,' I mumble into his shoulder. 'You cannot surely believe him?'

'Give the boy credit. He's not an idiot,' says Mama.

Charley rubs my back like a father soothing his child.

'Of course not. I saw them with my own eyes.'

I step back and look him in the face.

'Them?'

'Father and the girl.'

'Where? When?' I ask.

'Walking together on Hampstead Heath, a few weeks ago.'

'Parading her as bold as brass. Surrounded by mayhem and misery, but all water off a duck's back to him,' says Mama.

'Why didn't you tell me?' I ask.

Charley cups my face in his hands.

'It would have distressed you excessively, and you are already distressed too greatly.'

'Your father says that you agree with his arrangement.'

'I'm rather afraid I do,' he says.

I step further away from him—and almost trip backwards into one of the trunks.

Charley catches my arm and breaks my fall.

'Mother! I cannot bear to see you agitated in this way any longer. You have seen with your own eyes that he'll stop at nothing now. What you read in *The Times* spells it out. He is forcing Aunt Georgina to take an intimate examination to save his reputation. For the sake of your health, Mother, agree to what he wants and sign the deed of separation.'

'Poor Georgina,' I say. 'She cannot bear to be touched. She'll be terrified of such violation.'

'Serves her right,' says Mother.

'Charley, your grandmother and your aunt want me to fight your father in court,' I say. 'They want me to tell the truth, expose his wrongdoings and demand the children come to live with me.'

'Mother! Are you completely deluded? What possible good will that do any of us? Do you really believe that a judge will look favourably on a wife who speaks out against a husband, especially one who is a well-known philanthropist, and who contests his custody of his children? It's madness. Utter madness—and you risk getting locked up in an asylum with all the other women who have dared to question the law of the land.'

'Then I'm as bound and gagged as I would be in Bedlam,' I snarl. 'And to think it was your father who wrote "the law is an ass." It appears that you had better go back to live with him. I'll soon settle in here.'

'I don't want to live with him and Aunt Georgina, and neither do the others,' he says.

'I told you so,' says Mother. 'It's only natural for children to want to be with their mother. And please stop mentioning your aunt's name in my presence, Charley.'

She takes a cloth and starts polishing the already sparkling stove.

'Bide your time and maintain your dignity,' Charley says. 'Your day will come but, in the meantime, sign the deed and put an end to your misery. If you don't, it will only encourage him to publish again—and again. Do you want that? See even more lies laid bare in the press for the public to gobble up? Have your life and reputation defiled?'

He takes a piece of paper out of his pocket and lays it on the kitchen table.

Just a simple piece of paper but with such power.

'You should read it before putting your name to it, of course,' Charley says.

'Don't do it, Kate!' pleads Mama. She rinses the cloth under the tap and wrings it to within an inch of its life.

'You'll regret it all your living days,' says Helen.

'I've seen so many drafts; I don't suppose this one's much different. I just want to give your father more time. He's bound to come to his senses eventually . . . don't you think? You can't want me to abandon all hope? There'll be no going back once I've signed this. It will be like signing my own death warrant.'

Charley's face blurs. He helps me to a chair.

'Shall I read it to you, Mother?'

I try to say 'yes' but the word will not pass my lips. I fear igniting a charge that will reduce my marriage to a ruin. I nod and grunt '*Ja*' like Hans Christian Andersen.

Charley picks up the document and reads:

> 'Notwithstanding the marriage that has been had between them . . . it shall and may be lawful for the said Catherine Thomson Dickens . . . to live separate and apart from him the said Charles Dickens in such sort and manner as if she were sole and unmarried. And that he the said Charles Dickens shall not nor will compel or attempt to compel the said Catherine Thomson Dickens to cohabit and live with him by any legal proceedings . . . or in any manner assume claim or exercise any rule constraint authority or control over or upon the said Catherine Thomson Dickens or directly or indirectly . . . molest interrupt or disturb her . . . in her way of living or in her liberty or freedom of going to and staying in such place or places as she shall think fit or for any cause or under any pretence whatsoever sue or prosecute any person or persons for receiving harbouring protecting or assisting the said Catherine Thomson Dickens.'

'Ready to sign?' Charley asks.

'I don't want the "freedom" to live apart. I want the freedom to live at home with my husband and children,' I say.

'No question of that, Hen: he'd be the death of you there,' says Mother.

She hurls the cloth into the sink.

An energy builds at my core, spurts up to my stomach, erupts to my chest and forces from my lungs a terrible howl, like a beaten dog.

Charley looks close to tears.

'I know, I know, I know,' he says. 'But look: if you cannot sign to save yourself more pain, can you not sign to spare me from witnessing your pain?'

In my confusion, I wonder whether something of his father's talent for manipulation has entered my son's spirit. Or maybe that his father has sent him to win me round. Or that he is acting out of love for me and feels he must be cruel to be kind. I cannot tell.

I hesitate.

'The others are being torn apart too,' says Charley. 'Even Dora. She will always be your child too. Do it so she may rest in peace.'

No peace for me but peace for Charley, who has dark rings under his bloodshot eyes, flecks of grey in his lovely brown hair, hollow cheeks, a furrowed brow and bitten fingernails. Peace for all my children: those in this world and those in the next; and peace for Charles too. So much suffering assuaged by one stroke of my pen.

Mother and Helen stare at me with sunken eyes.

I pray to the Lord for guidance.

'Good Mothers do what is best for their children, however hard it is for them,' my sister Mary tells me, echoing the words she had spoken when Charley was a baby.

'Fetch me a pen, then,' I say, and sigh as if I'm blowing out all the candles in the world.

Saturday, 11th June 1870—4:20 am

SHE sighs again at the remembrance of that terrible day. Her sigh makes her single candle flutter. Kate wonders why men are so good at writing words that mask the truth. She gets up painfully and pulls a box of bad memories out from under the sideboard. Taking it into the dining room, she places it on the table and opens the lid. From inside she retrieves a bundle of documents tied with a black silk ribbon and spreads them out.

Charles had almost broken her, back then. He had lied to her and had then appealed to her better nature to believe him when he saw that she did not. He had probably done this throughout their marriage and yet Kate is still in two minds about him. He slapped her down so many times and yet she always believed it was her own fault for not doing more to please him.

Slap—forced her to move out.

Slap—forced Mama and Helen to sign what they knew to be false.

Slap—compelled her to agree to a separation when she had no wish to separate.

But she cannot resist a smirk when she reads a newspaper

review of Ellen's performance as Lydia, for which she had only been the understudy, in Sheridan's *The Rivals*. A critic in *The Manchester Guardian* writes:

> The comedy was completely successful, as far as the hearty enjoyment of the audience was concerned, although Miss E. Ternan being the Lydia there was the strongest reason for regretting the continued indisposition of Miss Amy Sedgwick.

She has another sneaky smile, recalling how misguided her husband had been in thinking his statement would put a stop to the rumours. It had, in fact, served only to add fuel to the fire that threatened to engulf him. Try as he may, he could not cut off all the heads of the Hydra. Kate reaches across the table to read the article by Mr Reynolds of *Reynolds's Weekly Newspaper*.

> *Reynolds's Weekly Newspaper*
> 13th June 1858
>
> The rumours alluded to by Mr. Dickens have, indeed been widely circulated, and generally credited in literary and artistic circles. The names of a female relative and of a professional young lady, have both been of late, so intimately associated with that of Mr. Dickens, as to excite suspicion and surprise in the minds of those who had hitherto looked upon the popular novelist as a very Joseph in all that regards morality, chastity, and decorum. The story in circulation is that his wife has left his roof—according to the mildest form of the narrative, 'on account of incompatibility of temper'—according to the worst form 'on account of that talented gentleman's preference of his wife's sister to herself,' a preference which has assumed a very definite and tangible shape. Mr. Dickens is in a fair way to figure in the new Matrimonial Court and in a mode which will add little to his laurels.

'Good for you, Mr Reynolds,' Kate says, 'and good for me too'.

Kate sees that *The Liverpool Mercury* was not impressed by Charles: it accuses him of 'unmanly selfishness and heartlessness.'

Elizabeth Barrett Browning, Kate's favourite poet, took her part too. Mrs Browning knew all about loving someone with all her soul. Kate goes to her bookcase and finds the sonnet that she needs to sustain her.

How do I love thee? Let me count the ways.
I love thee to the depth and breadth and height
My soul can reach, when feeling out of sight
For the ends of being and ideal grace.
I love thee to the level of every day's
Most quiet need, by sun and candle-light.
I love thee freely, as men strive for right.
I love thee purely as they turn from praise.
I love thee with the passion put to use
In my old griefs, and with my childhood's faith.
I love thee with a love I seemed to lose
With my lost saints. I love thee with the breath,
Smiles, tears of all my life; and, if God choose,
I shall but love thee better after death.

Kate smiles. Someone understands what, despite everything, she still feels for Charles. England's favourite poetess appreciated also how she suffered too—and said so when Kate dared not.

Elizabeth Barrett Browning
11th July 1858

What is this sad story about Dickens and his wife? Incompatibility of temper after twenty-three years of married life? What a plea!—Worse than irregularity of the passions it seems to me. Thinking of my own peace & selfish pleasure too, I would rather be beaten by my husband once a day than lose my child out of the house—yes, indeed. And the Dickens's have children younger than Penini!—Poor woman! She must suffer bitterly—that is for sure.

Not everyone was sympathetic to her plight. There were those who had bided their time and, with Kate wounded, now swooped in for the kill.

Kate takes the candle and walks round the room. Here is the letter from Charles's loyal old friend, Augusta De la Rue. She had been at pains to let Kate know that he had written to her to confide that his marital discord was even worse than it had been in the Villa Peschiere days, and that Kate could still not get on with him or their children. How blissfully relieved Augusta was to hear that Charles could rely on their aunt to take care of them.

She was in no doubt that it would be a great solace for Catherine to read his actual words on the subject:

> What we should do, or what the Girls would be, without Georgy, I cannot imagine. She is the active spirit of the house, and the children dote upon her.

Dear, sweet, sensitive Augusta was so distressed to discover that Catherine brought so much unhappiness upon herself with her insane distrust. Charles described her as 'excruciatingly jealous' without cause, having obtained positive proof that he had been 'on confidential terms with, at least Fifteen Thousand Women of various conditions in life, every condition in life', since they left Genoa. Dear kind, supportive Augusta.

Kate holds the candle high. She puffs out her cheeks and blows away her disdain. The flame falters but burns on, illuminating the truth without a flicker of uncertainty. She should not have been surprised—after all, Madame De la Rue had waited a long time to exact her revenge for being thwarted in her attempt to lure them back to Genoa all those years ago. And the Poison Pixie was not the only one to revel in Kate's misfortune.

June 1858

MOTHER and Helen are taking their leave.

'I don't know how I would have coped without you,' I say as I see them off and thank them for helping me to unpack. I open the front door to find Mrs Winter about to knock.

'Maria! How kind of you to call but I fear that I am not yet ready to receive,' I say.

'There need be no formality between us, my dear Mrs Dickens,' she says. 'I hope you might consider me a friend of yours, and a very dear friend at that, just as I consider you, and as you consider these two personages, no doubt.'

She hasn't changed, and just as I suppress a grin at her forwardness, she holds out her hand. I introduce them.

'Mrs Winter got to know Charles quite well many years ago: she was Miss Maria Beadnell then,' I say, trusting they will register the warning in my words, offer their courtesies and then enable me to shoo her away.

'I am quite charmed to make your acquaintance,' she says, standing her ground as if armed with an invitation. 'Of course I know your other daughter very well, having visited Tavistock House many times since I became reacquainted with your son-in-law, Mrs Hogarth. He may have mentioned me? No, no, of course not. No reason why he should. Such a very busy man. Far too busy for the likes of me, these days. Rich, world-famous author now. Just a penniless parliamentary reporter when I first met him—not that I was ever after his money. But how different his household is these days, Mrs Hogarth! And such a charming girl, your Georgina. As you are no doubt too, Miss Helen, but am I to take it that the "female relative" referred to in the rumours is her rather than you? Yes, yes it would be. You are far too young for Charles, although they do say that an eighteen-year-old actress is also involved in his *histoires de ménage*. And Charles must be, what, forty-six now?—just a little younger than I am, as I recall. I have to say I wasn't really surprised. Not with all that went on between Charles and me behind your back, Mrs Dickens. Actually, that's what I came to see you about. Things you should know which I didn't have the heart to tell you when we last met, you having not long lost your baby girl. And I seem to recall that you lost a daughter too, Mrs Hogarth, and that Charles was in love with that one too. My goodness, what a tangled web some weave when first they practise to deceive! . . .'

'Do come in, Maria,' I say, taking her arm and pulling her out of the path of my mother and sister so they can escape.

'What a shame you have to rush off,' Maria says to them. 'It made such an enjoyable change talking to you. Friends are so hard to find in London, is it not so? Or maybe not.'

'I do apologise,' I say, butting in as Helen and my mother hurry away. 'There is no furniture in the parlour as yet but I do have kitchen chairs.'

Maria surveys the pots and pans and open trunks with undisguised curiosity.

'Certainly not what you're used to but quite adequate for a spinster.'

'I am married,' I say rather loudly.

'Of course, of course, silly me! You're not a spinster, are you?'

She asks as if she cannot be sure. 'You were married once, weren't you? But not happily. That's the point.'

I tell myself that if I remain calm, she may tire of her taunting and leave me in peace.

'Married once, but now reduced to living as a single woman, quite on her own. Not that you'll be on your own, of course. Well, not all the time. There will be loyal friends such as myself, although, as I'm sure you know, acquaintances so often feel compelled to take sides when a couple parts and some, alas, side with the husband, even when his guilt is plain to see, while even close family members may waver in their allegiance, as you may have discovered to your own cost, for even sisters have been known to forget that blood is thicker than water . . . .'

My hands form into fists and my fingernails dig into my palms but I am a reluctant pugilist. I must not give this woman the satisfaction of goading me into a response.

'And your children visit? Sometimes? If he permits it? Even if he does, it's not the same as seeing them every day, is it? But I don't think that was ever your desire. Nevertheless, you must feel very put upon.'

Having no wish to discuss my desires or my feelings with this woman, I distract her with refreshments.

'A cup of tea, perhaps, before you leave?'

'You were always a most hospitable sort of person, Mrs Dickens. I won't say no.'

'I didn't think you would,' I mutter to myself as I fill the kettle and bang it down on the stove. 'I fear I cannot offer you any cake: there has been too little time for baking. We might hurry to the shops and purchase one, if you felt so inclined.'

'Don't trouble yourself on my account. I quite understand. You probably don't have the wherewithal to engage a cook now. Or a housemaid. Or even a lady's maid. Such a shame. You probably have to make do with a maid of all work. We all have to cut our coat according to our cloth, although it must be something of a come-down for you, but there we are. What can anyone do?'

I pour her tea into a cracked cup and admonish myself for enjoying this petty act of spite.

'You mentioned there were things I should know?'

'Quite so.' She takes letters from her reticule and hands them to me. 'I fear Mr Dickens has not been quite honest with you.

When I heard the rumours and read his statement in the papers, it was clear that you, my successor, had in turn been succeeded by another *amour*. I thought it incumbent upon myself to repay the kindness you had shown me when he discovered I had become a silly old woman, far too fat to be worth seeing, having responded over-enthusiastically when I first wrote to him—as you will see.'

'That is admirable, but I'm not sure what will be gained by dredging all this up now?' I say, as calmly as I can manage, and pass the letters back to her.

'Please humour me, Mrs Dickens. I trust that knowing something of his heart and how he yearns for his youth may free you from blaming yourself for his recent actions.'

She takes a seat beside me and holds the letters to her ample bosom. It pains me to acknowledge that we are a match.

'Look at this letter,' she says. 'He wrote it from your home at Tavistock House, on Thursday the twenty-second of February, 1855. "My Dear Maria", he calls me. "I have read your letter with great ease . . . and have not lost a word of it. I was obliged to leave Paris on Tuesday morning before the Post came in; but I took such precautions to prevent the possibility of any mischance"—he means any mischance of the letter being found by you, Mrs Dickens—"that the letter came close behind me. I arrived at home last night, and it followed me this morning. No one but myself has the slightest knowledge of my correspondence, I may add in this place. I could be nowhere addressed with stricter privacy or in more absolute confidence than at my own house."'

What call was there for such secrecy? I did not make a habit of prying—until, that is, he gave me such reason to do so. I would like to dwell on this a little longer, but Maria presses on.

'He goes on to say that he read my letter "with great emotion" and with "the old tenderness softened to a more sorrowful remembrance" than he could easily tell me. And then this: "if you had ever told me then what you tell me now, I know myself well enough to be thoroughly assured that the simple truth and energy which were in my love would have overcome everything." Are you not shocked, Mrs Dickens? I would be, in your place.'

I am. Despite what he told me, he is telling Maria that he would have married her. Or perhaps he was being truthful to me and merely being kind to her? With Charles, it is ever a challenge to discern where the truth ends and artfulness begins.

"'I remember well that long after I came of age,'" Maria continues, "'I wrote to you for the last time of all, with a dawn upon me of some sensible idea that we were changing into man and woman." I remember that, Mrs Dickens. He asked if I would forget our little differences and separations and let us begin again. I answered him very coldly and reproachfully, and so we parted. But look what follows:

> 'Nobody can ever know with what a sad heart I resigned you, or after what struggles and what a conflict. My entire devotion to you, and the wasted tenderness of those hard years which I have ever since half loved half dreaded to recall, made so deep an impression on me that I refer to it a habit of suppression which now belongs to me, which I know is no part of my original nature, but which makes me chary of shewing my affections, even to my children, except when they are very young.

'There: what do you think of that?' she says, and waves the letter in my face.

What I think is that Charles has confessed as much to me—his difficulty in laying his heart bare—and I have witnessed it with my own eyes. So I do not doubt he is being honest in this instance: heartbreakingly so, for himself, for me, and for our children.

'He loved me, Mrs Dickens. See? He goes on: "A few years ago (just before *Copperfield*) I began to write my life, intending the manuscript to be found among my papers when its subject should be concluded"—after his death, in other words. But as he got older, "I lost courage and burned the rest. I have never blamed you at all, but I have believed until now that you never had the stake in that serious game which I had." You see? He says he was more serious about me than I was about him.'

I'm astounded. He burnt his manuscript to obliterate his past with Maria, and he burnt my letters to obliterate any sign of having once enjoyed his time with me.

'And then look what he says, Mrs Dickens, when, after more than two decades of absence from each other, I wrote to him in the hope of our becoming reacquainted:

> 'All this mist passes away before your earnest words; and when I find myself to have been in your mind at that thoughtful crisis in

> your life which you so unaffectedly and feelingly describe, I am quite subdued and strangely enlightened.

'Then, after Charles's sister died, I went round to your house in Devonshire Terrace to pay my respects, as any proper person would—'

So fifteen years after they parted she took it upon herself to turn up at our house after Charles's sister Fanny's funeral! This woman is shameless!

'—but he didn't know because you were all out of town at the time, and no one told him, and so he didn't find out until I mentioned it in my letter to him. And so, over the course of time, he set his old passion aside, he says, and did not seek opportunities for us to see one another again.'

I want to laugh! Charles wanted not to see her again because she had turned against him. He has always been peerless in his ability to bear a grudge and will not hesitate to exorcise those who cross him as if they are troublesome ghosts.

'But look how he responds after I write to him, inviting him to renew our friendship:

> 'All this again you have changed and set right—at once so courageously, so delicately and gently, that you open the way to a confidence between us which once more, in perfect innocence and good faith, may be between ourselves alone. All that you propose, I accept with my whole heart. Whom can you ever trust if it be not your old lover! Lady Olliffe asked me in Paris the other day (we are, in our way, confidential you must know) whether it was really true that I used to love Maria Beadnell so very, very much? I told her that there was no woman in the world, and there were very few men, who could ever imagine how much.
>
> 'You are always the same in my remembrance. When you say you are 'toothless, fat, old and ugly' (which I don't believe), I fly away to the house in Lombard Street which is pulled down, as if it were necessary that the very bricks and mortar should go the way of my airy castles, and see you in a sort of raspberry coloured dress with a little black trimming at the top—black velvet it seems to be made of—cut into vandykes—an immense number of vandykes—with my boyish heart pinned like a captured butterfly on every one of them. I have never seen a girl play the harp, from that day to this, but my attention has been instantly arrested, and that

> drawing room has stood before me so plainly that I could write a most accurate description of it. I remember that there used to be a tendency in your eyebrows to join together, and sometimes in the most unlikely places—in Scotland, America, Italy—on the stateliest occasions and the unceremonious—when I have been talking to a strange face and have observed even such a slight association as this in it, I have suddenly been carried away at the rate of a thousand miles a second, and have thought 'Maria Beadnell!'"

It is my brows that knit together now. Was Charles thinking of Maria when I miscarried on the train in Scotland? And when he dragged me off to America? Has our whole life together been nothing but smoke and mirrors? Surely not in Genoa when his mind was full to the brim with Augusta De la Rue? It cannot be: he is telling Maria what she wants to hear. He has always been good at that.

'He says that when our feelings for one another were becoming less intense, he would often walk past where I then lived, at two or three in the morning, on his way home from the House of Commons, and that, in the last twelve months, has tried to restore his memory of his younger years by visiting the place again:

> 'You ask me to treasure what you tell me, in my heart of hearts. O see what I have cherished there, through all this time and of these changes!

'Is he not romantic, Mrs Dickens?' she says, pressing the letter to her heart.

Romantic? No. Self-deceiving? Yes. The fact is, Charles is seeking his lost youth rather than his lost love. He didn't find it with Maria and so he tried again with Ellen.

> 'In the course of Saturday I will write to you at Artillery Place, sending the little brooches and tell you when Catherine will come—I am a dangerous man to be seen with, for so many people know me. At St. Paul's, the Dean and the whole chapter know me. In Pasternoster Row of all places, the very tiles and chimney pots know me.'

'You see how amusing he can be?' Maria prattles. 'The tiles and chimney pots know him! Then he says:

> 'I should very much like to see you before we meet when others are by—I feel it is as it were, so necessary to our being at ease—and unless I hear from you to the contrary, you may expect to encounter a stranger whom you may suspect to be the right person if he wears a moustache. You would not like better to call here on Sunday, asking first for Catherine and then for me? It is almost a positive certainly that there will be no one here but I, between 3 and 4. I make this suggestion, knowing what odd coincidences take place in streets, when they are not wanted to happen; though I know them to be so unlikely, that I should not think of such a thing if any one but you were concerned. If you think you would not like to come here, make no change. I will come there.

So he sent me to invite Mr and Mrs Winter—Maria and her husband—to dinner to cover his true intentions of seeing her again, just as three years later he sent me to call on all the Ternans, to make his relationship with Ellen seem respectable and above board. That was bad enough, but then he lied to me when he told me he had written to Maria *after* our dinner party and suggested she meet him privately at our house, when I was away, to spare me from more of her prattle. This letter makes it clear that the tryst was arranged *before* that meal.

'There, you see, Mrs Dickens: it was all planned!' She places the letter in her lap and slaps her hand down upon it in a gesture of triumph. 'What do you think of that? Are you not outraged?'

I am certainly shocked by all the scheming and playacting but am I outraged? I may have been once. Now, I marvel more that Charles would squander his skills and his time as a writer to produce a mediocre melodrama in which he and his lost love take the leading but hardly starring roles. Whatever went on between them, however, was just a preliminary to the final scene in which the juvenile lead makes her entrance.

'It *is* a remarkable letter, is it not?' Maria adds, never one to allow a gap in her monologue. 'He ends by saying that starting up with me again would remind him of our separation, and of your house servant Anne wondering what state my affections were in, some time when he was feeling low, and telling him to be patient and let Time do its work. And see how he finishes up, Mrs Dickens:

> 'Well, well. It was not to be until Patience and Time should bring us together thus—
>
> 'Remember. I accept all with my whole soul, and reciprocate all.

'And he signs himself "ever your affectionate friend". Look, there, in his own script! I imagine it must be quite shocking for you to discover the true depth of his affection and undying love for me.'

Maria is unable to keep the smirk from her face, and although I had hoped that her peroration was over, she ploughs on. 'Though I have not wished to add one jot to your present upsets, I know you'll have wanted to acquire the fullest picture of your former husband's betrayal of you.'

I have maintained my dignity throughout all my trials, if one disregards unwrapping a bracelet on one occasion, and uprooting a few lavenders on another, and happening to glance over my husband's shoulder to read his riddler letter on a third, but I remain determined that Maria will not see me shaken.

'Well, you hinted at all this during your previous visit,' I say, with a shrug.

'You take it well, Mrs Dickens,' she says, fiddling with the ribbons on her bonnet. 'I am full of admiration at your stoic acceptance of your husband's deception and I wish to assure you, on my honour, that I was really only intending to pay a polite call on an old friend.'

'I'm sure you were,' I say, hoping to bring this unhappy reunion to a close.

'But will you forgive me if I venture that you may have been, not to put too fine a point on it, less than completely honest with me during our last interview?' she says.

Oh dear. Maria has untied her bonnet. Has she only just begun? I fear she may be about to take the bonnet off, preparatory to a more protracted stay but, to my relief, she begins to tie it up again.

'Whatever can you mean, Mrs Winter?' I ask, truly puzzled by her accusation of dishonesty on my part.

She runs her finger over the crack in her cup.

'Were I charitable, as I hope I always seem, I might admit the possibility of your duplicity being unintentional, but I gained the impression that you had been happily married, if not very happily married, and that you were equally content, in fact blessed, by all your girls and boys,' she says. 'But now I find that this was not the case . . . '

'Fie, now. Why do you say such things? You accuse me of falsehoods when I have never given you the least cause to do so.'

I snatch up her cup and saucer, run them under the tap and wonder how much water it would take to wash her right out of the door and my life.

'Some omissions are tantamount to untruths,' she says. 'I pitied your having to leave your children, for what could be a greater wrench for a loving mother, and I was sorry that he had forced you out of your home, but I have since discerned that you never wanted your children, let alone wanted to be with them, and that it was you who wanted to leave—you, in fact, who suggested it! You've made a fool of me, Mrs Dickens, just as your husband did before you.'

To my amazement, she bursts into tears.

I am nonplussed. We sit in a silence broken only by her snivelling. She takes a handkerchief out of her reticule along with another letter. She hands me the handkerchief, realises her mistake, snatches it back and passes me the letter. It is dated 31st May 1858 and is signed by my sister Georgina.

> I am now going to tell you something which will, I am sure, surprise you. There was no other way out of the separation: for my sister and Charles have lived unhappily for years—they were totally unsuited to each other in almost every respect—and as the children grew up this unsuitability developed itself more strongly and disagreements and miseries which used to be easily kept out of sight have forced themselves into notice.
>
> Unhappily, also, by some constitutional misfortune and incapacity, my sister always, from their infancy, threw her children upon other people, consequently as they grew up there was not the usual strong tie between them and her—in short, for many years, although we have put a good face upon it, we have been very miserable at home.
>
> My sister has often expressed a desire to go and live away, but Charles never agreed to it on the girls' account; but latterly he thought it must be to their advantage as well as to his own and Catherine's to consent to this and remodel their unhappy home.

So, by mutual consent and for the reasons I have told you, and no other, they have come to this arrangement.

The letter flutters to the floor. I have deluded myself all these years that I had the care and respect of my husband and, albeit to a lesser extent, of my sister too. I had nothing. I deserve nothing. I am nothing. I am drained.

'Mrs Dickens,' says Maria.

'All lies,' is all I can manage to say. 'All lies.'

'Of course, I knew all along it couldn't be true. I pride myself on being a good judge of character and, to be honest, I always suspected that Georgina of being two-faced,' Maria says. 'And, after all, you and I are soulmates.'

'Soulmates?'

'Indeed, Madam. We have both suffered rejection at the hands of your husband, have both been left heart-broken when he cast us off. I was almost destroyed, being a sensitive soul. You are obviously blessed with a tougher heart.'

I feel like opening one of the trunks, climbing inside and shutting the lid.

'Well, I must be off. Mr Winter will be wondering where I am,' she says. 'I'm truly blessed to have such a devoted husband. He hangs on my every word, you know.'

'I'm sure he does,' I say. Can you let yourself out? I'm not—'

'Do let me know if you ever need to talk again,' she says. 'Search high and low: you won't find a better listener than me in all London Town.'

'You are very kind, but I mostly want peace and quiet.'

I breathe a sigh of relief as the front door slams shut.

'Not in all of London,' shouts a voice through the letterbox.

Saturday, 11th June 1870—4:35 am

SEEING herself through her sister's eyes had set two Kates warring in her mind. Which was she?

Loving Kate?

Cold Kate?

Both?

Neither?

The loyal wife and loving mother she believed herself to be strove to defend herself against her sister's depiction of her as a cold-hearted shrew who had rejected her children and had wanted to escape from the home she had made miserable.

Severing familial ties cuts deep, and a sister's betrayal is one of the hardest to bear. Kate has not seen Georgina for twelve years but still hears her whispering 'totally unsuited, disagreements and miseries, no tie with children, no other reason' in her ear.

Kate has never really come to terms with the disregard for truth and the contempt shown by her husband and sister—and there was more to come.

Incensed by the failure of his first attempt to influence public opinion in his favour, Charles had released an even more damning statement in *The Morning Chronicle*, *The Morning Herald* and *The New York Tribune*. Kate is thankful that Harriet Martineau, their UK correspondent, was keen to set the record straight. 'I think it right to tell Mrs. Dickens's old friends in the U.S. that other old friends, who have been intimate in the family during her whole married life, feel towards her an unaltered respect & regard. – This can do no harm, & is required . . . by justice,' she wrote.

Kate wishes she could emulate her friend in the name of justice, but Charles's death is a double-edged sword. She can speak her mind at last but her voice is doomed to fall on deaf ears now. Nevertheless, she will have her say here on Earth and hope her words will wend their way to him in the afterlife, and that she will find her husband on his knees begging her forgiveness, should she meet him in Heaven.

She holds the *New York Tribune* up to the light and reads.

16 August 1858

Mrs Dickens and I have lived unhappily together for many years. Hardly any one who has known us intimately can fail to have known that we are, in all respects of character and temperament, wonderfully unsuited to each other. I suppose that no two people, not vicious in themselves, ever were joined together, who had a greater difficulty in understanding one another, or who had less in common.

'"Lived unhappily for years?" "Wonderfully unsuited"? "Had difficulty in understanding one another"? I understood you and your motives perfectly, Charles. Shame on you!' Kate shouts.

> An attached woman servant (more friend to both of us than a servant), who lived with us sixteen years, and is now married, and who was, and still is in Mrs Dickens's confidence and in mine, who had the closest familiar experience of this unhappiness, in London, in the country, in France, in Italy, wherever we have been, year after year, month after month, week after week, day after day, will bear testimony to this.

'Poor Anne—forced to bear false witness or lose her livelihood and later her daughter, Catherine's, school fees.'

> Nothing has, on many occasions, stood between us and a separation but Mrs Dickens's sister, Georgina Hogarth. From the age of fifteen, she has devoted herself to our house and our children. She has been their playmate, nurse, instructress, friend, protectress, adviser and companion. In the manly consideration toward Mrs Dickens which I owe to my wife, I will merely remark of her that the peculiarity of her character has thrown all the children on some one else. I do not know—I cannot by any stretch of fancy imagine—what would have become of them but for this aunt, who has grown up with them, to whom they are devoted, and who has sacrificed the best part of her youth and life to them.

'Really? My "peculiarity of character", Charles, which threw "all the children on some one else"? In truth, I was struggling to run a home and host dinner parties for you, after ten long, hard, painful confinements and the sadness that followed each of them. I was distressed at failing to nurse my babies and grief-stricken when I lost my sweet Dora. I was nineteen when we met and forty-three on the day you forced me out. It is I "who has sacrificed the best part of her youth and life"—to you, Charles: to you.'

> She has remonstrated, reasoned, suffered and toiled, again and again to prevent a separation between Mrs Dickens and me. Mrs Dickens has often expressed to her her sense of her affectionate care and devotion in the house—never more strongly than within the last twelve months.

'Yes, there's a grain of truth here—a sweetmeat thrown in to make your foul-tasting meal more palatable. I did thank Georgina for helping to keep house as I struggled to protect the children from your rage, but she repaid me by repeating your lies like a pet raven!'

> For some years past Mrs Dickens has been in the habit of representing to me that it would be better for her to go away and live apart; that her always increasing estrangement made a mental disorder under which she sometimes labours—more, that she felt herself unfit for the life she had to lead as my wife, and that she would be better far away. I have uniformly replied that we must bear our misfortune, and fight the fight out to the end; that the children were the first consideration, and that I feared they must bind us together 'in appearance'.

'"In appearance"? We were not bound "in appearance": twelve pregnancies testify against that Charles. And do enlighten me: when were our children ever your "first consideration"? When you insisted we leave them for a six-month tour of America; sent them off to school in France aged six; forced frightened Walter to fight on the other side of the world? Were they uppermost in your thoughts when you were walking on the Continent or visiting Augusta De la Rue, or hosting bachelor dinners at your office, or performing in theatricals, or shut away writing, or managing every detail of the lives of fallen women? Or was it when you devoted all your time and energies into covering up your attempts to turn Ellen Ternan into such a woman? Anyone would become mentally disordered if they were alternately praised and criticised, praised and criticised. I was either a saint or a sinner in your eyes—a well-baked sponge, for ever being yanked out of the oven to be told how I was not to your taste, until I believed you were right and that you might be better off without me, such was the selflessness of my love for you. You and our children were always my first consideration—it's a shame we were never yours!'

> At length, within these three weeks, it was suggested to me by Forster that even for their sakes, it would surely be better to reconstruct and rearrange their unhappy home. I empowered him to treat with Mrs Dickens, as the friend of both of us for one

> and twenty years. Mrs Dickens wished to add on her part, Mark Lemon, and did so. On Saturday last Lemon wrote to Forster that Mrs Dickens 'gratefully and thankfully accepted' the terms I proposed to her.

'Oh, so it was our friend Forster who persuaded you to end our unhappy marriage was it? So he was lying when he told me he had advised you to forget your infatuation with Ellen Ternan and be content with your wife and children? This cannot be the same Forster who just two years before looked forward to his own nuptials, on the strength of what he had witnessed of ours? He wrote that he had never felt so strongly how much of the happiness of past years he owed to me, and sent me a gift of jewellery for my forty-first birthday, imploring me to wear it for his sake, before wishing me and us all many, many happy returns of the day which for so many years we had passed together. And by the way, Charles, I was neither grateful nor thankful for what you proposed and I did not accept the deed of separation or your financial terms until you forced me to.'

> Of the pecuniary part of them, I will only say that I believe they are as generous as if Mrs Dickens were a lady of distinction and I a man of fortune. The remaining parts of them are easily described —my eldest boy to live with Mrs Dickens and take care of her; my eldest girl to keep my house; both my girls, and all my children but the eldest son, to live with me, in the continued companionship of their aunt Georgina, for whom they have all the tenderest affection that I have ever seen among young people, and who has a higher claim (as I have often declared for many years) upon my affection, respect and gratitude than anybody in this world.

'I *am* a "lady of distinction", Charles, and you *were* "a man of fortune", notwithstanding your unwillingness to share it with me. Where is the carriage you promised me? I needed money to furnish this house, but you would have left me to sit on the floor and sleep on bare boards. As for "Aunt Georgina", I would suggest that *affliction* rather than *affection* better stands for their feelings for her, nor was she the first of my sisters to receive the affection, respect and gratitude owing to your wife. You boosted them up that you might belittle me.'

> I hope that no one who may become acquainted with what I write here, can possibly be so cruel and unjust, as to put any misconstruction on our separation, so far. My elder children all understand it perfectly, and all accept it as inevitable. There is not a shadow of doubt or concealment among us—my eldest son and I are one, as to it all.

'Lucifer Box certainly did not misconstrue the reasons for our separation and Mamie dulled her senses to avoid accepting the inevitable. But Charley? You made me fearful that my dear boy had been hoodwinked by you, but he was never the naïve fool you took him for.'

> Two wicked persons who should have spoken very differently of me, in consideration of earned respect and gratitude, have . . . coupled with this separation the name of a young lady for whom I have a great attachment and regard. I will not repeat her name—I honour it too much. Upon my soul and honour, there is not on this earth a more virtuous and spotless creature than that young lady. I know her to be innocent and pure, and as good as my own dear daughters. Further, I am quite sure that Mrs Dickens, having received this assurance from me, must now believe it, in the respect I know her to have for me, and in the perfect confidence I know her in her better moment to repose in my truthfulness.

'I'll repeat her name for you, Charles: it's Ellen Ternan!' Kate cries, rising with a swiftness she has not known in years. She throws open the window. 'I shall call out "Nelly" to the street, to the town, to the world. Nothing remains to stop me—or my wicked mother, or my wicked sister. "Nelly! Nelly! Nelly!"'

> On this head, again, there is not a shadow of doubt or concealment between my children and me. All is open and plain among us, as though we were brothers and sisters. They are perfectly certain that I would not deceive them, and the confidence among us is without a fear.

'Liar! You punished my children for wishing to see me—banished my sons abroad, stopped speaking to Charley, drove Mamie to drink, pressed Lucifer Box into a loveless marriage, and consigned poor Walter to a certain death.'

She puts her head through the window again and shouts, 'To his death! To his death!'

'Oh my Lord! Madam, whatever is the matter?'

Matilda pulls her back into the room.

'He's dead!' Kate shouts.

'I know, Madam, 'tis very sad, Mr Dickens being no longer among us in this world, but you won't be far behind 'im if you take on so,' her maid warns. 'Come now.' Matilda takes her mistress's hand and tries to guide Kate back to her chair.

'Not Charles! Walter!' she shouts towards the window as Matilda leads her away. 'He killed my little boy. He died all alone in India. At twenty-two. Just twenty-two. And Dora just eight months. My baby girl! Dead! All dead! I died too. Don't bury me with my husband: I want to be with my babies!'

Kate slumps into the chair. Her spirits drain. Her vision swirls. Her head is so heavy, she has to support it in her hands.

A pretty woman with long brown ringlets sits across from her.

She smiles at Kate. 'What a dreadful letter that was,' she says. 'And what a crime, for a man to use his genius as a cudgel against the woman he promised to protect with his life and heart—taking advantage of his hold with the public to turn public opinion against her. I call it dreadful.'

'Why do you stand there gawping?' Kate asks Matilda. 'It is very kind of Mrs Browning to call and speak up for me. Please fetch us refreshments.'

Matilda glances about the empty room, her brow furrowing. She takes a step forward, then hesitates and draws back again, seemingly uncertain whether to rouse Kate from her reverie or indulge her daydream.

'And here is dear Aunt Helen,' says Kate, her gaze fixed on a chair that stands quite empty. 'I dare say she would enjoy a cup as well.'

Kate is pleased to see Matilda run out of the room to obey her instructions.

'Bring cake too,' she says, unsure whether it is breakfast, lunch or suppertime. Would eggs be better? Yes—they suit any hour. Let us have a picnic, as we did in the good old days. 'Matilda, bring hard-boiled eggs!' she calls out.

Kate is pleased to hear Aunt Helen exchanging confidences with the celebrated poet.

'Catherine was perfectly sound in mind. All that Georgina did was to teach the little boys to read and write until they went to school. While Catherine was having her family, was it not natural that she should lean upon the assistance of a sister in the care of her children?'

'Of course it was natural—and quite right too,' Mrs Browning says.

'Kate confessed to me that she still loved Charles and thought of him too much for her peace of mind,' says Aunt Helen. 'She trusted by God's assistance to be able to resign herself to His will, and lead a contented if not a happy life, although her position was a sad one. Time alone might blunt the keen pain that throbbed at her heart, but she would try to struggle against it. She hoped God would permit this page in her life's history eventually to be turned.'

'And you told me to be the author of my own story,' Kate says, as Mark Lemon arrives and sits next to her.

'Mark! He took my part too,' Kate tells the others. 'My dear friend negotiated a settlement with Charles on my behalf and refused to publish what Charles wrote about me in *Punch*.'

'Charles would have nothing more to do with me after that,' says Lemon, 'nor with Bradbury and Evans, our publishers, either, for that matter.'

'*Ja*, with me also,' says Hans Christian Andersen.

I didn't see Hans Christian arrive but he is most welcome nonetheless. I will ask Matilda to bring kippers.

'Jus becorse I say Georgina not nice person, unkind to me and made dear Kate cry, but ow appy rest of the family wos togezzer that summer.'

'He ostracised our whole family,' Aunt Helen says. 'Not only that, he stopped the children from seeing us. He even banned them from visiting their own grandparents! He threatened everyone that if they had anything to do with "the Hogarths", he'd never speak to them again.'

'I couldn't see the children either,' says Lemon.

'Cut me dead too!' says William Makepeace Thackeray.

Where did he spring from? Kate wonders. He doesn't seem to notice that Charles's mother is sitting on his lap.

'I didn't set out to upset the old boy,' Thackeray says.

'There wouldn't have been any of this trouble if Charles had taken my advice and married Maria Beadnell to begin with,' Mrs Dickens says.

'Knew he wasn't right in the head,' Thackeray says, 'and tried to set the record straight, but he took against me for it.'

Her words ignored, the senior Mrs Dickens takes umbrage and stomps off to the chair by the door.

'Yes, I recall that Garrick Club business,' Lemon says.

'Nice place *vor* lunch,' Hans Christian Andersen tells him.

'The poor matron: forced to leave her home, after twenty-two years of marriage,' Thackeray continues. 'Dickens's behaviour is a fatal story for our trade. Overheard one of the Garrick Club members saying Dickens was behaving like a scoundrel. Swapped his wife for her sister, don't you know? I put him straight. "Not Georgina Hogarth—some little actress," I said. Only trying to be helpful but no good trying to reason with Dickens, once he'd made up his mind. I was out and that was it. I recall he blocked his son's membership when the lad disagreed with him. Quite cast down about it, young Charles Dickens Jnr. was when he found himself blackballed by his own father.'

Charles walks in.

'Charles!' his mother shouts, 'I was just telling them how you should have married Maria, but no one ever listens to me.'

A pall of silence falls.

'I thought you were dead,' Kate says.

'No, that was just another of my stories,' he says.

Matilda is back but she's empty-handed.

'I'm afraid there are no eggs for our guests and no toasted cheese for you today, Charles,' Kate says. He doesn't seem to mind. There is a faraway look in her eyes. What is it she's been fretting over? Didn't she have a bothersome question? Something to do with red roses? It hovers on the periphery of her memory, tantalisingly close, until the clouds break.

'Did you ever love me Charles?' she asks her husband.

'*I love thee with a love I seemed to lose. With my lost saints. I love thee with the breath, Smiles, tears, of all my life!—and, if God choose, I shall but love thee better after death,*' he says.

Kate smiles, makes a pillow of the pile of newspapers on the table, lowers her head and drifts off to sleep, back in her husband's arms.

Saturday, 11th June 1870—5:15 AM

'HOW long has she been in this state?' someone whispers.

'I can't be sure but she was like this when I came down to see what all the commotion was about,' Matilda whispers back. 'She told me she was dead, and started talking to ghosts. That's when I sent for you.'

Ghosts? What ghosts? Kate opens her eyes just a slit to assess the situation. If there was a commotion, perhaps she has been attacked by burglars? Knocked senseless by them? Her head does feel as if it has been battered about. Through a haze of blurred vision, she perceives Lucifer Box and Matilda standing over her but the world has been drained of colour, and she sees through a veil of black and white.

'Should I open the curtains?' Matilda asks.

'Yes, that should rouse her gently. She's already had quite enough shock. We mustn't add to her distress, but she does need nourishment,' Lucifer Box says.

'I'm not hungry and I'm not distressed,' Kate says.

'Oh, Mother. I'm so sorry.' Her daughter puts an arm around her shoulders. 'I should have come sooner but there was so much to arrange,' she says.

'Don't trouble yourself on my account. Charley was here. At least I believe he was,' Kate says.

'Yes, he came yesterday, Ma'am,' Matilda confirms.

'Yesterday? Are you sure? What about the other visitors? When were they here?'

Matilda gives Lucifer Box a knowing look.

'Would you like to sit up, Mother?' she asks. She hands Kate a glass of water. 'Drink this while Matilda fetches your breakfast. We have a bath all ready for you. You'll feel more like your old self after that.'

Kate is not sure whether she wants to go back to being her old self, and is neither hungry nor thirsty, but does not want to appear ungrateful, and so she smiles—and drinks. The cool water washes over her tongue, which seems to have doubled in size and grown a fur coat. The liquid soothes her throat. Her stomach gurgles in gratitude. One glass is not enough after all. Lucifer Box fetches the jug and pours another.

The smell of toast makes Kate's mouth water. Matilda slices off a big slab of butter and slaps it on the golden bread. It gleams, spreads into a pool of liquid sunshine, soaks in but leaves a glow. There is a warm trickle on her tongue. Her teeth slide through its spongy surface to crunch the crust below.

'Well done, Mama,' Lucifer Box says. 'Can you stand?'

Kate is a knight whose armour has been battered out of shape in a long hard battle. Her joints need oiling but she manages to lever herself up. Her daughter takes one arm and her maid the other. She creaks and grinds along between them.

Steam rises from the bath. Kate slips in, stretches out, slides her head back under the water and feels her hair flow free like a mermaid's. Warmth seeps into her bones and eases her aching muscles. Light reflects on the ceiling like a sea lapping on the shore. The soap smells sweet. Bubbles float across the water and burst in little pops of pleasure. Soft towels embrace her. They have chosen a comfortable black day dress for her, rather than her formal mourning gown.

Tea is set out in the drawing room. Her daughter smiles at her from the armchair opposite.

'It's good to see you looking so much better. I thought I was going to lose both parents when Matilda sent word that I should come,' she says. There are tears in her eyes.

'I'm sorry she worried you unnecessarily. I was just a little over-tired. Now who would like a cup?'

Kate pours the tea, to make all seem normal.

Should she ask about the death?

No, her dear daughter looks so careworn that it would be cruel to make her relive the sorrow of her father's passing.

Perhaps just enquire about his last words? Casually slip a question into the conversation? 'I was wondering, by the by, if Aunt Georgina said whether my name was mentioned?' A passing thought. Nothing more than a passing thought.

But she knows that even if Charles had repeated her name a thousand thousand times and uttered one last 'Dearest Kate' with his dying breath, her sister would never admit it. Her sister would say that her husband had not given her a second thought since Georgina shut the door on her all those years ago.

Was Nelly with him? She doesn't think she could bear it, were it so. Kate was still his wife. It should have been *her* by his side, holding his hand, kissing his cheek, whispering 'Goodbye, my Love'.

She most definitely cannot venture into territory such as this with her daughter. If her father's mistress was with him at the end, Lucifer Box would be forced to choose between Scylla and Charybdis: either lie and spare her mother's feelings or tell the truth and lay extra hurts upon her, after having already suffered unendurable heartache in the last forty-eight hours.

A simpler question, then. Was he unhappy?

No—there is nothing to be gained from an answer to that question. Charles may have lied. Lucifer Box could lie. Georgina would definitely have lied to her if he was unhappy.

Did he love his wife? That's all she really wants to know, but she needs to work round to it.

'Charley said he didn't suffer,' Kate says vaguely, and busies herself with stirring her tea.

'That's right. Aunt Georgina said he collapsed and didn't come round again,' says Lucifer Box in a matter-of-fact manner, but her cup rattles against its saucer.

'Such a shame you didn't have the chance to say goodbye,' Kate says, hoping she will say if anyone was there at the end.

'Actually, we had a long talk the night before. I slept there. I don't think I got to bed until three in the morning.'

'Do you think he knew he was gravely ill?' Kate asks. That appears quite an innocuous question—but, if he did, he may have wanted to take his last opportunity to confess his true feelings.

'I wondered that too,' says Lucifer Box. 'He opened his heart to me and, as you know, that was most unlike Father.'

Her daughter would surely not mention this unless she wants to tell her mother what he confided. Dare Kate hope for a last-minute expression of his love for her?

'Most unlike him. His heart was broken by Maria Beadnell when he was young and he never quite recovered. That's why he kept his distance as you all grew up,' Kate says.

'I thank Heaven that I made my peace with him that night and that he told me of his abiding fear of the debtors' prison.' Tears well up in Lucifer Box's eyes.

'Deep inside him, he remained a fearful twelve-year-old and I felt sorry for him.' Kate lets out a sob. 'He couldn't help himself. That's why I always found it in my heart to forgive him.'

‘As the sun rose on the day he died, he confessed to feeling guilty for all the misery he’d caused and wished he had been a better father—and husband . . . .’ Her daughter’s voice trails away. She sips her tea. ‘He acknowledged I would never have wanted to leave home so urgently had you still been there, Mother.’

Saturday, 11th June 1870— 5:45 AM

A LIGHTNESS lifts Kate right out of her body. For the first time in twelve years her mind floods with peace. She is Kate, the loyal wife and caring mother, loved by her husband and children.

‘Everyone knew my marriage was a desperate attempt to escape from an unhappy house,’ says Lucifer Box. ‘Mamie caught him crying in my room after I’d set off on my honeymoon. He told her it was all his fault.’

‘All his fault, all his fault.’ This penitent Charles breaks Kate’s heart even more than the merciless Charles had when he sent her away.

She leads her daughter to the sofa where they can sit side by side.

‘The public had the inimitable author. We had the flawed patriarch,’ Kate says.

They weep in their grief for the charismatic man of genius whose books brought joy to hundreds of thousands of readers across the world. They will miss his exuberance, his laughter, his passion, the fun they had and the love they shared. They weep also for all those forced to suffer in silence at the hands of the spiteful, selfish monster hidden behind the scenes—their nine children, Kate’s family, his family—and for little Dora, who knew none of this.

Her precious baby girl’s cheeks dimple. Dora smiles and waves as Mary, seventeen years of age forever, passes her to Charles. He cradles her in his arms and whispers that Mama will be along soon.

SATURDAY, 11TH JUNE 1870—5:46 AM

A NEW day has dawned.

I take my daughter's hands and look into eyes that remind me so much of her father's.

'Promise me one thing, Lucifer Box' I say. 'When I die please give my letters to the British Museum so the world may know he loved me once . . . '[1]

THE END

[1] Kate's letters were given to the British Museum by Lucifer Box, in order to fulfil her mother's dying wish, and are now housed in the British Library.

AUTHOR'S NOTES

Mr & Mrs Charles Dickens is a novel, and thus a work of fiction, but tells a true story, and the entire narrative is based on historical facts and authentic documents, including Dickens's letters.

ACKNOWLEDGEMENTS

My thanks go to:

- Dr Stephen Games, my publisher, for his enthusiasm for my work, his professional advice, his meticulous editing and his wonderful cover design;
- The staff at the British Library for their help with my research;
- Emma Harper for her support in helping me gain access to the archives of the Charles Dickens Museum and the Ouvry papers (notably 25.4, 25.6 and 35);
- Jordan Evans-Hill, also of the Charles Dickens Museum, for incorporating the launch of this book into its exhibition, *Incredible Woman*, which opened on 11 February 2026.
- Charles Dickens Museum volunteers: Steven King, who escorted me to Gad's Hill and to the British Library, and Mally Scrutton, Sue Budge, Peter Thompson and Val Parks for fact-checking my manuscript;
- Edward Preston for reading an early draft and commending it;
- Peter and Theresa Clark for their encouragement and advice on historical detail;
- Martine and Roger Saunders for reading numerous versions of my manuscript and for listening to me talk about my writing, year in and year out;
- Members of the Frome Writers' Collective for their always helpful advice;
- Corsham Court Book Club members Huw Lewis and Kevin Lambert for their encouragement and Alison Woodhouse, Rowena Warwick, Irene Pinner and Becky Docton for their invaluable additional feedback on my manuscript;
- Anne Earley for proof reading many drafts;
- Hélèna Maclellan at Bath Spa University, Corsham Court Campus, who proof read my work in her lunch hour;

- Paula Bahadur, at Bath Spa University, who was my first fan;
- Lucy English, Nick Fox and Gavin Cologne-Brookes for championing me during my MA in creative writing;
- Tina Pepler, my BA dissertation supervisor, who told me I was a writer;
- My oldest friends, Gill Allen and Maureen Azulay, for their unwavering faith that I would one day be a published author;
- My sons Oliver and Matthew for their encouragement;
- My daughter Tulip and her husband Toby Sherman for their guidance and patience;
- Toby's mother, Jackie Sherman, whose reference gained me a place at Bath Spa University;
- Farzad Ali for being like a third son to me;
- Tom Kelly for designing my website;
- Nate Ashley for his work on publicity;
- My American friends John and Edith Rea who have sent me their blessings for this endeavour every year since its inception; and
- Ian Elliot for his lifelong love and friendship.

BIBLIOGRAPHY

I found the following books invaluable while writing my own:

Dexter, Walter (ed), *Mr. & Mrs. Charles Dickens: His Letters To Her. With A Foreword By Their Daughter, Kate Perugini* (Constable, 1935).

Lillian Nayder, *The Other Dickens, A Life of Catherine Hogarth* (Cornell University Press, 2011)

Christine Skelton, *Charles Dickens and Georgina Hogarth, A curious and Enduring Relationship* (Manchester University Press, 2023)

Claire Tomalin, *The Invisible Woman, the Story of Nelly Ternan and Charles Dickens* (Penguin Books, 2012).

I also made use of the following works:

Arnold, Gaynor, *Girl in a Blue Dress* (Birmingham: Tindal Street Press, 2008).

Barker, Katherine and Macready, William Charles, *The Sherborne Literary Institution and Charles Dickens* (Sherborne House: The Friends of Sherborne House, 2003).

Clark, Peter, *Dickens's Kent* (London: The Armchair Traveller, 2024).

Dickens, Charles,*American Notes* (London: Bradbury & Evans, 1842).

—*Pictures from Italy* (London: Bradbury & Evans, 1846).

Dickens, Ellie, *My Dearest Kate* (London: Grosvenor House, 2018).

Douglas-Fairhurst, Robert, *The Turning Point* (London: Penguin Random House, 2021).

Elena, Hebe, *Unwanted Wife: A defence of Mrs. Charles Dickens* (London: Jarrolds, 1963).

Forster, John, *The Life of Charles Dickens*, 3 Vols., (London: Chapman and Hall, 1872–24).

Gottlieb, Robert, *Great Expectations: The Sons and Daughters of Charles Dickens* (New York: Farrar, Straus and Giroux, 2012).

Hawksley, Lucinda Dickens, *Charles Dickens: Dickens' Bicentenary 1812-2012* (London: Andre Deutsch, 2011).

Kelly, Helena, *The Life & Lies of Charles Dickens* (London: Icon, 2023)

Mullan, John, *The Artful Dickens* (London: Bloomsbury, 2020).

Ramsden, Timothy, *A Handbook Of Charles Dickens Characters* (London: Creative Publishing, 1981).

Rootes, Andrew, *A History of Higham*, Vols. 1 & 2 (Higham Village History Group, 2011 & 2012).

Rossi-Wilcox, Susan M, *Dinner for Dickens: The Culinary History of Mrs Charles Dickens's Menu Books including a transcript of 'What Shall We Have for Dinner? by Lady Maria Clutterbuck'* (Totnes: Prospect Books, 2005).

Slater, Michael, *The Great Charles Dickens Scandal* (London: Yale University Press, 2012).

Watts, Alan S, *Dickens at Gads Hill* (Reading: Cedric Dickens & Elvendon Press, 1989).

More Fiction from EnvelopeBooks

WWW.ENVELOPEBOOKS.CO.UK

The Green Man | Dan Jones

After humiliating a fellow inquisitor at a trumped-up witch trial in Northern Italy, Brother Jacobus of Vienna is intrigued by rumours of strange events in Northern England. In defiance of the cardinals in Avignon, he travels to Berwick where he finds a land in disarray, beset by Scottish raiders, eccentric Franciscan friars and talk of demons in the woods. Can he solve the mystery and keep his faith and reason intact?

Mrs Woodbine's Prejudices | Michael Ladner

Prof. Arthur Lash, born Artur Lasch in pre-war Austria, takes his American wife and three sons back to Vienna, in 1960, to see how well his father is rebuilding a life interrupted by Nazi Germany's annexation of Austria in 1938. For Arthur, the trip helps to re-establish his links with the city he was brought up in; for the rest of his family, other emotions are awoken—all watched over by Mrs. Woodbine, their needy, disregarded but loyal nanny.

Belle Nash and the Bath Soufflé | William Keeling Esq.

In the first volume of *The Gay Street Chronicles*, bachelor Belle Nash attempts to navigate the bigotry and corruption of 1830s Bath without compromising his dearest confidante (the widow of Bath's greatest lawyer) and his boyfriend (the nephew of Immanuel Kant). Intrique and whimsy overflow after—horror!—the failure of a soufflé to rise.

Secrets of the Four-Chambered Heart | Steven Jay Griffel

In 1994 a group of Americans and Rwandans meet in the Rwandan capital of Kigali. The Americans have been sent by *The New York Times* to cover the ethnic violence; the Rwandans are there to treat the wounded and prepare them for interview. They need to collaborate, but the more they engage, the more their own conflicts surface, exposing unexpected and troublesome secrets. A deft piece of plotting that defies reader expectation.

The Train House on Lobengula Street | Fatima Kara

An anguished, folksy and life-affirming novel, set within the Indian community in Bulawayo, Rhodesia, from the 1940s to the 1960s, this novel focuses on female empowerment and the capacity of women to gain the same advantages as men in the modern world while remaining faithful to traditional Muslim values. Affectionate and passionate.

The Very Annoying Jew | Michael Kretzmer

Award-winning TV producer David Britton is enraged with the world of woke, but the world of woke is enraged with him too. Especially when he screws up the deal to sell the media company that's driving him crazy. But that's not the half of it. His wife wants a divorce, he's getting hate mail, and he's being harassed by religious freaks. Oh, and Sylvia Plath has died. In his kitchen. After he'd dropped her. It's not looking good.

The Lost Woman | Karen Mulvahill

When the Nazis arrest Nicole Cassin's parents and seize their art gallery in Paris in 1941, Nicole vows revenge and joins the Resistance. Years later, living in New York, she is haunted by her losses and hires an art historian to find her family's stolen paintings, among which is a portrait of her mother by Matisse. The whereabouts of the stolen art prove elusive but the search for them leads to another more unexpected discovery. A moving story of courage, determination and defiance.

Mustard Seed Itinerary | Robert Mullen

Po Cheng falls into a dream and finds himself on the road to the imperial Chinese capital. Once there he rises to the heights of the civil service, then finds that in addition to the ladders that helped him ascend, there are snakes facilitating his fall. An object lesson to all ambitious young men and a case study in Carrollian satire.

Frances Creighton: Found and Lost | Kirby Porter

Love demands trust, but trust is a lot to ask for from a victim of abuse. Having been bullied in Belfast at his school and at his church, Michael Roberts suppresses his childhood pains until a girlfriend's death years later forces him to revisit lost memories. A Northern Ireland reply to Sally Rooney's *Normal People*.

A Sin of Omission | Marguerite Poland
An emotionally intense novel, set in 1870s South Africa at a time of rising anti-colonial resistance. The book examines the tragedy of a black preacher, hand-picked for training in England as a missionary, only to be neglected by the Church he loves. Winner of the 2021 *Sunday Times* CNA 'Book of the Year' Award.

The Hopeful Traveller | Janina David
A collection of short stories about—and told by—single women who have put the past behind them but are still looking for their anchor in the present. It includes bitter-sweet accounts of the freedoms of postwar life, of foreign travel, of the rekindling of old friendships and of the search for new ones.

A Girl's Own War | K.J. Kelly
Flt. Lieut. Oliver Carmichael and Baron Julius von Stulpnagel have been living in Berlin, trying to sell forged paintings. So why are they now in run-down Ballingore, in wartime neutral Ireland in 1940, and will ex-convent-girl Mary Collins and her devoted red-headed sidekick Niamh Slattery play into their hands?

Belle Nash and the Bath Circus | William Keeling Esq.
In Volume Two of *The Gay Street Chronicles*, bachelor Belle Nash returns to Regency Bath from Grenada, inspired by a new love that leads him into various pretences that may compromise the ambitions of black circus impresario Pablo Fanque.

The Attraction of Cuba | Chris Hilton
Chris Hilton went to Cuba to escape the boredom of everyday life and make money, only to be entranced by the beauty of the country and of Yamilia, a street girl who brought him love and laughter but who could not help him from falling into an inevitable downward spiral.

Princess Brainy | Stephen Games
Raine couldn't help being hated for being clever, but it didn't help that her mother was modern and made her father (the king) ban the fairies. So what was she meant to do when disaster came to Rainland and the rivers dried up? Accept her fate or get sacrificed to the revolution?

Non-fiction from EnvelopeBooks

WWW.ENVELOPEBOOKS.CO.UK

Wembley Speaks: A Year in the Life of a London Suburb
How do people talk to each other, react to each other, give and ask for advice, conciliate, commiserate and laugh? In a modern reconstruction of Mayhew's landmark 19th-century social study, EnvelopeBooks turns to the *Nextdoor* social networking app to document a community engaging with itself on day-to-day issues. Full of revelation.

Lost Levant: A Journey of Ideas | Rupert de Borchgrave
In the last thousand years, cultural innovation has moved inexorably westwards, leaving us with a poor grasp of the turmoil out of which our own civilisation grew. In 2003 Rupert de Borchgrave went on a journey of ideas to the much-disputed grounds where many of the issues that shape us now were formed.

A Question of Paternity | David Tereshchuk
TV reporter David Tereshchuk traveled the world questioning the perpetrators of injustice and their victims, but could never prise one answer from his own mother: who his father was. Her evasion led to his life of insecurity and alcoholism. And a quest.

The West and the Rest | Ian Ross
Having worked in the oil and tobacco industries, Ian Ross argues that trade is objectively more creative than democracy in bridging cultural divisions. Where diplomats are held back by caution and principle, business executives are incentivised to be adaptable, forward-looking and trusting.

A Road to Extinction | Jonathan Lawley
When Britain colonised the Andamans in 1857, the welfare of its African pygmy inhabitants was of no concern. Nine tribes died out. Dr Lawley now assesses the survival prospects for the three remaining tribes and weighs up the legacy of his grandfather, a former colonial administrator

The Martyrdom of Ahmad Shawkat | Michael Goldfarb
When Gulf War II broke out in 2003, Ahmad Shawkat became guide and translator to NPR-reporter Michael Goldfarb. After the fall of Saddam, Ahmad set up a cultural magazine, published eleven issues and was killed for publicly decrying Islamic terror. This is his story.

Why My Wife Had To Die | Brian Verity
There is no known cure for Huntington's disease, a wasting condition that sufferers acquire from a parent. In this painful account, the author vents his rage at society, lawmakers, health services and the Church for not grasping the need, as he sees it, to legalise compulsory sterilisation and assisted dying.

Artist Spy Prisoner | George Tomaziu
Artist George Tomaziu was imprisoned and tortured for monitoring Nazi troop movements through Bucharest during the Second World War but imagined that his heroism would be recognised if Romania ever became free. He was terribly mistaken. Three years after the war ended he was imprisoned again—this time for thirteen years.

From Bedales to the Boche | Robert Best
Bedales, the progressive boarding school founded by J.H. Badley in 1893, instilled values that sustained many of its pupils for the rest of their lives. Robert Best recalls its influence on him as an enthusiastic army recruit in 1914 and in the Royal Flying Corps.

My Modern Movement | Robert Best
London's Festival of Britain in 1951 marked the belief that Modern design was visually and morally superior. Robert Best, at one time the UK's leading lighting manufacturer, thinks the dice were loaded. This is his memoir.

Postmark Africa | Michael Holman
Eye-witness reports on Eastern Africa for the *Financial Times* and other media provide rare insights into the region's post-colonial successes and setbacks, from accounts of atrocities by Rhodesian forces in the 1960s to interviews with those who aspired to lead Africa into its own future. Essential reading.

Printed in Great Britain
by Amazon

611e575b-bfb4-4b96-9b61-e20cd69607edR01